A Book of Myths

By Jeanie Lang

CONTENTS

PREFACE

Just as a little child holds out its hands to catch the sunbeams, to feel and to grasp what, so its eyes tell it, is actually there, so, down through the ages, men have stretched out their hands in eager endeavour to know their God. And because only through the human was the divine knowable, the old peoples of the earth made gods of their heroes and not unfrequently endowed these gods with as many of the vices as of the virtues of their worshippers. As we read the myths of the East and the West we find ever the same story. That portion of the ancient Aryan race which poured from the central plain of Asia, through the rocky defiles of what we now call "The Frontier," to populate the fertile lowlands of India, had gods who must once have been wholly heroic, but who came in time to be more degraded than the most vicious of lustful criminals. And the Greeks, Latins, Teutons, Celts, and Slavonians, who came of the same mighty Aryan stock, did even as those with whom they owned a common ancestry. Originally they gave to their gods of their best. All that was noblest in them, all that was strongest and most selfless, all the higher instincts of their natures were their endowment. And although their worship in time became corrupt and lost its beauty, there yet remains for us, in the old tales of the gods, a wonderful humanity that strikes a vibrant chord in the hearts of those who are the descendants of their worshippers. For though creeds and forms may change, human nature never changes. We are less simple than our fathers: that is all. And, as Professor York Powell most truly says: "It is not in a man's creed, but in his deeds; not in his knowledge, but in his sympathy, that there lies the essence of what is good and of what will last in human life."

The most usual habits of mind in our own day are the theoretical and analytical habits. Dissection, vivisection, analysis—those are the processes to which all things not conclusively historical and all things spiritual are bound to pass. Thus we find the old myths classified into Sun Myths and Dawn Myths, Earth Myths and Moon Myths, Fire Myths and Wind Myths, until, as one of the most sane and vigorous thinkers of the present day has justly observed: "If you take the rhyme of Mary and her little lamb, and call Mary the sun and the lamb the moon, you will achieve astonishing results, both in religion and astronomy, when you find that the lamb followed Mary to school one day."

In this little collection of Myths, the stories are not presented to the student of folklore as a fresh contribution to his knowledge. Rather is the book intended for those who, in the course of their reading, frequently come across names which possess for them no meaning, and who care to read some old stories, through which runs the same humanity that their own hearts know. For although the old worship has passed away, it is almost impossible for us to open a book that does not contain some mention of the gods of long ago. In our childhood we are given copies of Kingsley's *Heroes* and of Hawthorne's*Tanglewood Tales*. Later on, we find in Shakespeare, Spenser, Milton, Keats, Shelley, Longfellow, Tennyson, Mrs. Browning, and a host of other writers, constant allusion to the stories of the gods. Scarcely a poet has ever written but makes mention of them in one or other of his poems. It would seem as if there were no get-away from them. We might expect in this twentieth century that the old gods of Greece and of Rome, the gods of our Northern forefathers, the gods of Egypt, the gods of the British race, might be forgotten. But even when we read in a newspaper of aeroplanes, someone is more than likely to quote the story of Bellerophon and his winged steed, or of Icarus, the flyer, and in our daily speech the names of gods and goddesses continually crop up. We drive—or, at least, till lately we drove—in Phaetons. Not only schoolboys swear by Jove or by Jupiter. The silvery substance in our thermometers and barometers is named Mercury. Blacksmiths are accustomed to being referred to as "sons of Vulcan," and beautiful youths to being called "young Adonises." We accept the names of newspapers and debating societies as being the "Argus," without perhaps quite realising who was Argus, the many-eyed. We talk of "a panic," and forget that the great god Pan is father of the word. Even in our religious services we go back to heathenism. Not only are the crockets on our cathedral spires and church pews remnants of fire-worship, but one of our own most beautiful Christian blessings is probably of Assyrian origin. "The Lord bless thee and keep thee.... The Lord make His face to shine upon thee.... The Lord lift up the light of His countenance upon thee...." So did the priests of the sun-gods invoke blessings upon those who worshipped. We make many discoveries as we study the myths of the North and of the South. In the story of Baldur we find that the goddess Hel ultimately gave her name to the place of punishment precious to the Calvinistic mind. And because the Norseman very much disliked the bitter, cruel cold of the long winter, his heaven was a warm, well-fired abode, and his place of punishment one of terrible frigidity. Somewhere on the other side of the Tweed and Cheviots was the spot selected by the Celt of southern Britain. On the other hand, the eastern mind, which knew the terrors of a sun-smitten land and of a heat that was torture, had for a hell a fiery place of constantly burning flames.

In the space permitted, it has not been possible to deal with more than a small number of myths, and the well-known stories of Herakles, of Theseus, and of the Argonauts have been purposely omitted. These have been so perfectly told by great writers that to retell them would seem absurd. The same applies to the Odyssey and the Iliad, the translations of which probably take rank amongst the finest translations in any language. The writer will feel that her object has been gained should any readers of these stories feel that for a little while they have left the toilful utilitarianism of the present day behind them, and, with it, its hampering restrictions of sordid actualities that are so murderous to imagination and to all romance.

"Great God! I'd rather beA Pagan suckled in a creed outworn;So might I, standing on this pleasant lea,Have glimpses that would make me less forlorn;Have sight of Proteus rising from the sea;Or hear old Triton blow his wreathèd horn."

JEAN LANG.

"WHAT WAS HE DOING, THE GREAT GOD PAN,

DOWN IN THE REEDS BY THE RIVER?"

POSTSCRIPT

We have come, in those last long months, to date our happenings as they have never until now been dated by those of our own generation.

We speak of things that took place *"Before the War"*; and between that time and this stands a barrier immeasurable.

This book, with its Preface, was completed in 1914—*"Before the War."*

Since August 1914 the finest humanity of our race has been enduring Promethean agonies. But even as Prometheus unflinchingly bore the cruelties of pain, of heat and of cold, of hunger and of thirst, and the tortures inflicted by an obscene bird of prey, so have endured the men of our nation and of those nations with whom we are proud to be allied. Much more remote than they seemed one little year ago, now seem the old stories of sunny Greece. But if we have studied the strange transmogrification of the ancient gods, we can look with interest, if with horror, at the Teuton representation of the GOD in whom we believe as a GOD of perfect purity, of honour, and of love. According to their interpretation of Him, the God of the Huns would seem to be as much a confederate of the vicious as the most degraded god of ancient worship. And if we turn with shame from the Divinity so often and so glibly referred to by blasphemous lips, and look on a picture that tears our hearts, and yet makes our hearts big with pride, we can understand how it was that those heroes who fought and died in the Valley of the Scamander came in time to be regarded not as men, but as gods.

There is no tale in all the world's mythology finer than the tale that began in August 1914. How future generations will tell the tale, who can say?

But we, for whom Life can never be the same again, can say with all earnestness: "It is the memory that the soldier leaves behind him, like the long train of light that follows the sunken sun—that is all which is worth caring for, which distinguishes the death of the brave or the ignoble."

And, surely, to all those who are fighting, and suffering, and dying for a noble cause, the GOD of gods, the GOD of battles, who is also the GOD of peace, and the GOD of Love, has become an ever near and eternally living entity.

"Our little systems have their day;They have their day and cease to be,They are but broken lights of Thee,And Thou, oh Lord, art more than they."

JEAN LANG.

PROMETHEUS AND PANDORA

Those who are interested in watching the mental development of a child must have noted that when the baby has learned to speak even a little, it begins to show its growing intelligence by asking questions. "What is this?" it would seem at first to ask with regard to simple things that to it are still mysteries. Soon it arrives at the more far-reaching inquiries—"Why is this so?" "How did this happen?" And as the child's mental growth continues, the painstaking and conscientious parent or guardian is many times faced by questions which lack of knowledge, or a sensitive honesty, prevents him from answering either with assurance or with ingenuity.

As with the child, so it has ever been with the human race. Man has always come into the world asking "How?" "Why?" "What?" and so the Hebrew, the Greek, the Maori, the Australian blackfellow, the Norseman—in a word, each race of mankind—has formed for itself an explanation of existence, an answer to the questions of the groping child-mind—"Who made the world?" "What is God?" "What made a God think of fire and air and water?" "Why am I, *I*?"

Into the explanation of creation and existence given by the Greeks come the stories of Prometheus and of Pandora. The world, as first it was, to the Greeks was such a world as the one of which we read in the Book of Genesis—"without form, and void." It was a sunless world in which land, air, and sea were mixed up together, and over which reigned a deity called Chaos. With him ruled the goddess of Night and their son was Erebus, god of Darkness. When the two beautiful children of Erebus, Light and Day, had flooded formless space with their radiance, Eros, the god of Love, was born, and Light and Day and Love, working together, turned discord into harmony and made the earth, the sea, and the sky into one perfect whole. A giant race, a race of Titans, in time populated this newly-made earth, and of these one of the mightiest was Prometheus. To him, and to his brother Epimethus, was entrusted by Eros the

1

distribution of the gifts of faculties and of instincts to all the living creatures in the world, and the task of making a creature lower than the gods, something less great than the Titans, yet in knowledge and in understanding infinitely higher than the beasts and birds and fishes. At the hands of the Titan brothers, birds, beasts, and fishes had fared handsomely. They were Titanic in their generosity, and so prodigal had they been in their gifts that when they would fain have carried out the commands of Eros they found that nothing was left for the equipment of this being, to be called Man. Yet, nothing daunted, Prometheus took some clay from the ground at his feet, moistened it with water, and fashioned it into an image, in form like the gods. Into its nostrils Eros breathed the spirit of life, Pallas Athené endowed it with a soul, and the first man looked wonderingly round on the earth that was to be his heritage. Prometheus, proud of the beautiful thing of his own creation, would fain have given Man a worthy gift, but no gift remained for him. He was naked, unprotected, more helpless than any of the beasts of the field, more to be pitied than any of them in that he had a soul to suffer.

Surely Zeus, the All Powerful, ruler of Olympus, would have compassion on Man? But Prometheus looked to Zeus in vain; compassion he had none. Then, in infinite pity, Prometheus bethought himself of a power belonging to the gods alone and unshared by any living creature on the earth.

"We shall give Fire to the Man whom we have made," he said to Epimethus. To Epimethus this seemed an impossibility, but to Prometheus nothing was impossible. He bided his time and, unseen by the gods, he made his way into Olympus, lighted a hollow torch with a spark from the chariot of the Sun and hastened back to earth with this royal gift to Man. Assuredly no other gift could have brought him more completely the empire that has since been his. No longer did he tremble and cower in the darkness of caves when Zeus hurled his lightnings across the sky. No more did he dread the animals that hunted him and drove him in terror before them.

Armed with fire, the beasts became his vassals. With fire he forged weapons, defied the frost and cold, coined money, made implements for tillage, introduced the arts, and was able to destroy as well as to create.

From his throne on Olympus, Zeus looked down on the earth and saw, with wonder, airy columns of blue-grey smoke that curled upwards to the sky. He watched more closely, and realised with terrible wrath that the moving flowers of red and gold that he saw in that land that the Titans shared with men, came from fire, that had hitherto been the gods' own sacred power. Speedily he assembled a council of the gods to mete out to Prometheus a punishment fit for the blasphemous daring of his crime. This council decided at length to create a thing that should for evermore charm the souls and hearts of men, and yet, for evermore, be man's undoing.

To Vulcan, god of fire, whose province Prometheus had insulted, was given the work of fashioning out of clay and water the creature by which the honour of the gods was to be avenged. "The lame Vulcan," says Hesiod, poet of Greek mythology, "formed out of the earth an image resembling a chaste virgin. Pallas Athené, of the blue eyes, hastened to ornament her and to robe her in a white tunic. She dressed on the crown of her head a long veil, skilfully fashioned and admirable to see; she crowned her forehead with graceful garlands of newly-opened flowers and a golden diadem that the lame Vulcan, the illustrious god, had made with his own hands to please the puissant Jove. On this crown Vulcan had chiselled the innumerable animals that the continents and the sea nourish in their bosoms, all endowed with a marvellous grace and apparently alive. When he had finally completed, instead of some useful work, this illustrious masterpiece, he brought into the assembly this virgin, proud of the ornaments with which she had been decked by the blue-eyed goddess, daughter of a powerful sire." To this beautiful creature, destined by the gods to be man's destroyer, each of them gave a gift. From Aphrodite she got beauty, from Apollo music, from Hermes the gift of a winning tongue. And when all that great company in Olympus had bestowed their gifts, they named the woman Pandora—"Gifted by all the Gods." Thus equipped for victory, Pandora was led by Hermes to the world that was thenceforward to be her home. As a gift from the gods she was presented to Prometheus.

But Prometheus, gazing in wonder at the violet blue eyes bestowed by Aphrodite, that looked wonderingly back into his own as if they were indeed as innocent as two violets wet with the morning dew, hardened his great heart, and would have none of her. As a hero—a worthy descendant of Titans—said in later years, "Timeo Danaos et dona ferentes,"—"I fear the Greeks, even when they bring gifts." And Prometheus, the greatly-daring, knowing that he merited the anger of the gods, saw treachery in a gift outwardly so perfect. Not only would he not accept this exquisite creature for his own, but he hastened to caution his brother also to refuse her.

But well were they named Prometheus (Forethought) and Epimethus (Afterthought). For Epimethus it was enough to look at this peerless woman, sent from the gods, for him to love her and to believe in her utterly. She was the fairest thing on earth, worthy indeed of the deathless gods who had created her. Perfect, too, was the happiness that she brought with her to Epimethus. Before her coming, as he well knew now, the fair world had been incomplete. Since she came the fragrant flowers had grown more sweet for him, the song of the birds more full of melody. He found new life in Pandora and marvelled how his brother could ever have fancied that she could bring to the world aught but peace and joyousness.

Now when the gods had entrusted to the Titan brothers the endowment of all living things upon the earth, they had been careful to withhold everything that might bring into the world pain, sickness, anxiety, bitterness of heart, remorse, or soul-crushing sorrow. All these hurtful things were imprisoned in a coffer which was given into the care of the trusty Epimethus.

To Pandora the world into which she came was all fresh, all new, quite full of unexpected joys and delightful surprises. It was a world of mystery, but mystery of which her great, adoring, simple Titan held the golden key. When she saw the coffer which never was opened, what then more natural than that she should ask Epimethus what it contained? But the contents were known only to the gods. Epimethus was unable to answer. Day by day, the curiosity of Pandora increased. To her the gods had never given anything but good. Surely there must be here gifts more precious still. What if the Olympians had destined her to be the one to open the casket, and had sent her to earth in order that she might bestow on this dear world, on the men who lived on it, and on her own magnificent Titan, happiness and blessings which only the minds of gods could have conceived? Thus did there come a day when Pandora, unconscious instrument in the hands of a vengeful Olympian, in all faith, and with the courage that is born of faith and of love, opened the lid of the prison-house of evil. And as from coffers in the old Egyptian tombs, the live plague can still rush forth and slay, the long-imprisoned evils rushed forth upon the fair earth and on the human beings who lived on it—malignant, ruthless, fierce, treacherous, and cruel—poisoning, slaying, devouring. Plague and pestilence and murder, envy and malice and revenge and all viciousness—an ugly wolf-pack indeed was that one let loose by Pandora. Terror, doubt, misery, had all rushed straightway to attack her heart, while the evils of which she had never dreamed stung mind and soul into dismay and horror, when, by hastily shutting the lid of the coffer, she tried to undo the evil she had done.

And lo, she found that the gods had imprisoned one good gift only in this Inferno of horrors and of ugliness. In the world there had never been any need of Hope. What work was there for Hope to do where all was perfect, and where each creature possessed the desire of body and of heart? Therefore Hope was thrust into the chest that held the evils, a star in a black night, a lily growing on a dung-heap. And as Pandora, white-lipped and trembling, looked into the otherwise empty box, courage came back to her heart, and Epimethus let fall to his side the arm that would have slain the woman of his love because there came to him, like a draught of wine to a warrior spent in battle, an imperial vision of the sons of men through all the aeons to come, combatting all evils of body and of soul, going on conquering and to conquer. Thus, saved by Hope, the Titan and the woman faced the future, and for them the vengeance of the gods was stayed.

"Yet I argue notAgainst Heav'n's hand or will, nor bate a jotOf heart or hope; but still bear up and steerRight onward."

So spoke Milton, the blind Titan of the seventeenth century; and Shakespeare says:

"True hope is swift, and flies with swallow's wings;Kings it makes gods, and meaner creatures kings."

Upon the earth, and on the children of men who were as gods in their knowledge and mastery of the force of fire, Jupiter had had his revenge. For Prometheus he reserved another punishment. He, the greatly-daring, once the dear friend and companion of Zeus himself, was chained to a rock on Mount Caucasus by the vindictive deity. There, on a dizzy height, his body thrust against the sun-baked rock, Prometheus had to endure the torment of having a foul-beaked vulture tear out his liver, as though he were a piece of carrion lying on the mountain side. All day, while the sun mercilessly smote him and the blue sky turned from red to black before his pain-racked eyes, the torture went on. Each night, when the filthy bird of prey that worked the will of the gods spread its dark wings and flew back to its eyrie, the Titan endured the cruel mercy of having his body grow whole once more. But with daybreak there came again the silent shadow, the smell of the unclean thing, and again with fierce beak and talons the vulture greedily began its work.

Thirty thousand years was the time of his sentence, and yet Prometheus knew that at any moment he could have brought his torment to an end. A secret was his—a mighty secret, the revelation of which would have brought him the mercy of Zeus and have reinstated him in the favour of the all-powerful god. Yet did he

6

prefer to endure his agonies rather than to free himself by bowing to the desires of a tyrant who had caused Man to be made, yet denied to Man those gifts that made him nobler than the beasts and raised him almost to the heights of the Olympians. Thus for him the weary centuries dragged by—in suffering that knew no respite—in endurance that the gods might have ended. Prometheus had brought an imperial gift to the men that he had made, and imperially he paid the penalty.

"Three thousand years of sleep-unsheltered hours,And moments aye divided by keen pangsTill they seemed years, torture and solitude,Scorn and despair,—these are mine empire.More glorious far than that which thou surveyestFrom thine unenvied throne, O, Mighty God!Almighty, had I deigned to share the shameOf thine ill tyranny, and hung not hereNailed to this wall of eagle-baffling mountain,Black, wintry, dead, unmeasured; without herb,Insect, or beast, or shape or sound of life.Ah me! alas, pain, pain ever, for ever!"

SHELLEY.

"Titan! to whose immortal eyesThe sufferings of mortalitySeen in their sad reality, Were not as things that gods despise;What was thy pity's recompense?A silent suffering, and intense;The rock, the vulture, and the chain,All that the proud can feel of pain,The agony they do not show,The suffocating sense of woe,Which speaks but in its loneliness,And then is jealous lest the skyShould have a listener, nor will sighUntil its voice is echoless."

BYRON.

"Yet, I am still Prometheus, wiser grownBy years of solitude,—that holds apartThe past and future, giving the soul roomTo search into itself,—and long communeWith this eternal silence;—more a god,In my long-suffering and strength to meetWith equal front the direst shafts of fate,Than thou in thy faint-hearted despotism ...Therefore, great heart, bear up! thou art but typeOf what all lofty spirits endure that fainWould win men back to strength and peace through love:Each hath his lonely peak, and on each heartEnvy, or scorn or hatred tears lifelongWith vulture beak; yet the high soul is left;And faith, which is but hope grown wise, and loveAnd patience, which at last shall overcome."

LOWELL.

PYGMALION

In days when the world was young and when the gods walked on the earth, there reigned over the island of Cyprus a sculptor-king, and king of sculptors, named Pygmalion. In the language of our own day, we should call him "wedded to his art." In woman he only saw the bane of man. Women, he believed, lured men from the paths to which their destiny called them. While man walked alone, he walked free—he had given no "hostages to fortune." Alone, man could live for his art, could combat every danger that beset him, could escape, unhampered, from every pitfall in life. But woman was the ivy that clings to the oak, and throttles the oak in the end. No woman, vowed Pygmalion, should ever hamper him. And so at length he came to hate women, and, free of heart and mind, his genius wrought such great things that he became a very perfect sculptor. He had one passion, a passion for his art, and that sufficed him. Out of great rough blocks of marble he would hew the most perfect semblance of men and of women, and of everything that seemed to him most beautiful and the most worth preserving.

When we look now at the Venus of Milo, at the Diana of Versailles, and at the Apollo Belvidere in the Vatican, we can imagine what were the greater things that the sculptor of Cyprus freed from the dead blocks of marble. One day as he chipped and chiselled there came to him, like the rough sketch of a great picture, the semblance of a woman. How it came he knew not. Only he knew that in that great mass of pure white stone there seemed to be imprisoned the exquisite image of a woman, a woman that he must set free. Slowly, gradually, the woman came. Soon he knew that she was the most beautiful thing that his art had ever wrought. All that he had ever thought that a woman *should* be, this woman was. Her form and features were all most perfect, and so perfect were they, that he felt very sure that, had she been a woman indeed, most perfect would have been the soul within. For her he worked as he had never worked before. There came, at last, a day when he felt that another touch would be insult to the exquisite thing he had created. He laid his chisel aside and sat down to gaze at the Perfect Woman. She seemed to gaze back at him. Her parted lips were ready to speak–to smile. Her hands were held out to hold his hands. Then Pygmalion covered his eyes. He, the hater of women, loved a woman–a woman of chilly marble. The women he had scorned were avenged.

Day by day his passion for the woman of his own creation grew and grew. His hands no longer wielded the chisel. They grew idle. He would stand under the great pines and gaze across the sapphire-blue sea, and dream strange dreams of a marble woman who walked across the waves with arms outstretched, with smiling lips, and who became a woman of warm flesh and blood when her bare feet touched the yellow sand, and the bright sun of Cyprus touched her marble hair and turned it into hair of living gold. Then he would hasten back to his studio to find the miracle still unaccomplished, and would passionately kiss the little cold hands, and lay beside the little cold feet the presents he knew that young girls loved–bright shells and exquisite precious stones, gorgeous-hued birds and fragrant flowers, shining amber, and beads that sparkled and flashed with all the most lovely combinations of colour that the mind of artist could devise. Yet more he did, for he spent vast sums on priceless pearls and hung them in her ears and upon her cold white breast; and the merchants wondered who could be the one upon whom Pygmalion lavished the money from his treasury.

To his divinity he gave a name–"Galatea"; and always on still nights the myriad silver stars would seem to breathe to him "Galatea" … and on those days when the tempests blew across the sandy wastes of Arabia and churned up the fierce white surf on the rocks of Cyprus, the very spirit of the storm seemed to moan through the crash of waves in longing, hopeless and unutterable–"Galatea!… Galatea!…" For her he decked a couch with Tyrian purple, and on the softest of pillows he laid the beautiful head of the marble woman that he loved.

So the time wore on until the festival of Aphrodite drew near. Smoke from many altars curled out to sea, the odour of incense mingled with the fragrance of the great pine trees, and garlanded victims lowed and bleated as they were led to the sacrifice. As the leader of his people, Pygmalion faithfully and perfectly performed all his part in the solemnities and at last he was left beside the altar to pray alone. Never before had his words faltered as he laid his petitions before the gods, but on this day he spoke not as a sculptor-king, but as a child who was half afraid of what he asked.

"O Aphrodite!" he said, "who can do all things, give me, I pray you, one like my Galatea for my wife!"

"Give me my Galatea," he dared not say; but Aphrodite knew well the words he would fain have uttered, and smiled to think how Pygmalion at last was on his knees. In token that his prayer was answered, three times she made the flames on the altar shoot up in a fiery point, and Pygmalion went home, scarcely daring to hope, not allowing his gladness to conquer his fear.

The shadows of evening were falling as he went into the room that he had made sacred to Galatea. On the purple-covered couch she lay, and as he entered it seemed as though she met his eyes with her own; almost it seemed that she smiled at him in welcome. He quickly went up to her and, kneeling by her side, he pressed his lips on those lips of chilly marble. So many times he had done it before, and always it was as though the icy lips that could never live sent their chill right through his heart, but now it surely seemed to him that the lips were cold no longer. He felt one of the little hands, and no more did it remain heavy and cold and stiff in his touch, but lay in his own hand, soft and living and warm. He softly laid his fingers on the marble hair, and lo, it was the soft and wavy burnished golden hair of his desire. Again, reverently as he had laid his offerings that day on the altar of Venus, Pygmalion kissed her lips. And then did Galatea, with warm and rosy cheeks, widely open her eyes, like pools in a dark mountain stream on which the sun is shining, and gaze with timid gladness into his own.

There are no after tales of Pygmalion and Galatea. We only know that their lives were happy and that to them was born a son, Paphos, from whom the city sacred to Aphrodite received its name. Perhaps Aphrodite may have smiled sometimes to watch Pygmalion, once the scorner of women, the adoring servant of the woman that his own hands had first designed.

THEN PYGMALION COVERED HIS EYES

PHAETON

"The road, to drive on which unskilled were Phaeton's hands."

DANTE—*Purgatorio.*

To Apollo, the sun-god, and Clymene, a beautiful ocean-nymph, there was born in the pleasant land of Greece a child to whom was given the name of Phaeton, the Bright and Shining One. The rays of the sun seemed to live in the curls of the fearless little lad, and when at noon other children would seek the cool shade of the cypress groves, Phaeton would hold his head aloft and gaze fearlessly up at the brazen sky from whence fierce heat beat down upon his golden head.

"Behold, my father drives his chariot across the heavens!" he proudly proclaimed. "In a little while I, also, will drive the four snow-white steeds."

His elders heard the childish boast with a smile, but when Epaphos, half-brother to Apollo, had listened to it many times and beheld the child, Phaeton, grow into an arrogant lad who held himself as though he were indeed one of the Immortals, anger grew in his heart. One day he turned upon Phaeton and spoke in fierce scorn:

"Dost say thou art son of a god? A shameless boaster and a liar art thou! Hast ever spoken to thy divine sire? Give us some proof of thy sonship! No more child of the glorious Apollo art thou than are the vermin his children, that the sun breeds in the dust at my feet."

For a moment, before the cruel taunt, the lad was stricken into silence, and then, his pride aflame, his young voice shaking with rage and with bitter shame, he cried aloud: "Thou, Epaphos, art the liar. I have but to ask my father, and thou shalt see me drive his golden chariot across the sky."

To his mother he hastened, to get balm for his hurt pride, as many a time he had got it for the little bodily wounds of childhood, and with bursting heart he poured forth his story.

"True it is," he said, "that my father has never deigned to speak to me. Yet I know, because thou hast told me so, that he is my sire. And now my word is pledged. Apollo must let me drive his steeds, else I am for evermore branded braggart and liar, and shamed amongst men."

Clymene listened with grief to his complaint. He was so young, so gallant, so foolish.

"Truly thou art the son of Apollo," she said, "and oh, son of my heart, thy beauty is his, and thy pride the pride of a son of the gods. Yet only partly a god art thou, and though thy proud courage would dare all things, it were mad folly to think of doing what a god alone can do."

But at last she said to him, "Naught that I can say is of any avail. Go, seek thy father, and ask him what thou wilt." Then she told him how he might find the place in the east where Apollo rested ere the labours of the day began, and with eager gladness Phaeton set out upon his journey. A long way he travelled, with never a stop, yet when the glittering dome and jewelled turrets and minarets of the Palace of the Sun came into view, he forgot his weariness and hastened up the steep ascent to the home of his father.

Phœbus Apollo, clad in purple that glowed like the radiance of a cloud in the sunset sky, sat upon his golden throne. The Day, the Month, and the Year stood by him, and beside them were the Hours. Spring was there, her head wreathed with flowers; Summer, crowned with ripened grain; Autumn, with his feet empurpled by the juice of the grapes; and Winter, with hair all white and stiff with hoar-frost. And when Phaeton walked up the golden steps that led to his father's throne, it seemed as though incarnate Youth had come to join the court of the god of the Sun, and that Youth was so beautiful a thing that it must surely live forever. Proudly did Apollo know him for his son, and when the boy looked in his eyes with the arrogant fearlessness of boyhood, the god greeted him kindly and asked him to tell him why he came, and what was his petition.

As to Clymene, so also to Apollo, Phaeton told his tale, and his father listened, half in pride and amusement, half in puzzled vexation. When the boy stopped, and then breathlessly, with shining eyes and flushed cheeks, ended up his story with: "And, O light of the boundless world, if I am indeed thy son, let it be as I have said, and for one day only let me drive thy chariot across the heavens!" Apollo shook his head and answered very gravely:

"In truth thou art my dear son," he said, "and by the dreadful Styx, the river of the dead, I swear that I will give thee any gift that thou dost name and that will give proof that thy father is the immortal Apollo. But never to thee nor to any other, be he mortal or immortal, shall I grant the boon of driving my chariot."

But the boy pled on:

"I am shamed for ever, my father," he said. "Surely thou wouldst not have son of thine proved liar and braggart?"

"Not even the gods themselves can do this thing," answered Apollo. "Nay, not even the almighty Zeus. None but I, Phœbus Apollo, may drive the flaming chariot of the sun, for the way is beset with dangers and none know it but I."

"Only tell me the way, my father!" cried Phaeton. "So soon I could learn."

Half in sadness, Apollo smiled.

"The first part of the way is uphill," he said. "So steep it is that only very slowly can my horses climb it. High in the heavens is the middle, so high that even I grow dizzy when I look down upon the earth and the sea. And the last piece of the way is a precipice that rushes so steeply downward that my hands can scarce check the mad rush of my galloping horses. And all the while, the heaven is spinning round, and the stars with it. By the horns of the Bull I have to drive, past the Archer whose bow is taut and ready to slay, close to where the Scorpion stretches out its arms and the great Crab's claws grope for a prey...."

"I fear none of these things, oh my father!" cried Phaeton. "Grant that for one day only I drive thy white-maned steeds!"

Very pitifully Apollo looked at him, and for a little space he was silent.

"The little human hands," he said at length, "the little human frame!—and with them the soul of a god. The pity of it, my son. Dost not know that the boon that thou dost crave from me is Death?"

"Rather Death than Dishonour," said Phaeton, and proudly he added, "For once would I drive like the god, my father. I have no fear."

So was Apollo vanquished, and Phaeton gained his heart's desire.

From the courtyard of the Palace the four white horses were led, and they pawed the air and neighed aloud in the glory of their strength. They drew the chariot whose axle and pole and wheels were of gold, with spokes of silver, while inside were rows of diamonds and of chrysolites that gave dazzling reflection of the sun. Then Apollo anointed the face of Phaeton with a powerful essence that might keep him from being smitten by the flames, and upon his head he placed the rays of the sun. And then the stars went away, even to the Daystar that went last of all, and, at Apollo's signal, Aurora, the rosy-fingered, threw open the purple gates of the east, and Phaeton saw a path of pale rose-colour open before him.

With a cry of exultation, the boy leapt into the chariot and laid hold of the golden reins. Barely did he hear Apollo's parting words: "Hold fast the reins, and spare the whip. All thy strength will be wanted to hold the horses in. Go not too high nor too low. The middle course is safest and best. Follow, if thou canst, in the old tracks of my chariot wheels!" His glad voice of thanks for the godlike boon rang back to where Apollo stood and watched him vanishing into the dawn that still was soft in hue as the feathers on the breast of a dove.

Uphill at first the white steeds made their way, and the fire from their nostrils tinged with flame-colour the dark clouds that hung over the land and the sea. With rapture, Phaeton felt that truly he was the son of a god, and that at length he was enjoying his heritage. The day for which, through all his short life, he had longed, had come at last. He was driving the chariot whose progress even now was awaking the sleeping earth. The radiance from its wheels and from the rays he wore round his head was painting the clouds, and he laughed aloud in rapture as he saw, far down below, the sea and the rivers he had bathed in as a human boy, mirroring the green and rose and purple, and gold and silver, and fierce crimson, that he, Phaeton, was placing in the sky. The grey mist rolled from the mountain tops at his desire. The white fog rolled up from the valleys. All living things awoke; the flowers opened their petals; the grain grew golden; the fruit grew ripe. Could but Epaphos see him now! Surely he must see him, and realise that not Apollo but Phaeton was guiding the horses of his father, driving the chariot of the Sun.

Quicker and yet more quick grew the pace of the white-maned steeds. Soon they left the morning breezes behind, and very soon they knew that these were not the hands of the god, their master, that held the golden reins. Like an air-ship without its accustomed ballast, the chariot rolled unsteadily, and not only the boy's light weight but his light hold on their bridles made them grow mad with a lust for speed. The white foam flew from their mouths like the spume from the giant waves of a furious sea, and their pace was swift as that of a bolt that is cast by the arm of Zeus.

Yet Phaeton had no fear, and when they heard him shout in rapture, "Quicker still, brave ones! more swiftly still!" it made them speed onwards, madly, blindly, with the headlong rush of a storm.

17

There was no hope for them to keep on the beaten track, and soon Phaeton had his rapture checked by the terrible realisation that they had strayed far out of the course and that his hands were not strong enough to guide them. Close to the Great Bear and the Little Bear they passed, and these were scorched with heat. The Serpent which, torpid, chilly and harmless, lies coiled round the North Pole, felt a warmth that made it grow fierce and harmful again. Downward, ever downward galloped the maddened horses, and soon Phaeton saw the sea as a shield of molten brass, and the earth so near that all things on it were visible. When they passed the Scorpion and only just missed destruction from its menacing fangs, fear entered into the boy's heart. His mother had spoken truth. He was only partly a god, and he was very, very young. In impotent horror he tugged at the reins to try to check the horses' descent, then, forgetful of Apollo's warning, he smote them angrily. But anger met anger, and the fury of the immortal steeds had scorn for the wrath of a mortal boy. With a great toss of their mighty heads they had torn the guiding reins from his grasp, and as he stood, giddily swaying from side to side, Phaeton knew that the boon he had craved from his father must in truth be death for him.

And, lo, it was a hideous death, for with eyes that were like flames that burned his brain, the boy beheld the terrible havoc that his pride had wrought. That blazing chariot of the Sun made the clouds smoke, and dried up all the rivers and water-springs. Fire burst from the mountain tops, great cities were destroyed. The beauty of the earth was ravished, woods and meadows and all green and pleasant places were laid waste. The harvests perished, the flocks and they who had herded them lay dead. Over Libya the horses took him, and the desert of Libya remains a barren wilderness to this day, while those sturdy Ethiopians who survived are black even now as a consequence of that cruel heat. The Nile changed its course in order to escape, and nymphs and nereids in terror sought for the sanctuary of some watery place that had escaped destruction. The face of the burned and blackened earth, where the bodies of thousands of human beings lay charred to ashes, cracked and sent dismay to Pluto by the lurid light that penetrated even to his throne.

All this Phaeton saw, saw in impotent agony of soul. His boyish folly and pride had been great, but the excruciating anguish that made him shed tears of blood, was indeed a punishment even too heavy for an erring god.

From the havoc around her, the Earth at last looked up, and with blackened face and blinded eyes, and in a voice that was harsh and very, very weary, she called to Zeus to look down from Olympus and behold the ruin that had been wrought by the chariot of the Sun. And Zeus, the cloud-gatherer, looked down and beheld. And at the sight of that piteous devastation his brow grew dark, and terrible was his wrath against him who had held the reins of the chariot. Calling upon Apollo and all the other gods to witness him, he seized a lightning bolt, and for a moment the deathless Zeus and all the dwellers in Olympus looked on the fiery chariot in which stood the swaying, slight, lithe figure of a young lad, blinded with horror, shaken with agony. Then, from his hand, Zeus cast the bolt, and the chariot was dashed into fragments, and Phaeton, his golden hair ablaze, fell, like a bright shooting star, from the heavens above, into the river Eridanus. The steeds returned to their master, Apollo, and in rage and grief Apollo lashed them. Angrily, too, and very rebelliously did he speak of the punishment meted to his son by the ruler of the Immortals. Yet in truth the punishment was a merciful one. Phaeton was only half a god, and no human life were fit to live after the day of dire anguish that had been his.

Bitter was the mourning of Clymene over her beautiful only son, and so ceaselessly did his three sisters, the Heliades, weep for their brother, that the gods turned them into poplar trees that grew by the bank of the river, and, when still they wept, their tears turned into precious amber as they fell. Yet another mourned for Phaeton— Phaeton "dead ere his prime." Cycnus, King of Liguria, had dearly loved the gallant boy, and again and yet again he dived deep in the river and brought forth the charred fragments of what had once been the beautiful son of a god, and gave to them honourable burial. Yet he could not rest satisfied that he had won all that remained of his friend from the river's bed, and so he continued to haunt the stream, ever diving, ever searching, until the gods grew weary of his restless sorrow and changed him into a swan.

And still we see the swan sailing mournfully along, like a white-sailed barque that is bearing the body of a king to its rest, and ever and anon plunging deep into the water as though the search for the boy who would fain have been a god were never to come to an end.

To Phaeton the Italian Naiades reared a tomb, and inscribed on the stone these words:

"Driver of Phœbus' chariot, Phaëton, Struck by Jove's thunder, rests beneath this stone, He could not rule his father's car of fire, Yet was it much, so nobly to aspire."

OVID.

ENDYMION

To the modern popular mind perhaps none of the goddesses of Greece—not even Venus herself—has more appeal than has the huntress goddess, Diana. Those who know but little of ancient statuary can still brighten to intelligent recognition of the huntress with her quiver and her little stag when they meet with them in picture gallery or in suburban garden. That unlettered sportsman in weather-worn pink, slowly riding over the fragrant dead leaves by the muddy roadside on this chill, grey morning, may never have heard of Artemis, but he is quite ready to make intelligent reference to Diana to the handsome young sportswoman whom he finds by the covert side; and Sir Walter's Diana Vernon has helped the little-read public to realise that the original Diana was a goddess worthy of being sponsor to one of the finest heroines of fiction.

But not to the sportsman alone, but also to the youth or maid who loves the moon—they know not why—to those whom the shadows of the trees on a woodland path at night mean a grip of the heart, while "pale Dian" scuds over the dark clouds that are soaring far beyond the tree-tops and is peeping, chaste and pale, through the branches of the firs and giant pines, there is something arresting, enthralling, in the thought of the goddess Diana who now has for hunting-ground the blue firmament of heaven where the pale Pleiades

"Glitter like a swarm of fire-flies tangled in a silver braid."

TENNYSON.

"She gleans her silvan trophies; down the woldShe hears the sobbing of the stags that fleeMixed with the music of the hunting roll'd,But her delight is all in archery,And naught of ruth and pity wotteth sheMore than her hounds that follow on the flight;The goddess draws a golden bow of mightAnd thick she rains the gentle shafts that slay.She tosses loose her locks upon the night,And through the dim wood Dian threads her way."

21

ANDREW LANG.

Again and again in mythological history we come on stories of the goddess, sometimes under her best known name of Diana, sometimes under her older Greek name of Artemis, and now and again as Selene, the moon-goddess, the Luna of the Romans. Her twin brother was Apollo, god of the sun, and with him she shared the power of unerringly wielding a bow and of sending grave plagues and pestilences, while both were patrons of music and of poetry.

When the sun-god's golden chariot had driven down into the west, then would his sister's noiseless-footed silver steeds be driven across the sky, while the huntress shot from her bow at will silent arrows that would slay without warning a joyous young mother with her newly-born babe, or would wantonly pierce, with a lifelong pain, the heart of some luckless mortal.

Now one night as she passed Mount Latmos, there chanced to be a shepherd lad lying asleep beside his sleeping flock. Many times had Endymion watched the goddess from afar, half afraid of one so beautiful and yet so ruthless, but never before had Diana realised the youth's wonderful beauty. She checked her hounds when they would have swept on in their chase through the night, and stood beside Endymion. She judged him to be as perfect as her own brother, Apollo—yet more perfect, perhaps, for on his upturned sleeping face was the silver glamour of her own dear moon. Fierce and burning passion could come with the sun's burning rays, but love that came in the moon's pale light was passion mixed with gramarye. She gazed for long, and when, in his sleep, Endymion smiled, she knelt beside him and, stooping, gently kissed his lips. The touch of a moonbeam on a sleeping rose was no more gentle than was Diana's touch, yet it was sufficient to wake Endymion. And as, while one's body sleeps on, one's half-waking mind, now and again in a lifetime seems to realise an ecstasy of happiness so perfect that one dares not wake lest, by waking, the wings of one's realised ideal should slip between grasping fingers and so escape forever, so did Endymion realise the kiss of the goddess. But before

22

his sleepy eyes could be his senses' witnesses, Diana had hastened away. Endymion, springing to his feet, saw only his sleeping flock, nor did his dogs awake when he heard what seemed to him to be the baying of hounds in full cry in a forest far up the mountain. Only to his own heart did he dare to whisper what was this wonderful thing that he believed had befallen him, and although he laid himself down, hoping that once again this miracle might be granted to him, no miracle came; nor could he sleep, so great was his longing.

All the next day, through the sultry hours while Apollo drove his chariot of burnished gold through the land, Endymion, as he watched his flocks, tried to dream his dream once more, and longed for the day to end and the cool, dark night to return. When night came he tried to lie awake and see what might befall, but when kind sleep had closed his tired eyes,

"There came a lovely vision of a maid,Who seemed to step as from a golden carOut of the low-hung moon."

LEWIS MORRIS.

Always she kissed him, yet when her kiss awoke him he never could see anything more tangible than a shaft of silver moonlight on the moving bushes of the mountain side, never hear anything more real than the far-away echo of the baying of pursuing hounds, and if, with eager, greatly-daring eyes, he looked skywards, a dark cloud, so it seemed to him, would always hasten to hide the moon from his longing gaze.

In this manner time passed on. The days of Endymion were filled by longing day-dreams. His sleeping hours ever brought him ecstasy. Ever, too, to the goddess, the human being that she loved seemed to her to grow more precious. For her all the joy of day and of night was concentrated in the moments she spent by the side of the sleeping Endymion. The flocks of the shepherd flourished like those of no other herd. No wild beast dared come near them; no storm nor disease assailed them. Yet for Endymion the things of earth no longer held any value. He lived only for his dear dream's sake. Had he been permitted to grow old and worn and tired, and still a dreamer, who knows how his story might have ended? But to Diana there came the fear that with age his beauty might wane, and from her father, Zeus, she obtained for the one she loved the gifts of unending youth and of eternal sleep.

There came a night when the dreams of Endymion had no end. That was a night when the moon made for herself broad silver paths across the sea, from far horizon to the shore where the little waves lapped and curled in a radiant, ever-moving silver fringe. Silver also were the leaves of the forest trees, and between the branches of the solemn cypresses and of the stately dark pines, Diana shot her silver arrows. No baying of hounds came then to make Endymion's flocks move uneasily in their sleep, but the silver stars seemed to sing in unison together. While still those gentle lips touched his, hands as gentle lifted up the sleeping Endymion and bore him to a secret cave in Mount Latmos. And there, for evermore, she came to kiss the mouth of her sleeping lover. There, forever, slept Endymion, happy in the perfect bliss of dreams that have no ugly awaking, of an ideal love that knows no ending.

SHE CHECKED HER HOUNDS, AND STOOD BESIDE ENDYMION

ORPHEUS

"Orpheus with his lute made trees,And the mountain tops that freeze,Bow themselves when he did sing;To his music plants and flowersEver sprung, as sun and showersThere had made a lasting spring.Everything that heard him play,Even the billows of the sea,Hung their heads, and then lay by,In sweet music is such art,Killing care and grief of heartFall asleep, or hearing die."

SHAKESPEARE.

"Are we not all lovers as Orpheus was, loving what is gone from us forever, and seeking it vainly in the solitudes and wilderness of the mind, and crying to Eurydice to come again? And are we not all foolish as Orpheus was, hoping by the agony of love and the ecstasy of will to win back Eurydice; and do we not all fail, as Orpheus failed, because we forsake the way of the other world for the way of this world?"

FIONA MACLEOD.

It is the custom nowadays for scientists and for other scholarly people to take hold of the old myths, to take them to pieces, and to find some deep, hidden meaning in each part of the story. So you will find that some will tell you that Orpheus is the personification of the winds which "tear up trees as they course along, chanting their wild music," and that Eurydice is the morning "with its short-lived beauty." Others say that Orpheus is "the mythological expression of the delight which music gives to the primitive races," while yet others accept without hesitation the idea that Orpheus is the sun that, when day is done, plunges into the black abyss of night, in the vain hope of overtaking his lost bride, Eurydice, the rosy dawn. And, whether they be right or wrong, it would seem that the sadness that comes to us sometimes as the day dies and the last of the sun's rays vanish to leave the hills and valleys dark and cold, the sorrowful feeling that we cannot understand when, in country places, we hear music coming from far away, or listen to

27

the plaintive song of the bird, are things that very specially belong to the story of Orpheus.

In the country of Thrace, surrounded by all the best gifts of the gods, Orpheus was born. His father was Apollo, the god of music and of song, his mother the muse Calliope. Apollo gave his little son a lyre, and himself taught him how to play it. It was not long before all the wild things in the woods of Thrace crept out from the green trees and thick undergrowth, and from the holes and caves in the rocks, to listen to the music that the child's fingers made. The coo of the dove to his mate, the flute-clear trill of the blackbird, the song of the lark, the liquid carol of the nightingale— all ceased when the boy made music. The winds that whispered their secrets to the trees owned him for their lord, and the proudest trees of the forest bowed their heads that they might not miss one exquisite sigh that his fingers drew from the magical strings. Nor man nor beast lived in his day that he could not sway by the power of his melody. He played a lullaby, and all things slept. He played a love-lilt, and the flowers sprang up in full bloom from the cold earth, and the dreaming red rosebud opened wide her velvet petals, and all the land seemed full of the loving echoes of the lilt he played. He played a war-march, and, afar off, the sleeping tyrants of the forest sprang up, wide awake, and bared their angry teeth, and the untried youths of Thrace ran to beg their fathers to let them taste battle, while the scarred warriors felt on their thumbs the sharpness of their sword blades, and smiled, well content. While he played it would seem as though the very stones and rocks gained hearts. Nay, the whole heart of the universe became one great, palpitating, beautiful thing, an instrument from whose trembling strings was drawn out the music of Orpheus.

He rose to great power, and became a mighty prince of Thrace. Not his lute alone, but he himself played on the heart of the fair Eurydice and held it captive. It seemed as though, when they became man and wife, all happiness must be theirs. But although Hymen, the god of marriage, himself came to bless them on the day they wed, the omens on that day were against them. The torch that

Hymen carried had no golden flame, but sent out pungent black smoke that made their eyes water. They feared they knew not what; but when, soon afterwards, as Eurydice wandered with the nymphs, her companions, through the blue-shadowed woods of Thrace, the reason was discovered. A bold shepherd, who did not know her for a princess, saw Eurydice, and no sooner saw her than he loved her. He ran after her to proclaim to her his love, and she, afraid of his wild uncouthness, fled before him. She ran, in her terror, too swiftly to watch whither she went, and a poisonous snake that lurked amongst the fern bit the fair white foot that flitted, like a butterfly, across it. In agonised suffering Eurydice died. Her spirit went to the land of the Shades, and Orpheus was left broken-hearted.

The sad winds that blow at night across the sea, the sobbing gales that tell of wreck and death, the birds that wail in the darkness for their mates, the sad, soft whisper of the aspen leaves and the leaves of the heavy clad blue-black cypresses, all now were hushed, for greater than all, more full of bitter sorrow than any, arose the music of Orpheus, a long-drawn sob from a broken heart in the Valley of the Shadow of Death.

Grief came alike to gods and to men as they listened, but no comfort came to him from the expression of his sorrow. At length, when to bear his grief longer was impossible for him, Orpheus wandered to Olympus, and there besought Zeus to give him permission to seek his wife in the gloomy land of the Shades. Zeus, moved by his anguish, granted the permission he sought, but solemnly warned him of the terrible perils of his undertaking.

But the love of Orpheus was too perfect to know any fear; thankfully he hastened to the dark cave on the side of the promontory of Taenarus, and soon arrived at the entrance of Hades. Stark and grim was the three-headed watchdog, Cerberus, which guarded the door, and with the growls and the furious roaring of a wild beast athirst for its prey it greeted Orpheus. But Orpheus touched his lute, and the brute, amazed, sank into silence. And still he played, and the dog would gently have licked the player's feet, and looked up in his face with its savage eyes full of the light that we see in the eyes of the dogs of this earth as they gaze with love at their masters. On, then, strode Orpheus, playing still, and the melody he drew from his lute passed before him into the realms of Pluto.

Surely never were heard such strains. They told of perfect, tender love, of unending longing, of pain too great to end with death. Of all the beauties of the earth they sang—of the sorrow of the world—of all the world's desire—of things past—of things to come. And ever, through the song that the lute sang, there came, like a thread of silver that is woven in a black velvet pall, a limpid melody. It was as though a bird sang in the mirk night, and it spoke of peace and of hope, and of joy that knows no ending.

Into the blackest depths of Hades the sounds sped on their way, and the hands of Time stood still. From his bitter task of trying to quaff the stream that ever receded from the parched and burning lips, Tantalus ceased for a moment. The ceaseless course of Ixion's wheel was stayed, the vulture's relentless beak no longer tore at the Titan's liver; Sisyphus gave up his weary task of rolling the stone and sat on the rock to listen, the Danaïdes rested from their labour of drawing water in a sieve. For the first time, the cheeks of the Furies were wet with tears, and the restless shades that came and went in the darkness, like dead autumn leaves driven by a winter gale, stood still to gaze and listen. Before the throne where Pluto and his queen Proserpine were seated, sable-clad and stern, the relentless Fates at their feet, Orpheus still played on. And to Proserpine then came the living remembrance of all the joys of her girlhood by the blue Ægean Sea in the fair island of Sicily. Again she knew the fragrance and the beauty of the flowers of spring. Even into Hades the scent of the violets seemed to come, and fresh in her heart was the sorrow that had been hers on the day on which the ruthless King of Darkness tore her from her mother and from all that she held most dear. Silent she sat beside her frowning, stern-faced lord, but her eyes grew dim.

When, with a quivering sigh, the music stopped, Orpheus fearlessly pled his cause. To let him have Eurydice, to give him back his more than life, to grant that he might lead her with him up to "the light of Heaven"—that was his prayer.

The eyes of Pluto and Proserpine did not dare to meet, yet with one accord was their answer given. Eurydice should be given back to him, but only on one condition. Not until he had reached the light of earth again was he to turn round and look upon the face for a sight of which his eyes were tired with longing. Eagerly Orpheus complied, and with a heart almost breaking with gladness he heard the call for Eurydice and turned to retrace his way, with the light footfall of the little feet that he adored making music behind him. Too good a thing it seemed—too unbelievable a joy. She was there— quite close to him. Their days of happiness were not ended. His love had won her back, even from the land of darkness. All that he had not told her of that love while yet she was on earth he would tell her now. All that he had failed in before, he would make perfect now. The little limping foot—how it made his soul overflow with adoring tenderness. So near she was, he might even touch her were he to stretch back his hand....

And then there came to him a hideous doubt. What if Pluto had played him false? What if there followed him not Eurydice, but a mocking shade? As he climbed the steep ascent that led upwards to the light, his fear grew more cruelly real. Almost he could imagine that her footsteps had stopped, that when he reached the light he would find himself left once more to his cruel loneliness. Too overwhelming for him was the doubt. So nearly there they were that the darkness was no longer that of night, but as that of evening when the long shadows fall upon the land, and there seemed no reason for Orpheus to wait.

Swiftly he turned, and found his wife behind him, but only for a moment she stayed. Her arms were thrown open and Orpheus would fain have grasped her in his own, but before they could touch each other Eurydice was borne from him, back into the darkness.

"Farewell!" she said—"Farewell!" and her voice was a sigh of hopeless grief. In mad desperation Orpheus sought to follow her, but his attempt was vain. At the brink of the dark, fierce-flooded Acheron the boat with its boatman, old Charon, lay ready to ferry across to the further shore those whose future lay in the land of Shades. To him ran Orpheus, in clamorous anxiety to undo the evil he had wrought. But Charon angrily repulsed him. There was no place for such as Orpheus in his ferry-boat. Those only who went, never to return, could find a passage there. For seven long days and seven longer nights Orpheus waited beside the river, hoping that Charon would relent, but at last hope died, and he sought the depths of the forests of Thrace, where trees and rocks and beasts and birds were all his friends.

He took his lyre again then and played:

"Such strains as would have won the earOf Pluto, to have quite set freeHis half-regained Eurydice."

MILTON.

Day and night he stayed in the shadow of the woodlands, all the sorrow of his heart expressing itself in the song of his lute. The fiercest beasts of the forest crawled to his feet and looked up at him with eyes full of pity. The song of the birds ceased, and when the wind moaned through the trees they echoed his cry, "Eurydice! Eurydice!"

In the dawning hours it would seem to him that he saw her again, flitting, a thing of mist and rising sun, across the dimness of the woods. And when evening came and all things rested, and the night called out the mystery of the forest, again he would see her. In the long blue shadows of the trees she would stand—up the woodland paths she walked, where her little feet fluttered the dry leaves as she passed. Her face was white as a lily in the moonlight, and ever she held out her arms to Orpheus:

"At that elm-vista's end I trace,Dimly thy sad leave-taking face,Eurydice! Eurydice!The tremulous leaves repeat to meEurydice! Eurydice!"

LOWELL.

For Orpheus it was a good day when Jason, chief of the Argonauts, sought him out to bid him come with the other heroes and aid in the quest of the Golden Fleece.

"Have I not had enough of toil and of weary wandering far and wide," sighed Orpheus. "In vain is the skill of the voice which my goddess mother gave me; in vain have I sung and laboured; in vain I went down to the dead, and charmed all the kings of Hades, to win back Eurydice, my bride. For I won her, my beloved, and lost her again the same day, and wandered away in my madness even to Egypt and the Libyan sands, and the isles of all the seas.... While I charmed in vain the hearts of men, and the savage forest beasts, and the trees, and the lifeless stones, with my magic harp and song, giving rest, but finding none."

But in the good ship *Argo*, Orpheus took his place with the others and sailed the watery ways, and the songs that Orpheus sang to his shipmates and that tell of all their great adventures are called the Songs of Orpheus, or the Orphics, to this day.

Many were the mishaps and disasters that his music warded off. With it he lulled monsters to sleep; more powerful to work magic on the hearts of men were his melodies than were the songs of the sirens when they tried to capture the Argonauts by their wiles, and in their downward, destroying rush his music checked mountains.

When the quest of the Argonauts was ended, Orpheus returned to his own land of Thrace. As a hero he had fought and endured hardship, but his wounded soul remained unhealed. Again the trees listened to the songs of longing. Again they echoed, "Eurydice! Eurydice!"

As he sat one day near a river in the stillness of the forest, there came from afar an ugly clamour of sound. It struck against the music of Orpheus' lute and slew it, as the coarse cries of the screaming gulls that fight for carrion slay the song of a soaring lark. It was the day of the feast of Bacchus, and through the woods poured Bacchus and his Bacchantes, a shameless rout, satyrs capering around them, centaurs neighing aloud. Long had the Bacchantes hated the loyal poet-lover of one fair woman whose dwelling was with the Shades. His ears were ever deaf to their passionate voices, his eyes blind to their passionate loveliness as they danced through the green trees, a riot of colour, of fierce beauty, of laughter and of mad song. Mad they were indeed this day, and in their madness the very existence of Orpheus was a thing not to be borne. At first they stoned him, but his music made the stones fall harmless at his feet. Then in a frenzy of cruelty, with the maniac lust to cause blood to flow, to know the joy of taking life, they threw themselves upon Orpheus and did him to death. From limb to limb they tore him, casting at last his head and his blood-stained lyre into the river. And still, as the water bore them on, the lyre murmured its last music and the white lips of Orpheus still breathed of her whom at last he had gone to join in the shadowy land, "Eurydice! Eurydice!"

"Combien d'autres sont morts de même! C'est la lutte éternelle de la force brutale contre l'intelligence douce et sublime inspirée du ciel, dont le royaume n'est pas de ce monde."

In the heavens, as a bright constellation called Lyra, or Orpheus, the gods placed his lute, and to the place of his martyrdom came the Muses, and with loving care carried the fragments of the massacred body to Libetlera, at the foot of Mount Olympus, and there buried them. And there, unto this day, more sweetly than at any other spot in any other land, the nightingale sings. For it sings of a love that knows no ending, of life after death, of a love so strong that it can conquer even Death, the all-powerful.

SWIFTLY HE TURNED, AND FOUND HIS WIFE BEHIND HIM

APOLLO AND DAPHNE

Conqueror of all conquerable earth, yet not always victorious over the heart of a maid was the golden-locked Apollo.

As mischievous Eros played one day with his bow and arrows, Apollo beheld him and spoke to him mockingly.

"What hast thou to do with the weapons of war, saucy lad?" he said. "Leave them for hands such as mine, that know full well how to wield them. Content thyself with thy torch, and kindle flames, if indeed thou canst, but such bolts as thy white young arms can drive will surely not bring scathe to god nor to man."

Then did the son of Aphrodite answer, and as he made answer he laughed aloud in his glee. "With thine arrows thou mayst strike all things else, great Apollo, a shaft of mine shall surely strike thy heart!"

Carefully, then, did Eros choose two arrows from his quiver. One, sharp-pointed and of gold, he fitted carefully to his bow, drew back the string until it was taut, and then let fly the arrow, that did not miss its mark, but flew straight to the heart of the sun-god. With the other arrow, blunt, and tipped with lead, he smote the beautiful Daphne, daughter of Peneus, the river-god. And then, full joyously did the boy-god laugh, for his roguish heart knew well that to him who was struck by the golden shaft must come the last pangs that have proved many a man's and many a god's undoing, while that leaden-tipped arrow meant to whomsoever it struck, a hatred of Love and an immunity from all the heart weakness that Love can bring. Those were the days when Apollo was young. Never before had he loved.

But as the first fierce storm that assails it bends the young, supple tree with its green budding leaves before its furious blast, so did the first love of Apollo bend low his adoring heart. All day as he held the golden reins of his chariot, until evening when its fiery wheels were cooled in the waters of the western seas, he thought of Daphne. All night he dreamed of her. But never did there come to Daphne a time when she loved Love for Love's sake. Never did she look with gentle eye on the golden-haired god whose face was as the face of all the exquisite things that the sunlight shows, remembered in a dream. Her only passion was a passion for the chase. One of Diana's nymphs was she, cold and pure and white in soul as the virgin goddess herself.

There came a day when Apollo could no longer put curbing hands on his fierce longing. The flames from his chariot still lingered in reflected glories on sea and hill and sky. The very leaves of the budding trees of spring were outlined in gold. And through the dim wood walked Daphne, erect and lithe and living as a sapling in the early spring.

With beseeching hands, Apollo followed her. A god was he, yet to him had come the vast humility of passionate intercession for the gift of love to a little nymph. She heard his steps behind her and turned round, proud and angry that one should follow her when she had not willed it.

"Stay!" he said, "daughter of Peneus. No foe am I, but thine own humble lover. To thee alone do I bow my head. To all others on earth am I conqueror and king."

But Daphne, hating his words of passionate love, sped on. And when his passion lent wings to his feet and she heard him gaining on her as she fled, not as a lover did Daphne look on deathless Apollo, but as a hateful foe. More swiftly than she had ever run beside her mistress Diana, leaving the flying winds behind her as she sped, ran Daphne now. But ever did Apollo gain upon her, and almost had he grasped her when she reached the green banks of the river of which her father, Peneus, was god.

"Help me, Peneus!" she cried. "Save me, oh my father, from him whose love I fear!"

As she spoke the arms of Apollo seized her, yet, even as his arms met around her waist, lissome and slight as a young willow, Daphne the nymph was Daphne the nymph no longer. Her fragrant hair, her soft white arms, her tender body all changed as the sun-god touched them. Her feet took root in the soft, damp earth by the river. Her arms sprouted into woody branches and green leaves. Her face vanished, and the bark of a big tree enclosed her snow-white body. Yet Apollo did not take away his embrace from her who had been his dear first love. He knew that her cry to Peneus her father had been answered, yet he said, "Since thou canst not be my bride, at least thou shalt be my tree; my hair, my lyre, my quiver shall have thee always, oh laurel tree of the Immortals!"

So do we still speak of laurels won, and worn by those of deathless fame, and still does the first love of Apollo crown the heads of those whose gifts have fitted them to dwell with the dwellers on Olympus.

"I espouse thee for my tree:Be thou the prize of honour and renown;The deathless poet, and the poem, crown;Thou shalt the Roman festivals adorn,And, after poets, be by victors worn."

OVID (*Dryden's translation*).

.

PSYCHE

Those who read for the first time the story of Psyche must at once be struck by its kinship to the fairy tales of childhood. Here we have the three sisters, the two elder jealous and spiteful, the youngest beautiful and gentle and quite unable to defend herself against her sisters' wicked arts. Here, too, is the mysterious bridegroom who is never seen and who is lost to his bride because of her lack of faith. Truly it is an old, old tale—older than all fairy tales—the story of love that is not strong enough to believe and to wait, and so to "win through" in the end—the story of seeds of suspicion sown by one full of malice in an innocent heart, and which bring to the hapless reaper a cruel harvest.

Once upon a time, so goes the tale, a king and queen had three beautiful daughters. The first and the second were fair indeed, but the beauty of the youngest was such that all the people of the land worshipped it as a thing sent straight from Olympus. They awaited her outside the royal palace, and when she came, they threw chaplets of roses and violets for her little feet to tread upon, and sang hymns of praise as though she were no mortal maiden but a daughter of the deathless gods.

There were many who said that the beauty of Aphrodite herself was less perfect than the beauty of Psyche, and when the goddess found that men were forsaking her altars in order to worship a mortal maiden, great was her wrath against them and against the princess who, all unwittingly, had wrought her this shameful harm.

In her garden, sitting amongst the flowers and idly watching his mother's fair white doves as they preened their snowy feathers in the sun, Aphrodite found her son Eros, and angrily poured forth to him the story of her shame.

"Thine must be the task of avenging thy mother's honour," she said. "Thou who hast the power of making the loves of men, stab with one of thine arrows the heart of this presumptuous maiden, and

41

shame her before all other mortals by making her love a monster from which all others shrink and which all despise." With wicked glee Eros heard his mother's commands. His beautiful face, still the face of a mischievous boy, lit up with merriment. This was, in truth, a game after his own heart. In the garden of Aphrodite is a fountain of sweet, another of bitter water, and Eros filled two amber vases, one from each fountain, hung them from his quiver, and

"Straight he rose from earth and down the windWent glittering 'twixt the blue sky and the sea."

In her chamber Psyche lay fast asleep, and swiftly, almost without a glance at her, Eros sprinkled some of the bitter drops upon her lips, and then, with one of his sharpest arrows, pricked her snowy breast. Like a child who half awakes in fear, and looks up with puzzled, wondering eyes, Psyche, with a little moan, opened eyes that were bluer than the violets in spring and gazed at Eros. He knew that he was invisible, and yet her gaze made him tremble.

"They spoke truth!" said the lad to himself. "Not even my mother is as fair as this princess."

For a moment her eyelids quivered, and then dropped. Her long dark lashes fell on her cheeks that were pink as the hearts of the fragile shells that the waves toss up on western beaches, her red mouth, curved like the bow of Eros, smiled happily, and Psyche slept again. With heart that beat as it had never beaten before, Eros gazed upon her perfect loveliness. With gentle, pitying finger he wiped away the red drop where his arrow had wounded her, and then stooped and touched her lips with his own, so lightly that Psyche in her dreams thought that they had been brushed by a butterfly's wings. Yet in her sleep she moved, and Eros, starting back, pricked himself with one of his arrows. And with that prick, for Eros there passed away all the careless ease of the heart of a boy, and he knew that he loved Psyche with the unquenchable love of a deathless god. Now, with bitter regret, all his desire was to undo the wrong he had done to the one that he loved. Speedily he sprinkled her with the sweet water that brings joy, and when

42

Psyche rose from her couch she was radiant with the beauty that comes from a new, undreamed-of happiness.

"From place to place Love followed her that dayAnd ever fairer to his eyes she grew,So that at last when from her bower he flew,And underneath his feet the moonlit seaWent shepherding his waves disorderly, He swore that of all gods and men, no oneShould hold her in his arms but he alone;That she should dwell with him in glorious wiseLike to a goddess in some paradise;Yea, he would get from Father Jove this graceThat she should never die, but her sweet faceAnd wonderful fair body should endureTill the foundations of the mountains sureWere molten in the sea; so utterlyDid he forget his mother's cruelty."

WILLIAM MORRIS.

Meantime it came to be known all over that land, and in other lands to which the fame of the fair Psyche had spread, that the mighty goddess Aphrodite had declared herself the enemy of the princess. Therefore none dared seek her in marriage, and although many a noble youth sighed away his heart for love of her, she remained in her father's palace like an exquisite rose whose thorns make those who fain would have it for their own, fear to pluck it from the parent stem. Her sisters married, and her father marvelled why so strange a thing should come about and why the most beautiful by far of his three daughters should remain unwed.

At length, laden with royal gifts, an embassy was sent by the king to the oracle of Apollo to inquire what might be the will of the dwellers on Olympus concerning his fairest daughter. In a horror of anxiety the king and his queen and Psyche awaited the return of the ambassadors. And when they returned, before ever a word was spoken, they knew that the oracle had spoken Psyche's doom.

"No mortal lover shall fair Psyche know," said the oracle. "For bridegroom she shall have a monster that neither man nor god can resist. On the mountain top he awaits her coming. Woe unutterable shall come to the king and to all the dwellers in his land if he dares to resist the unalterable dictum of the deathless gods!"

"... Of dead corpses shalt thou be the king,And stumbling through the dark land shalt thou go,Howling for second death to end thy woe."

WILLIAM MORRIS.

Only for a little while did the wretched king strive to resist the decrees of fate. And in her own chamber, where so short a time before the little princess had known the joy of something inexpressible—something most exquisite—intangible—unknown—she sat, like a flower broken by the ruthless storm, sobbing pitifully, dry-eyed, with sobs that strained her soul, for the shameful, hideous fate that the gods had dealt her.

All night, until her worn-out body could no longer feel, her worn-out mind think, and kind sleep came to bring her oblivion, Psyche faced the horror for the sake of her father and of his people, that she knew she could not avoid. When morning came, her handmaids, white-faced and red-eyed, came to deck her in all the bridal magnificence that befitted the most beautiful daughter of a king, and when she was dressed right royally, and as became a bride, there started up the mountain a procession at sight of which the gods themselves must have wept. With bowed heads the king and queen walked before the litter upon which lay their daughter in her marriage veil of saffron colour, with rose wreath on her golden hair. White, white were the faces of the maidens who bore the torches, and yet rose red were they by the side of Psyche. Minstrels played wedding hymns as they marched onwards, and it seemed as though the souls of unhappy shades sobbed through the reeds and moaned through the strings as they played.

At length they reached the rocky place where they knew they must leave the victim bride, and her father dared not meet her eyes as he turned his head to go. Yet Psyche watched the procession wending its way downhill. No more tears had she to shed, and it seemed to her that what she saw was not a wedding throng, but an assembly of broken-hearted people who went back to their homes with heavy feet after burying one that they loved. She saw no sign of the monster who was to be her bridegroom, yet at every little sound her heart grew sick with horror, and when the night wind swept through the craggy peaks and its moans were echoed in loneliness, she fell on her face in deadly fear and lay on the cold rock in a swoon.

Yet, had Psyche known it, the wind was her friend. For Eros had used Zephyrus as his trusty messenger and sent him to the mountain top to find the bride of him "whom neither man nor god could resist." Tenderly—very tenderly—he was told, must he lift her in his arms, and bear her to the golden palace in that green and pleasant land where Eros had his home. So, with all the gentleness of a loving nurse to a tired little child Zephyrus lifted Psyche, and sped with her in his strong arms to the flowery meadows behind which towered the golden palace of Eros, like the sun behind a sky of green and amber and blue and rose. Deeply, in the weariness of her grief, Psyche slept, and when she awoke it was to start up with the chill hands of the realisation of terrible actualities on her heart. But when her eyes looked round to find the barren rocks, the utter forsakenness, the coming of an unnameable horror, before her she saw only fair groves with trees bedecked with fruit and blossom, fragrant meadows, flowers whose beauty made her eyes grow glad. And from the trees sang birds with song more sweet than any that Psyche had ever known, and with brilliant plumage which they preened caressingly when they had dipped their wings in crystal-sparkling fountains. There, too, stood a noble palace, golden fronted, and with arcades of stainless marble that shone like snow in the sun. At first all seemed like part of a dream from which she dreaded to awake, but soon there came to her the joy of knowing that all the exquisite things that made appeal to her senses were indeed realities. Almost holding her breath, she walked forward to the open golden doors. "It is a trap," she thought. "By this means does the monster subtly mean to lure me into his golden cage." Yet, even as she thought, there seemed to be hovering round her winged words, like little golden birds with souls. And in her ears they whispered, "Fear not. Doubt not. Recall the half-formed dreams that so short a time ago brought to thy heart such unutterable joy. No evil shall come to thee—only the bliss of loving and of being loved."

Thus did Psyche lose her fear, and enter the golden doors. And inside the palace she found that all the beautiful things of which she had ever dreamed, all the perfect things for which she had ever longed, were there to greet her. From one to another she flitted, like a humming-bird that sucks honey from one and then from another gorgeous flower. And then, when she was tired with so much wearing out of her thankful mind, she found a banquet ready spread for her, with all the dainties that her dainty soul liked best; and, as she ate, music so perfect rejoiced her ears that all her soul was soothed and joyous and at peace. When she had refreshed herself, a soft couch stood before her, ready for her there to repose, and when that strange day had come to an end, Psyche knew that, monster or not, she was beloved by one who had thought for her every thought, and who desired only her desire.

Night came at last, and when all was dark and still, and Psyche, wide awake, was full of forebodings and fears lest her happy dreams might only be misleading fancies, and Horror incarnate might come to crown her peaceful day, Eros softly entered the palace that was his own. Even as he had gone to the palace of her father he went now, and found Psyche lying with violet eyes that stared into the velvety darkness, seeking something that she hoped for, trembling before something that brought her dread.

His voice was as the voice of spring when it breathes on the sleeping earth; he knew each note in Love's music, every word in the great thing that is Love's vocabulary. Love loved, and Psyche listened, and soon she knew that her lover was Love himself.

Thus, for Psyche, did a time of perfect happiness begin. All through the day she roamed in her Love's dominion, and saw on every side the signs of his passion and of his tenderness. All through the night he stayed by her, and satisfied all the longing of her heart. Yet always, ere daybreak, Eros left her, and when she begged him to stay he only made answer:

"I am with thee only while I keepMy visage hidden; and if thou once shouldst seeMy face, I must forsake thee; the high godsLink Love with Faith, and he withdraws himselfFrom the full gaze of knowledge."

LEWIS MORRIS.

So did time glide past for Psyche, and ever she grew more in love with Love; always did her happiness become more complete. Yet, ever and again, there returned to her the remembrance of those sorrowful days when her father and mother had broken their hearts over her martyrdom, and her sisters had looked askance at her as at one whose punishment must assuredly have come from her own misdoing. Thus at length she asked Eros to grant her, for love's sake, a boon—to permit her to have her sisters come to see for themselves the happiness that was hers. Most unwillingly was her request granted, for the heart of Eros told him that from their visit no good could come. Yet he was unable to deny anything to Psyche, and on the following day Zephyrus was sent to bring the two sisters to the pleasant valley where Psyche had her home. Eagerly, as she awaited them, Psyche thought she might make the princely palace wherein she dwelt yet fairer than it was. And almost ere she could think, her thoughts became realities. When the two sisters came, they were bewildered with the beauty and the magnificence of it all. Beside this, their own possessions were paltry trifles indeed. Quickly, in their little hearts, black envy grew. They had always been jealous of their younger sister, and now that they found her, whom all the world believed to have been slain by a horrible monster, more beautiful than ever, decked with rare jewels, radiant in her happiness, and queen of a palace fit for the gods, their envy soon turned to hatred, and they sought how best to wreak their malice upon the joyous creature who loaded them with priceless gifts. They began to ply Psyche with questions. He who was her lord, to whom she owed all her happiness, where was he? Why did he stay away when her sisters came to be presented to him? What manner of man was he? Was he fair or dark? Young or old? And as they questioned her, Psyche grew like a bewildered child and answered in frightened words that contradicted one another. And well the wicked sisters, who brooded evil in their hearts, knew that this husband whom Psyche had never seen must indeed be one of the deathless gods. Wily words they spoke to her then.

"Alas! unhappy one," they said, "dost think to escape the evil fate the gods meted out for thee? Thy husband is none other than the monster of which the oracle spake! Oh, foolish Psyche! canst not understand that the monster fears the light? Too great horror would it mean for thee to see the loathsome thing that comes in the blackness of night and speaks to thee words of love."

White-lipped and trembling, Psyche listened. Drop by drop the poisonous words passed into her soul. She had thought him king of all living things—worthy to rule over gods as well as men. She was so sure that his body was worthy sheath for the heart she knew so well.... She had pictured him beautiful as Eros, son of Aphrodite—young and fair, with crisp, golden locks—a husband to glory in—a lover to adore. And now she knew, with shame and dread, that he who had won her love between the twilight and the dawn was a thing to shame her, a monster to be shunned of men.

"What, then, shall I do?" piteously she asked of her sisters. And the women, pitilessly, and well content, answered:

"Provide thyself with a lamp and a knife sharp enough to slay the man or monster. And when this creature to whom, to thy undying shame, thou belongest, sleeps sound, slip from thy couch and in the rays of the lamp have courage to look upon him in all his horror. Then, when thou hast seen for thyself that what we say is truth, with thy knife swiftly slay him. Thus shalt thou free thyself from the pitiless doom meted out by the gods."

Shaking with sobs, Psyche made answer:

48

"I love him so!... I love him so!"

And her sisters turned upon her with furious scorn and well-simulated wrath.

"Shameless one!" they cried; "and does our father's daughter confess to a thing so unutterable! Only by slaying the monster canst thou hope to regain thy place amongst the daughters of men."

They left her when evening fell, carrying with them their royal gifts. And while she awaited the coming of her lord, Psyche, provided with knife and lamp, crouched with her head in her hands, a lily broken by a cruel storm. So glad was Eros to come back to her, to find her safely there—for greatly had he feared the coming of that treacherous pair—that he did not note her silence. Nor did the dark night show him that her eyes in her sad face looked like violets in a snow wreath. He wanted only to hold her safely in his arms, and there she lay, passive and still, until sleep came to lay upon him an omnipotent hand. Then, very gently, she withdrew herself from his embrace, and stole to the place where her lamp was hidden. Her limbs shook under her as she brought it to the couch where he lay asleep; her arm trembled as she held it aloft.

As a martyr walks to death, so did she walk. And when the yellow light fell upon the form of him who lay there, still she gazed steadily.

And, lo, before her she saw the form of him who had ever been the ideal of her dreams. Love himself, incarnate Love, perfect in beauty and in all else was he whom her sisters had told her was a monster—he, of whom the oracle had said that neither gods nor men could resist him. For a moment of perfect happiness she gazed upon his beauty. Then he turned in his sleep, and smiled, and stretched out his arms to find the one of his love. And Psyche started, and, starting, shook the lamp; and from it fell a drop of burning oil on the white shoulder of Eros. At once he awoke, and with piteous, pitying eyes looked in those of Psyche. And when he

49

spoke, his words were like daggers that pierced deep into her soul. He told her all that had been, all that might have been. Had she only had faith and patience to wait, an immortal life should have been hers.

"Farewell! though I, a god, can never knowHow thou canst lose thy pain, yet time will goOver thine head, and thou mayst mingle yetThe bitter and the sweet, nor quite forget,Nor quite remember, till these things shall seemThe wavering memory of a lovely dream."

WILLIAM MORRIS.

He left her alone then, with her despair, and as the slow hours dragged by, Psyche, as she awaited the dawn, felt that in her heart no sun could ever rise again. When day came at last, she felt she could no longer endure to stay in the palace where everything spoke to her of the infinite tenderness of a lost love. Through the night a storm had raged, and even with the day there came no calm. And Psyche, weary and chill, wandered away from the place of her happiness, onward and ever on, until she stood on the bank of a swift-flowing river. For a little she stayed her steps and listened to the sound of its wash against the rocks and tree roots as it hurried past, and to her as she waited came the thought that here had she found a means by which to end her woe.

"I have lost my Love," she moaned. "What is Life to me any longer! Come to me then, O Death!"

So then she sprang into the wan water, hoping that very swiftly it might bear her grief-worn soul down to the shades. But the river bore her up and carried her to its shallows in a fair meadow where Pan himself sat on the bank and merrily dabbled his feet in the flowing water. And when Psyche, shamed and wet, looked at him with sad eyes, the god spoke to her gently and chid her for her folly. She was too young and much too fair to try to end her life so rudely, he said. The river gods would never be so unkind as to drive so beautiful a maiden in rough haste down to the Cocytus valley.

50

"Thou must dree thy weird like all other daughters of men, fair Psyche," he said. "He or she who fain would lose their lives, are ever held longest in life. Only when the gods will it shall thy days on earth be done."

And Psyche, knowing that in truth the gods had spared her to endure more sorrow, looked in his face with a very piteous gaze, and wandered on. As she wandered, she found that her feet had led her near the place where her two sisters dwelt.

"I shall tell them of the evil they have wrought," she thought. "Surely they must sorrow when they know that by their cruel words they stole my faith from me and robbed me of my Love and of my happiness."

Gladly the two women saw the stricken form of Psyche and looked at her face, all marred by grief. Well, indeed, had their plot succeeded; their malice had drunk deep, yet deeper still they drank, for with scornful laughter they drove her from their palace doors. Very quickly, when she had gone, the elder sought the place where she had stood when Zephyrus bore her in safety to that palace of pleasure where Psyche dwelt with her Love. Now that Psyche was no longer there, surely the god by whom she had been beloved would gladly have as her successor the beautiful woman who was now much more fair than the white-faced girl with eyes all red with weeping. And such certainty did the vengeful gods put in her heart that she held out her arms, and calling aloud:

"Bear me to him in thine arms, Zephyrus! Behold I come, my lord!" she sprang from the high cliff on which she stood, into space. And the ravens that night feasted on her shattered body. So also did it befall the younger sister, deluded by the Olympians to her own destruction, so that her sin might be avenged.

For many a weary day and night Psyche wandered, ever seeking to find her Love, ever longing to do something by which to atone for the deed that had been her undoing. From temple to temple she went, but nowhere did she come near him, until at length in

Cyprus she came to the place where Aphrodite herself had her dwelling. And inasmuch as her love had made her very bold, and because she no longer feared death, nor could think of pangs more cruel than those that she already knew, Psyche sought the presence of the goddess who was her enemy, and humbly begged her to take her life away.

With flaming scorn and anger Aphrodite received her.

"O thou fool," she said, "I will not let thee die!But thou shalt reap the harvest thou hast sown,And many a day that wretched lot bemoan;Thou art my slave, and not a day shall beBut I will find some fitting task for thee."

There began then for Psyche a time of torturing misery of which only those could speak who have knowledge of the merciless stripes with which the goddess can scourge the hearts of her slaves. With cruel ingenuity, Aphrodite invented labours for her.

In uncountable quantity, and mingled in inextricable and bewildering confusion, there lay in the granary of the goddess grains of barley and of wheat, peas and millet, poppy and coriander seed. To sort out each kind and lay them in heaps was the task allotted for one day, and woe be to her did she fail. In despair, Psyche began her hopeless labour. While the sun shone, through a day that was for her too short, she strove to separate the grains, but when the shadows of evening made it hard for her to distinguish one sort from another, only a few very tiny piles were the result of her weary toil. Very soon the goddess would return, and Psyche dared not think what would be the punishment meted out to her. Rapidly the darkness fell, but while the dying light still lingered in some parts of the granary, it seemed to Psyche as though little dark trickles of water began to pour from underneath the doors and through the cracks in the wall. Trembling she watched the ceaseless motion of those long, dark lines, and then, in amazement, realised that what she saw were unending processions of ants. And as though one who loved her directed their labours, the millions of busy little toilers swiftly did for Psyche what she herself had failed to do. When at length they went away, in those long dark lines that looked like the flow of a thread-like stream, the grains were all piled up in high heaps, and the sad heart of Psyche knew not only thankful relief, but had a thrill of gladness.

"Eros sent them to me:" she thought. "Even yet his love for me is not dead."

And what she thought was true.

Amazed and angry, Aphrodite looked at the task she had deemed impossible, well and swiftly performed. That Psyche should possess such magic skill only incensed her more, and next day she said to her new slave:

"Behold, on the other side of that glittering stream, my golden-fleeced sheep crop the sweet flowers of the meadow. To-day must thou cross the river and bring me back by evening a sample of wool pulled from each one of their shining fleeces."

Then did Psyche go down to the brink of the river, and even as her white feet splashed into the water, she heard a whisper of warning from the reeds that bowed their heads by the stream.

"Beware! O Psyche," they said. "Stay on the shore and rest until the golden-fleeced sheep lie under the shade of the trees in the evening and the murmur of the river has lulled them to sleep."

But Psyche said, "Alas, I must do the bidding of the goddess. It will take me many a weary hour to pluck the wool that she requires."

And again the reeds murmured, "Beware! for the golden-fleeced sheep, with their great horns, are evil creatures that lust for the lives of mortals, and will slay thee even as thy feet reach the other bank. Only when the sun goes down does their vice depart from them, and while they sleep thou canst gather of their wool from the bushes and from the trunks of the trees."

And again the heart of Psyche felt a thrill of happiness, because she knew that she was loved and cared for still. All day she rested in the wood by the river and dreamt pleasant day-dreams, and when the sun had set she waded to the further shore and gathered the golden wool in the way that the reeds had told her. When in the evening she came to the goddess, bearing her shining load, the brow of Aphrodite grew dark.

"If thou art so skilled in magic that no danger is danger to thee, yet another task shall I give thee that is worthy of thy skill," she said, and laid upon Psyche her fresh commands.

Sick with dread, Psyche set out next morning to seek the black stream out of which Aphrodite had commanded her to fill a ewer. Part of its waters flowed into the Styx, part into the Cocytus, and well did Psyche know that a hideous death from the loathly creatures that protected the fountain must be the fate of those who risked so proud an attempt. Yet because she knew that she must "dree her weird," as Pan had said, she plodded onward, towards that dark mountain from whose side gushed the black water that she sought. And then, once again, there came to her a message of love. A whirring of wings she heard, and

"O'er her head there flew the bird of Jove, The bearer, of his servant, friend of Love, Who, when he saw her, straightway towards her flew, And asked her why she wept, and when he knew, And who she was, he said, 'Cease all thy fear, For to the black waves I thy ewer will bear, And fill it for thee; but, remember me, When thou art come unto thy majesty.'"

And, yet once again, the stricken heart of Psyche was gladdened, and when at nightfall she came with her ewer full of water from the dread stream and gave it to Aphrodite, although she knew that a yet more arduous task was sure to follow, her fear had all passed away.

With beautiful, sullen eyes, Aphrodite received her when she brought the water. And, with black brow, she said: "If thou art so skilled in magic that no danger is known to thee, I shall now give thee a task all worthy of thy skill."

Thereon she told her that she must seek that dark valley where no silver nor golden light ever strikes on the black waters of Cocytus and of the Styx; and where Pluto reigns in gloomy majesty over the restless shades. From Proserpine she was to crave for Aphrodite the gift of a box of magical ointment, the secret of which was known to the Queen of Darkness alone, and which was able to bring to those who used it, beauty more exquisite than any that the eyes of gods or of men had as yet looked upon.

"I grow weary and careworn," said Aphrodite, and she looked like a rose that has budded in Paradise as she spoke. "My son was wounded by a faithless slave in whom, most weakly, he put his trust, and in tending to his wound, my beauty has faded."

And at these scornful words, the heart of Psyche leaped within her.

"In helping his mother, I shall help him!" she thought. And again she thought, "I shall atone." And so, when day was come, she took her way along the weary road that leads to that dark place from whence no traveller can ever hope to return, and still with gladness in her heart. But, as she went onward, "cold thoughts and dreadful fears" came to her.

"Better were it for me to hasten my journey to the shades," she thought.

And when she came to an old grey tower, that seemed like an old man that Death has forgotten, she resolved to throw herself down from it, and thus swiftly to find herself at her journey's end. But as she stood on the top of the tower, her arms outstretched, like a white butterfly that poises its wings for flight, a voice spoke in her ear.

"Oh, foolish one," it said, "why dost thou strive to stay the hope that is not dead?" And while she held her breath, her great eyes wide open, the voice spoke on, and told her by what means she might speedily reach Hades and there find means to face with courage the King of Darkness himself and his fair wife, Proserpine.

All that she was bidden to do, Psyche did, and so at last did she come before the throne of Proserpine, and all that Psyche endured, all that she saw, all that through which she came with bleeding heart and yet with unscathed soul, cannot here be written.

To her Proserpine gave the box of precious ointment that Aphrodite described, and gladly she hastened homeward. Good, indeed, it was to her when again she reached the fair light of day. Yet, when she had won there, there came to Psyche a winged thought, that beat against the stern barriers of her mind like a little moth against a window.

"This ointment that I carry with me," said Psyche to herself, "is an ointment that will bring back to those all faded by time, or worn by suffering, a beauty greater than any beauty that has joyed the Immortals!" And then she thought:

"For my beauty, Eros—*Love*—loved me; and now my beauty is worn and wasted and well-nigh gone. Were I to open this box and make use of the ointment of Proserpine, then indeed I should be fair enough to be the bride of him who, even now, believes that he loves me—of Eros whose love is my life!"

So it came to pass that she opened the fateful box. And out of it there came not Beauty, but Sleep, that put his gyves upon her limbs, and on her eyelids laid heavy fingers. And Psyche sank down by the wayside, the prisoner of Sleep.

But Eros, who had loved her ever, with a love that knew the ebb and flow of no tides, rose from his bed and went in search of her who had braved even the horrors of Hades for his dear sake. And by the wayside he found her, fettered by sleep. Her little oval face was white as a snowdrop. Like violets were her heavy eyelids, and underneath her sleeping eyes a violet shadow lay. Once had her mouth been as the bow of Eros, painted in carmine. Now either end of the bow was turned downwards, and its colour was that of a faded rose-leaf.

And as Eros looked at her that he loved, pity stirred his heart, as the wind sweeps through the sighing, grey leaves of the willow, or sings through the bowing reeds.

"My *Belovèd!*" he said, and he knew that Psyche was indeed his beloved. It was her fair soul that he loved, nor did it matter to him whether her body was like a rose in June or as a wind-scourged tree in December. And as his lips met hers, Psyche awoke, and heard his soft whisper:

"Dear, unclose thine eyes.Thou mayst look on me now. I go no more,But am thine own forever."

LEWIS MORRIS.

Then did there spring from the fair white shoulders of Psyche, wings of silver and of gold, and, hand in hand with Eros, she winged her way to Olympus.

And there all the deathless gods were assembled, and Aphrodite no longer looked upon her who had once been her slave with darkened brows, but smiled upon her as the sun smiles upon a new-born flower. And when into the hand of Psyche there was placed a cup of gold, the voice of the great Father and King of Olympus rang out loud and clear:

"Drink now, O beautiful, and have no fear!For with this draught shalt thou be born again,And live for ever free from care and pain."

WILLIAM MORRIS.

In this wise did Psyche, a human soul, attain by bitter suffering to the perfect happiness of purified love.

And still do we watch the butterfly, which is her emblem, bursting from its ugly tomb in the dark soil, and spreading joyous white and gold-powdered wings in the caressing sunshine, amidst the radiance and the fragrance of the summer flowers. Still, too, do we sadly watch her sister, the white moth, heedlessly rushing into pangs unutterable, thoughtlessly seeking the anguish that brings her a cruel death.

THUS DID PSYCHE LOSE HER FEAR, AND ENTER THE GOLDEN DOORS

THE CALYDONIAN HUNT

Œneus and Althæa were king and queen of Calydon, and to them was born a son who was his mother's joy and yet her bitterest sorrow. Meleager was his name, and ere his birth his mother dreamed a dream that the child that she bore was a burning firebrand. But when the baby came he was a royal child indeed, a little fearless king from the first moment that his eyes, like unseeing violets, gazed steadily up at his mother. To the chamber where he lay by his mother's side came the three Fates, spinning, ceaselessly spinning.

"He shall be strong," said one, as she span her thread. "He shall be fortunate and brave," said the second. But the third laid a billet of wood on the flames, and while her withered fingers held the fatal threads, she looked with old, old, sad eyes at the new-born child.

"To thee, O New-Born," she said, "and to this wood that burns, do we give the same span of days to live."

From her bed sprang Althæa, and, heedless of the flames, she seized the burning wood, trod on it with her fair white feet, and poured on it water that swiftly quenched its red glow. "Thou shalt live forever, O Beloved," she said, "for never again shall fire char the brand that I have plucked from the burning."

And the baby laughed.

"Those grey women with bound hairWho fright the gods frighted not him; he laughedSeeing them, and pushed out hands to feel and haulDistaff and thread."

The years sped on, and from fearless and beautiful babyhood, Meleager grew into gallant boyhood, and then into magnificent youth. When Jason and his heroes sailed away into a distant land to win the Golden Fleece, Meleager was one of the noble band. From all men living he won great praise for his brave deeds, and when the tribes of the north and west made war upon Ætolia, he fought against their army and scattered it as a wind in autumn drives the fallen leaves before it.

But his victory brought evil upon him. When his father Œneus, at the end of a fruitful year, offered sacrifices to the gods, he omitted to honour the goddess Diana by sacrificing to her, and to punish his neglect, she had sent this destroying army. When Meleager was victor, her wrath against his father grew yet more hot, and she sent a wild boar, large as the bulls of Epirus, and fierce and savage to kill and to devour, that it might ravage and lay waste the land of Calydon. The fields of corn were trampled under foot, the vineyards laid waste, and the olive groves wrecked as by a winter hurricane. Flocks and herds were slaughtered by it, or driven hither and thither in wild panic, working havoc as they fled. Many went out to slay it, but went only to find a hideous death. Then did Meleager resolve that he would rid the land of this monster, and called on all his friends, the heroes of Greece, to come to his aid. Theseus and his friend Pirithous came; Jason; Peleus, afterwards father of Achilles; Telamon, the father of Ajax; Nestor, then but a youth; Castor and Pollux, and Toxeus and Plexippus, the brothers of Althæa, the fair queen-mother. But there came none more fearless nor more ready to fight the monster boar of Calydon than Atalanta, the daughter of the king of Arcadia. When Atalanta was born, her father heard of her birth with anger. He desired no daughter, but only sturdy sons who might fight for him, and in the furious rage of bitter disappointment he had the baby princess left on the Parthenian Hill that she might perish there. A she-bear heard the baby's piteous cries, and carried it off to its lair, where she suckled it along with her young, and there the little Atalanta tumbled about and played with her furry companions and grew strong and vigorous as any other wild young creature of the forest.

Some hunters came one day to raid the den and kill the foster-mother, and found, amazed, a fearless, white-skinned thing with rosy cheeks and brave eyes, who fought for her life and bit them as did her fierce foster-brothers, and then cried human tears of rage and sorrow when she saw the bear who had been her mother lying bloody and dead. Under the care of the hunters Atalanta grew into a maiden, with all the beauty of a maid and all the strength and the courage of a man. She ran as swiftly as Zephyrus runs when he rushes up from the west and drives the white clouds before him like a flock of timid fawns that a hound is pursuing. The shafts that her strong arm sped from her bow smote straight to the heart of the beast that she chased, and almost as swift as her arrow was she there to drive her spear into her quarry. When at length her father the king learned that the beautiful huntress, of whom all men spoke as of one only a little lower than Diana, was none other than his daughter, he was not slow to own her as his child. So proud was he of her beauty and grace, and of her marvellous swiftness of foot and skill in the chase, that he would fain have married her to one of the great ones of Greece, but Atalanta had consulted an oracle. "Marry not," said the oracle. "To thee marriage must bring woe."

So, with untouched heart, and with the daring and the courage of a young lad, Atalanta came along with the heroes to the Calydonian Hunt. She was so radiantly lovely, so young, so strong, so courageous, that straightway Meleager loved her, and all the heroes gazed at her with eyes that adored her beauty. And Diana, looking down at her, also loved the maiden whom from childhood she had held in her protection—a gallant, fearless virgin dear to her heart.

The grey mist rose from the marshes as the hunt began, and the hunters of the boar had gone but a little way when they came upon traces of the hated boar. Disembowelled beasts marked its track. Here, in a flowery meadow, had it wallowed. There, in rich wheat land, had it routed, and the marks of its bestial tusks were on the gashed grey trunks of the trees that had once lived in the peace of a fruitful olive grove.

In a marsh they found their enemy, and all the reeds quivered as it heaved its vast bulk and hove aside the weed in which it had wallowed, and rooted with its tusks amongst the wounded water-lilies before it leapt with a snort to meet and to slay the men who had come against it. A filthy thing it was, as its pink snout rose above the green ooze of the marshes, and it looked up lustingly, defying the purity of the blue skies of heaven, to bring to those who came against it a cruel, shameful death.

Upon it, first of all, Jason cast his spear. But the sharp point only touched it, and unwounded, the boar rushed on, its gross, bristly head down, to disembowel, if it could, the gallant Nestor. In the branches of a tree Nestor found safety, and Telamon rushed on to destroy the filthy thing that would have made carrion of the sons of the gods. A straggling cypress root caught his fleeting foot and laid him prone, a helpless prey for the rooting brute. His hounds fell before it, but ere it could reach him, Atalanta, full of vengeful rage—the pure angered against the filthy and cruel—let draw her bow, with a prayer to Diana to guide her shaft aright. Into the boar's smoking flank sped the arrow.

"The sudden stringRang, and sprang inward, and the waterish airHissed, and the moist plumes of the songless reedsMoved as a wave which the wind moves no more.But the boar heaved half out of ooze and slime,His tense flank trembling round the barbed wound,Hateful; and fiery with invasive eyesAnd bristling with intolerable hairPlunged, and the hounds clung, and green flowers and whiteReddened and broke all round them where they came. And charging with sheer tusk he drove, and smoteHyleus; and sharp death caught his sudden soul,And violent sleep shed night upon his eyes."

SWINBURNE.

More than ever terrible was the monster now that it was wounded. One after the other the hunters fell before its mad rage, and were sent to the shades by a bloody and merciless death.

Before its furious charge even the heart of a hero might have been stricken. Yet Meleager, like a mighty oak of the forest that will not sway even a little before the rush of a storm, stood full in its way and met its onslaught.

"Aimed on the left side his well-handled spearGrasped where the ash was knottiest hewn, and smote,And with no missile wound, the monstrous boarRight in the hairiest hollow of his hideUnder the last rib, sheer through bulk and bone,Deep in; and deeply smitten, and to death,The heavy horror with his hanging shafts,Leapt, and fell furiously, and from raging lipsFoamed out the latest wrath of all his life." Great was the shout that rose from those who still lived when that grim hunt thus came to an end. And when, with his keen blade, Meleager struck off the head, even as the quivering throat drew its last agonised breath, louder still shouted the men of Greece. But not for himself did Meleager despoil the body of his foe. He laid the ugly thing at the feet of Atalanta.

"This is thy spoil, not mine," he said. "The wounding shaft was sped by thee. To thee belongs the praise."

And Atalanta blushed rosily, and laughed low and gladly, not only because Diana had heard her prayer and helped her slay the beast, but for happiness that Meleager was so noble in his giving.

At that the brows of the heroes grew dark, and angrily one cried:

"Lo, now,Shall not the Arcadian shoot out lips at us,Saying all we were despoiled by this one girl."

Like a spark that kindles the dry grass, their kindling anger spread, and they rushed against Atalanta, seized the trophy she had been given, and smote her as though she were but a shameless wanton and not the noble daughter of a king. And because the heart of Meleager was given very wholly to the fair huntress, and because those whom he deemed his friends had not only dishonoured her, but had done him a very grievous wrong, a great rage seized him. Right and left he smote, and they who had been most bitter in their jealousy of Atalanta, the two brothers of his own mother, were laid low in death. Tidings of the slaying of the boar had been brought to Althæa by swift messengers, and she was on her way to the temples bearing gifts to the gods for the victory of her son, when she beheld the slow-footed procession of those who bore the bodies of the dead. And when she saw the still faces of her two dear brothers, quickly was her joy turned into mourning. Terrible was her grief and anger when she learned by whose hand they were slain, and her mother's love and pride dried up in her heart like the clear water of a fountain before the scorching of a devouring fire. No sacrifices to the gods would she offer, but her dead brothers should have the greatest sacrifice that mother could make to atone for the guilt of her son. Back to the palace she went, and from its safe hiding-place drew out the brand that she had rescued from the flames when Meleager the hero was but a babe that made his mother's heart sing for joy. She commanded a fire to be prepared, and four times, as its flames blazed aloft, she tried to lay the brand upon the pile. Yet four times she drew back, and then at last she threw into the reddest of the ashes the charred brand that for a little she held so close to her breast that it seemed as though she fondled her child.

A wreath of leaves as sign of victory was being placed on Atalanta's beautiful head by the adoring hands of Meleager when his mother gave him his doom. Through his body there rushed a pang of mortal agony. His blood turned to fire, and the hand of Death that smote him was as a hand of molten lead. In torture his gallant spirit passed away, uncomplaining, loving through his pain the maid for whose dear sake he had brought woe upon himself. As the last white ashes in the fire crumbled and fell away into nothingness, the soul of Meleager departed. Swiftly through the dark valley his mother's shade followed him, for she fell upon a sword and so perished. And Diana, looking down on the grief-stricken sisters of Meleager and on the bitter sorrow of his father, had compassion on them and turned them into birds. So ended the Calydonian Hunt, and Atalanta returned to Arcadia, heavy at heart for the evil she had wrought unwittingly. And still the Three Fates span on, and the winds caught up the cold wood ashes and blew them across the ravaged land that Meleager had saved and that quickly grew fertile again.

ATALANTA

Atalanta, daughter of the king of Arcadia, returned sad at heart to her own land. Only as comrades, as those against whose skill in the chase she was wont to pit her own skill, had she looked upon men. But Meleager, the hero who loved her and her fair honour more than life itself, and whose love had made him haste in all his gallant strength and youthful beauty to the land of the Shades, was one to touch her as never before had she been touched. Her father, proud of her triumph in Calydon, again besought her to marry one of her many noble suitors.

"If indeed they love me as thou sayest," said Atalanta to her father, "then must they be ready to face for my sake even the loss of dear life itself. I shall be the prize of him who outruns me in a foot-race. But he who tries and fails, must pay to Death his penalty."

Thereafter, for many days, a strange sight was to be seen in Arcadia. For one after another the suitors came to race with the maiden whose face had bewitched them, though truly the race was no more fair to him who ran than would be a race with Death. No mortal man was as fleet as Atalanta, who had first raced with the wild things of the mountains and the forests, and who had dared at last to race with the winds and leave even them behind. To her it was all a glorious game. Her conquest was always sure, and if the youths who entered in the contest cared to risk their lives, why should they blame her? So each day they started, throbbing hope and fierce determination to win her in the heart of him who ran— fading hope and despairing anger as he saw her skimming ahead of him like a gay-hued butterfly that a tired child pursues in vain. And each day, as the race ended, another man paid the price of his defeat.

Daily, amongst those who looked on, stood her cousin Milanion. He would fain have hated Atalanta for her ruthlessness and her joyousness as he saw his friends die for her sake, yet daily her beauty, her purity, and her gallant unconsciousness took a firmer hold upon his heart. To himself he vowed that he would win Atalanta, but not without help from the gods was this possible. Therefore he sought Aphrodite herself and asked her aid.

Milanion was a beautiful youth, and to Aphrodite, who loved beauty, he pled his cause as he told her how Atalanta had become to him more than life, so that he had ceased to pity the youths, his friends, who had died for love of her. The goddess smiled upon him with gentle sympathy.

In the garden of her temple grew a tree with branches and twigs of gold, and leaves as yellow as the little leaves of the silver birch when the autumn sun kisses them as it sets. On this tree grew golden apples, and Aphrodite plucked three of them and gave them to the youth who had not feared to ask her to aid him to win the maid he loved. How he was to use the apples she then told him, and, well content, Milanion returned home.

Next day he spoke to Atalanta.

"So far has victory been thine, Fairest on earth," he said, "but so far have thy little winged white feet had only the heavy-footed laggards to outrun. Wilt have me run a race with thee? for assuredly I shall win thee for my own."

And Milanion looked into the eyes of Atalanta with a smile as gay and fearless as that with which a hero is wont to look in the eyes of his fellow.

Look for look did the virgin huntress give him.

Then her cheeks grew red, as though the rosy-fingered dawn had touched them, and the dawning of love came into her heart.

Even Meleager was not quite so goodly a youth as this. Not even Meleager had been so wholly fearless.

"Thou art tempted by the deathless gods," she said, but her long lashes drooped on her cheek as she spoke. "I pity you, Milanion, for when thou dost race with me, the goal is assuredly the meadows of asphodel near where sit Pluto and Persephone on their gloomy thrones."

But Milanion said, "I am ready, Atalanta. Wilt race with me now?" And steadily he looked in her eyes until again they fell as though at last they had found a conqueror.

Like two swallows that skim across a sunny sea, filled with the joyousness of the coming of spring, Atalanta and Milanion started. Scarcely did their feet seem to touch the solid earth, and all those who stood by vowed that now, at length, was a race indeed, a race worthy for the gods to behold.

But as they ran, almost abreast, so that none could tell which was the gainer, Milanion obeyed the bidding of Aphrodite and let fall one of the golden apples. Never before had Atalanta dreamed of such a thing—an apple of glistening gold! She stopped, poised on one foot as a flying bird poises for a moment on the wing, and picked up the treasure. But Milanion had sped several paces ahead ere she was again abreast of him, and even as she gained on him, he dropped the second apple. Again Atalanta was tempted. Again she stopped, and again Milanion shot ahead of her. Her breath came short and fast, as once more she gained the ground that she had lost. But, yet a third time, Milanion threw in her way one of the golden illusions of the gods. And, yet again, Atalanta stooped to pick up the apple of gold.

Then a mighty shout from those who watched rent the air, and Atalanta, half fearful, half ashamed, yet wholly happy, found herself running, vanquished, into the arms of him who was indeed her conqueror. For not only had Milanion won the race, but he had won the heart of the virgin huntress, a heart once as cold and remote as the winter snow on the peak of Mount Olympus.

SHE STOPPED, AND PICKED UP THE TREASURE

ARACHNE

The hay that so short a time ago was long, lush grass, with fragrant meadow-sweet and gold-eyed marguerites growing amongst it in the green meadow-land by the river, is now dry hay—fragrant still, though dead, and hidden from the sun's warm rays underneath the dark wooden rafters of the barn. Occasionally a cat on a hunting foray comes into the barn to look for mice, or to nestle cosily down into purring slumber. Now and then a hen comes furtively tip-toeing through the open door and makes for itself a secret nest in which to lay the eggs which it subsequently heralds with such loud clucks of proud rejoicing as to completely undo all its previous precautions. Sometimes children come in, pursuing cat or hen, or merely to tumble each other over amongst the soft hay which they leave in chaotic confusion, and when they have gone away, a little more of the sky can be seen through the little window in the roof, and through the wooden bars of the window lower down. Yet, whatever other living creatures may come or go, by those windows of the barn, and high up on its dark rafters, there is always a living creature working, ceaselessly working. When, through the skylight, the sun-god drives a golden sunbeam, and a long shaft of dancing dust-atoms passes from the window to what was once a part of the early summer's glory, the work of the unresting toiler is also to be seen, for the window is hung with shimmering grey tapestries made by Arachne, the spider, and from rafter to rafter her threads are suspended with inimitable skill.

She was a nymph once, they say—the daughter of Idmon the dyer, of Colophon, a city of Lydia. In all Lydia there was none who could weave as wove the beautiful Arachne. To watch her card the wool of the white-fleeced sheep until in her fingers it grew like the soft clouds that hang round the hill tops, was pleasure enough to draw nymphs from the golden river Pactolus and from the vineyards of Tymolus. And when she drove her swift shuttle hither and thither, still it was joy to watch her wondrous skill. Magical was the growth of the web, fine of woof, that her darting fingers span, and yet more magical the exquisite devices that she then wrought upon it. For birds and flowers and butterflies and pictures of all the beautiful things on earth were limned by Arachne, and old tales grew alive again under her creative needle.

To Pallas Athené, goddess of craftsmen, came tidings that at Colophon in Lydia lived a nymph whose skill rivalled that of the goddess herself, and she, ever jealous for her own honour, took on herself the form of a woman bent with age, and, leaning on her staff, joined the little crowd that hung round Arachne as she plied her busy needle. With white arms twined round each other the eager nymphs watched the flowers spring up under her fingers, even as flowers spring from the ground on the coming of Demeter, and Athené was fain to admire, while she marvelled at the magic skill of the fair Arachne.

Gently she spoke to Arachne, and, with the persuasive words of a wise old woman, warned her that she must not let her ambition soar too high. Greater than all skilled craftswomen was the great goddess Athené, and were Arachne, in impious vanity, to dream that one day she might equal her, that were indeed a crime for any god to punish.

Glancing up for a moment from the picture whose perfect colours grew fast under her slim fingers, Arachne fixed scornful eyes on the old woman and gave a merry laugh.

"Didst say *equal* Athené? old mother," she said. "In good sooth thy dwelling must be with the goat-herds in the far-off hills and thou art not a dweller in our city. Else hadst thou not spoken to Arachne of *equalling* the work of Athené; *excelling* were the better word."

In anger Pallas Athené made answer.

"Impious one!" she said, "to those who would make themselves higher than the gods must ever come woe unutterable. Take heed what thou sayest, for punishment will assuredly be thine."

Laughing still, Arachne made reply:

"I fear not, Athené, nor does my heart shake at the gloomy warning of a foolish old crone." And turning to the nymphs who, half afraid, listened to her daring words, she said: "Fair nymphs who watch me day by day, well do ye know that I make no idle boast. My skill is as great as that of Athené, and greater still it shall be. Let Athené try a contest with me if she dare! Well do I know who will be the victor."

Then Athené cast off her disguise, and before the frightened nymphs and the bold Arachne stood the radiant goddess with eyes that blazed with anger and insulted pride.

"Lo, Athené is come!" she said, and nymphs and women fell on their knees before her, humbly adoring. Arachne alone was unabashed. Her cheeks showed how fast her heart was beating. From rosy red to white went the colour in them, yet, in firm, low voice she spoke.

"I have spoken truth," she said. "Not woman, nor goddess, can do work such as mine. Ready am I to abide by what I have said, and if I did boast, by my boast I stand. If thou wilt deign, great goddess, to try thy skill against the skill of the dyer's daughter and dost prove the victor, behold me gladly willing to pay the penalty."

The eyes of Athené, the grey-eyed goddess, grew dark as the sea when a thunder-cloud hangs over it and a mighty storm is coming. Not for one moment did she delay, but took her place by the side of Arachne. On the loom they stretched out two webs with a fine warp, and made them fast on the beam.

"The sley separates the warp, the woof is inserted in the middle with sharp shuttles, which the fingers hurry along, and, being drawn within the warp, the teeth notched in the moving sley strike it. Both hasten on, and girding up their garments to their breasts, they move their skilful arms, their eagerness beguiling their fatigue. There both the purple is being woven, which is subjected to the Tyrian brazen vessel, and fine shades of minute difference; just as the rainbow, with its mighty arch, is wont to tint a long tract of sky by means of the rays reflected by the shower; in which, though a thousand different colours are shining, yet the very transition eludes the eyes that look upon it.... There, too, the pliant gold is mixed with the threads."

OVID.

Their canvases wrought, then did Athené and Arachne hasten to cover them with pictures such as no skilled worker of tapestry has ever since dreamed of accomplishing. Under the fingers of Athené grew up pictures so real and so perfect that the watchers knew not whether the goddess was indeed creating life. And each picture was one that told of the omnipotence of the gods and of the doom that came upon those mortals who had dared in their blasphemous presumption to struggle as equals with the immortal dwellers in Olympus. Arachne glanced up from her web and looked with eyes that glowed with the love of beautiful things at the creations of Athené. Yet, undaunted, her fingers still sped on, and the goddess saw, with brow that grew yet more clouded, how the daughter of Idmon the dyer had chosen for subjects the tales that showed the weaknesses of the gods. One after another the living pictures grew beneath her hand, and the nymphs held their breath in mingled fear and ecstasy at Arachne's godlike skill and most arrogant daring. Between goddess and mortal none could have chosen, for the colour and form and exquisite fancy of the pictures of the daughter of Zeus were equalled, though not excelled, by those of the daughter of the dyer of Colophon.

Darker and yet more dark grew the eyes of Athené as they looked on the magical beauty of the pictures, each one of which was an insult to the gods. What picture had skilful hand ever drawn to compare with that of Europa who,

"riding on the back of the divine bull, with one hand clasped the beast's great horn, and with the other caught up her garment's purple fold, lest it might trail and be drenched in the hoar sea's infinite spray. And her deep robe was blown out in the wind, like the sail of a ship, and lightly ever it wafted the maiden onward."

MOSCHUS.

Then at last did the storm break, and with her shuttle the enraged goddess smote the web of Arachne, and the fair pictures were rent into motley rags and ribbons. Furiously, too, with her shuttle of boxwood she smote Arachne. Before her rage, the nymphs fled back to their golden river and to the vineyards of Tymolus, and the women of Colophon in blind terror rushed away. And Arachne, shamed to the dust, knew that life for her was no longer worth possessing. She had aspired, in the pride of her splendid genius, to a contest with a god, and knew now that such a contest must ever be vain. A cord hung from the weaver's beam, and swiftly she seized it, knotted it round her white neck, and would have hanged herself. But ere the life had passed out of her, Athené grasped the cord, loosened it, and spoke Arachne's doom:

"Live!" she said, "O guilty and shameless one! For evermore shalt thou live and hang as now, thou and thy descendants, that men may never forget the punishment of the blasphemous one who dared to rival a god."

Even as she spoke, Arachne's fair form dried up and withered. Her straight limbs grew grey and crooked and wiry, and her white arms were no more. And from the beam where the beautiful weaver of Lydia had been suspended, there hung from a fine grey thread the creature from which, to this day, there are but few who do not turn with loathing. Yet still Arachne spins, and still is without a compeer.

"Not anie damzell, which her vaunteth mostIn skilfull knitting of soft silken twyne,Nor anie weaver, which his worke doth boastIn dieper, in damaske, or in lyne,Nor anie skil'd in workmanship embost,Nor anie skil'd in loupes of fingring fine,Might in their divers cunning ever dareWith this so curious networke to compare."

SPENSER.

Thus, perhaps, does Arachne have her compensations, and in days that followed long after the twilight of the gods, did she not gain eternal honour in the heart of every Scot by the tale of how she saved a national hero? Kindly, too, are her labours for men as she slays their mortal enemies, the household flies, and when the peasant—practical, if not favoured by Æsculapius and Hygeia—runs to raid the loom of Arachne in order to staunch the quick-flowing blood from the cut hand of her little child, much more dear to her heart is Arachne the spider than the unknown Athené.

"Also in spinners be tokens of divination, and of knowing what weather shall fall—for oft by weathers that shall fall, some spin or weave higher or lower. Also multitude of spinners is token of much rain."

BARTHOLOMEW.

The sun has not long enough shown his face to dry up the dew in the garden, and behold on the little clipped tree of boxwood, a great marvel! For in and out, and all over its twigs and leaves, Arachne has woven her web, and on the web the dew has dropped a million diamond drops. And, suddenly, all the colours in the sky are mirrored dazzlingly on the grey tapestry of her making. Arachne has come to her own again.

IDAS AND MARPESSA

By day, while the sun-god drove his chariot in the high heavens and turned the blue-green Ægean Sea into the semblance of a blazing shield of brass, Idas and Marpessa sat together in the trees' soft shades, or walked in shadowy valleys where violets and wild parsley grew, and where Apollo rarely deigned to come. At eventide, when, in royal splendour of purple and crimson and gold, Apollo sought his rest in the western sky, Idas and Marpessa wandered by the seashore watching the little wavelets softly kissing the pebbles on the beach, or climbed to the mountain side from whence they could see the first glimpse of Diana's silver crescent and the twinkling lights of the Pleiades breaking through the blue canopy of the sky. While Apollo sought in heaven and on earth the best means to gratify his imperial whims, Idas, for whom all joys had come to mean but one, sought ever to be by the side of Marpessa. Shadowy valley, murmuring sea, lonely mountain side, or garden where grew the purple amaranth and where roses of pink and amber-yellow and deepest crimson dropped their radiant petals on the snowy marble paths, all were the same to Idas—Paradise for him, were Marpessa by his side; without her, dreary desert.

More beautiful than any flower that grew in the garden was Marpessa. No music that Apollo's lute could make was as sweet in the ears of Idas as her dear voice. Its music was ever new to him—a melody to make his heart more quickly throb. New, too, ever was her beauty. For him it was always the first time that they met, always the same fresh ravishment to look in her eyes. And when to Idas came the knowledge that Marpessa gave him love for love, he had indeed won happiness so great as to draw upon him the envy of the gods.

"The course of true love never did run smooth," and, like many and many another father since his day, Evenos, the father of Marpessa, was bitterly opposed to a match where the bridegroom was rich only in youth, in health, and in love. His beautiful daughter naturally seemed to him worthy of something much more high. Thus it was an unhappy day for Marpessa when, as she sat alone by the fountain which dripped slowly down on the marble basin, and dreamed of her lover, Idas, Apollo himself, led by caprice, noiselessly walked through the rose bushes, whose warm petals dropped at his feet as he passed, and beheld a maiden more fair than the fairest flower that grew. The hum of bees, the drip, drip of the fountain, these lulled her mind and heart and soothed her day-dreams, and Marpessa's red lips, curved like the bow of Eros, smiled as she thought of Idas, the man she loved. Silently Apollo watched her. This queen of all the roses was not fit to be the bride of mortal man—Marpessa must be his.

To Evenos Apollo quickly imparted his desire. He was not used to having his imperial wishes denied, nor was Evenos anxious to do so. Here, indeed, was a match for his daughter. No insignificant mortal, but the radiant sun-god himself! And to Marpessa he told what Apollo wished, and Marpessa shyly looked at her reflection in the pool of the fountain, and wondered if she were indeed beautiful enough to win the love of a god.

"Am I in truth so wondrous fair?" she asked her father.

"Fair enough to mate with Apollo himself!" proudly answered Evenos.

And joyously Marpessa replied, "Ah, then am I happy indeed! I would be beautiful for my Idas' sake!"

An angry man was her father. There was to be no more pleasant dallying with Idas in the shadowy wood or by the seashore. In the rose garden Apollo took his place and charmed Marpessa's ears with his music, while her eyes could not but be charmed by his beauty. The god had no doubts or fears. Only a little time he would give her, for a very little only would he wait, and then undoubtedly this mortal maiden would be his, her heart conquered as assuredly as the rays from his chariot conquered the roses, whose warm crimson petals they strewed at his feet. Yet as Marpessa looked and listened, her thoughts were often far away and always her heart was with Idas. When Apollo played most exquisitely to her it seemed that he put her love for Idas into music. When he spoke to her of his love she thought, "Thus, and thus did Idas speak," and a sudden memory of the human lad's halting words brought to her heart a little gush of tenderness, and made her eyes sparkle so that Apollo gladly thought, "Soon she will be mine."

And all this while Idas schemed and plotted and planned a way in which he could save his dear one from her obdurate father, and from the passion of a god. He went to Neptune, told his tale, and begged him to lend him a winged chariot in which he could fly away with Marpessa. Neptune good-naturedly consented, and when Idas flew up from the seashore one day, like a great bird that the tempests have blown inland, Marpessa joyously sprang up beside her lover, and swiftly they took flight for a land where in peace they might live and love together. No sooner did Evenos realise that his daughter was gone, than, in furious anger against her and her lover, he gave chase. One has watched a hawk in pursuit of a pigeon or a bird of the moors and seen it, a little dark speck at first, gradually growing larger and more large until at length it dominated and conquered its prey, swooping down from above, like an arrow from a bow, to bring with it sudden death.

So at first it seemed that Evenos must conquer Idas and Marpessa in the winged chariot of Neptune's lending. But onwards Idas drove the chariot, ever faster and faster, until before the eyes of Marpessa the trees of the forest grew into blurs of blue and brown, and the streams and rivers as they flew past them were streaks of silver. Not until he had reached the river Lycormas did the angry father own that his pursuit had been in vain. Over the swift-flowing stream flew the chariot driven by Idas, but Evenos knew that his horses, flecked with white foam, pumping each breath from hearts that were strained to breaking-point, no longer could go on with the chase. The passage of that deep stream would destroy them. The fierce water would sweep the wearied beasts down in its impelling current, and he with them. A shamed man would he be forever. Not for a moment did he hesitate, but drew his sharp sword from his belt and plunged it into the breast of one steed and then of the other who had been so willing and who yet had failed him in the end. And then, as they, still in their traces, neighed shrilly aloud, and then fell over and died where they lay, Evenos, with a great cry, leaped into the river. Over his head closed the eddies of the peat-brown water. Once only did he throw up his arms to ask the gods for mercy; then did his body drift down with the stream, and his soul hastened downwards to the Shades. And from that day the river Lycormas no more was known by that name, but was called the river *Evenos* forever.

Onwards, triumphantly, drove Idas, but soon he knew that a greater than Evenos had entered in the chase, and that the jealous sun-god's chariot was in pursuit of the winged car of Neptune. Quickly it gained on him—soon it would have swept down on him—a hawk indeed, this time, striking surely its helpless prey—but even as Apollo saw the white face of Marpessa and knew that he was the victor, a mighty thunderbolt that made the mountains shake, and rolled its echoes through the lonely fastnesses of a thousand hills, was sent to earth by Jupiter. While the echoes still re-echoed, there came from Olympus the voice of Zeus himself.

"Let her decide!" he said.

Apollo, like a white flame blown backward by the wind, withheld his hands that would have seized from Idas the woman who was his heart's desire.

And then he spoke, and while his burning gaze was fixed upon her, and his face, in beautiful fury, was more perfect than any exquisite picture of her dreams, his voice was as the voice of the sea as it calls to the shore in the moonlit hours, as the bird that sings in the darkness of a tropic night to its longing mate.

"Marpessa!" he cried, "Marpessa! wilt thou not come to me? No woe nor trouble, never any pain can touch me. Yet woe indeed was mine when first I saw thy fairest face. For even now dost thou hasten to sorrow, to darkness, to the dark-shadowed tomb. Thou art but mortal! thy beauty is short-lived. Thy love for mortal man shall quickly fade and die. Come to me, Marpessa, and my kisses on your lips shall make thee immortal! Together we shall bring the sunbeams to a cold, dark land! Together shall we coax the spring flowers from the still, dead earth! Together we shall bring to men the golden harvest, and deck the trees of autumn in our liveries of red and gold. I love thee, Marpessa—not as mere mortal loves do I love thee. Come to me, Marpessa—my Love—my Desire!"

When his voice was silent, it seemed as if the very earth itself with all its thousand echoes still breathed his words: "Marpessa—my Love—my Desire."

Abashed before the god's entreaties stood Idas. And the heart of Marpessa was torn as she heard the burning words of the beautiful Apollo still ringing through her head, and saw her mortal lover, silent, white-lipped, gazing first at the god and then into her own pale face. At length he spoke:

"After such argument what can I plead?Or what pale promise make? Yet since it isIn woman to pity rather than to aspire,A little I will speak. I love thee thenNot only for thy body packed with sweetOf all this world, that cup of brimming June,That jar of violet wine set in the air,That palest rose sweet in the night of life;Nor for that stirring bosom all besiegedBy drowsing lovers, or thy perilous hair;Nor for that face that might indeed provokeInvasion of old cities; no, nor allThy freshness stealing on me like strange sleep.Nor for this only do I love thee, butBecause Infinity upon thee broods;And thou art full of whispers and of shadows.Thou meanest what the sea has striven to saySo long, and yearned up the cliffs to tell;Thou art what all the winds have uttered not,What the still night suggesteth to the heart.Thy voice is like to music heard ere birth,Some spirit lute touched on a spirit sea;Thy face remembered is from other worlds,It has been died for, though I know not when,It has been sung of, though I know not where.It has the strangeness of the luring West,And of sad sea-horizons; beside theeI am aware of other times and lands,Of birth far-back, of lives in

79

many stars.O beauty lone and like a candle clearIn this dark country of the world! Thou artMy woe, my early light, my music dying."

STEPHEN PHILLIPS.

Then Idas, in the humility that comes from perfect love, drooped low his head, and was silent. In silence for a minute stood the three—a god, a man, and a woman. And from on high the watching stars looked down and marvelled, and Diana stayed for a moment the course of her silver car to watch, as she thought, the triumph of her own invincible brother.

From man to god passed the eyes of Marpessa, and back from god to man. And the stars forgot to twinkle, and Diana's silver-maned horses pawed the blue floor of the sky, impatient at the firm hand of the mistress on the reins that checked their eager course.

Marpessa spoke at last, in low words that seemed to come "remembered from other worlds."

For all the joys he offered her she thanked Apollo. What grander fate for mortal woman than to rule the sunbeams—to bring bliss to the earth and to the sons of men? What more could mortal woman crave than the gift of immortality shared with one whose power ruled the vast universe, and who still had stooped to lay the red roses of his passionate love at her little, human feet? And yet—and yet—in that sorrow-free existence that he promised, might there not still be something awanting to one who had once known tears?

"Yet I, being human, human sorrow miss."

Then were he indeed to give her the gift of immortal life, what value were life to one whose beauty had withered as the leaves in autumn, whose heart was tired and dead? What uglier fate than this, to endure an endless existence in which no life was, yoked to one whose youth was immortal, whose beauty was everlasting?

Then did she turn to Idas, who stood as one who awaits the judgment of the judge in whose hands lies the power of meting out life or death. Thus she spoke:

"But if I live with Idas, then we twoOn the low earth shall prosper hand in handIn odours of the open field, and liveIn peaceful noises of the farm, and watchThe pastoral fields burned by the setting sun.And he shall give me passionate children, notSome radiant god that will despise me quite,But clambering limbs and little hearts that err.... So shall we live,And though the first sweet sting of love be past,The sweet that almost venom is; though youth,With tender and extravagant delight,The first and secret kiss by twilight hedge,The insane farewell repeated o'er and o'er,Pass off; there shall succeed a faithful peace;Beautiful friendship tried by sun and wind,Durable from the daily dust of life."

The sun-god frowned as her words fell from her lips. Even now, as she looked at him, he held out his arms. Surely she only played with this poor mortal youth. To him she must come, this rose who could own no lesser god than the sun-god himself.

But Marpessa spoke on:

"And thou beautiful god, in that far time,When in thy setting sweet thou gazest downOn his grey head, wilt thou remember thenThat once I pleased thee, that I once was young?"

So did her voice cease, and on the earth fell sudden darkness. For to Apollo had come the shame of love rejected, and there were those who said that to the earth that night there came no sunset, only the sullen darkness that told of the flight of an angry god. Yet, later, the silver moonbeams of Diana seemed to greet the dark earth with a smile, and, in the winged car of Neptune, Idas and Marpessa sped on, greater than the gods, in a perfect harmony of human love that feared nor time, nor pain, nor Death himself.

MARPESSA SAT ALONE BY THE FOUNTAIN

ARETHUSA

"We have victualled and watered," wrote Nelson from Syracuse in 1798, "and surely, watering at the fountain of Arethusa, we must have victory. We shall sail with the first breeze; and be assured I will return either crowned with laurel or covered with cypress." Three days later, he won the Battle of the Nile, one of the greatest sea-fights of history.

Here in our own land the tales of the Greek gods seem very remote. Like the colours in an old, old portrait, the humanity of the stories seems to have faded. But in Sicily they grow vivid at once. Almost, as we stand above Syracuse, that long yellow town by the sea—a blue-green sea, with deep purple shadows where the clouds above it grow dark, and little white-sailed boats, like white butterflies, wing their way across to the far horizon—can we

"Have glimpse of Proteus rising from the sea,Or hear old Triton blow his wreathèd horn."

Here, to this day, one of the myths most impossible of acceptance to the scientific modern mind lives on, and Arethusa is not yet forgotten. "In Ortygia," says Cicero, "is a fountain of sweet water, the name of which is Arethusa, of incredible flow, very full of fish, which would be entirely overwhelmed by the sea, were its waters not protected from the waves by a rampart and a wall of stone." White marble walls have taken the place of the protecting barrier, but the spring bubbles up to this day, and Ortygia (Quail Island) is the name still given to that part of Syracuse. Fluffy-headed, long, green stalks of papyrus grow in the fountain, and red and golden fish dart through its clear water. Beyond lie the low shores of Plemmgrium, the fens of Lysimeleia, the hills above the Anapus, and above all towers Etna, in snowy and magnificent serenity and indifference to the changes wrought by the centuries to gods and to men. Yet here the present is completely overshadowed by the past, and even the story of Arethusa knocks loudly at the well-barricaded doors of twentieth-century incredulity.

The beautiful Arethusa was a nymph in Diana's train, and many a time in the chase did she thread her way through the dim woodland, as a stream flows down through the forest from the mountains to the sea. But to her, at last, there came a day when she was no longer the huntress but the hunted.

The flaming wheels of the chariot of Apollo had made the whole land scintillate with heat, and the nymph sought the kind shelter of a wood where she might bathe in the exquisite coolness of the river that still was chilled by the snows of the mountain. On the branch of a tree that bent over the stream she hung her garments, and joyously stepped into the limpid water. A ray of the sun glanced through the leaves above her and made the soft sand in the river's bed gleam like gold and the beautiful limbs of the nymph seem as though carved from pure white marble by the hand of Pygmalion himself. There was no sound there but the gentle sound of the stream that murmured caressingly to her as it slowly moved on through the solitude, and so gently it flowed that almost it seemed to stand still, as though regretful to leave for the unknown forest so beautiful a thing as Arethusa.

"The Earth seemed to love herAnd Heaven smiled above her."

But suddenly the stillness of the stream was ruffled. Waves, like the newly-born brothers of the billows of the sea, swept both down-stream and up-stream upon her, and the river no longer murmured gently, but spoke to her in a voice that thrilled with passionate longing. Alpheus, god of the river, had beheld her, and, beholding her, had loved her once and forever. An uncouth creature of the forest was he, unversed in all the arts of love-making. So not as a supplicant did he come to her, but as one who demanded fiercely love for love. Terror came upon Arethusa as she listened, and hastily she sprang from the water that had brought fear upon her, and hastened to find shelter in the woodlands. Then the murmur, as of the murmur of a river before a mighty flood comes to seize it and

84

hold it for its own, took form in a voice that pled with her, in tones that made her tremble as she heard.

"Hear me, Arethusa!" it said. "I am Alpheus, god of the river that now thou hast made sacred. I am the god of the rushing streams— the god of the thundering cataracts. Where the mountain streams crash over the rocks and echo through the shadowy hollows of the hills, I hold my kingship. Down from Etna I come, and the fire of Etna is in my veins. I love thee! I love but thee, and thou shalt be mine, and I thine forever."

Then Arethusa, in blind panic, fled before the god who loved her. Through the shadowy forest she sped, while he swiftly gained upon her. The asphodel bent under her flying feet, and the golden flowers of the *Fiori Maggio* were swept aside as she fled. Yet ever Alpheus gained upon her, until at length she felt that the chase was ended, and cried to Diana to save her. Then a cloud, grey and thick and blinding as the mist that wraps the mountain tops, suddenly descended and enfolded her, and Alpheus groped for her in vain.

"Arethusa!" she heard him cry, in a voice of piteous longing— "Arethusa!—my belovèd!"

Patiently he waited, with the love that makes uncouth things beautiful, until at length a little breath from Zephyrus blew aside the soft grey veil that hid his beloved from his sight, and he saw that the nymph had been transformed into a fountain. Not for a moment did Alpheus delay, but, turning himself into a torrent in flood, he rushed on in pursuit of Arethusa. Then did Diana, to save her votary, cleave a way for her through the dark earth even into the gloomy realm of Pluto himself, and the nymph rushed onward, onward still, and then upward, until at length she emerged again to the freedom of the blue sky and green trees, and beheld the golden orange groves and the grey olives, the burning red geranium flowers and the great snow-capped mountain of Sicily.

But Alpheus had a love for her that cast out all fear. Through the terrible blackness of the Cocytus valley he followed Arethusa, and

85

found a means of bursting through the encumbering earth and joining her again. And in a spring that rises out of the sea near the shore he was able at last to mingle his waters with those of the one for whom he had lost his godship.

"And now from their fountainsIn Enna's mountains,Down one vale where the morning basks,Like friends once partedGrown single-hearted,They ply their watery tasks,At sunrise they leapFrom their cradles steepIn the cave of the shelving hill;At noontide they flowThrough the woods belowAnd the meadows of asphodel;And at night they sleepIn the rocking deepBeneath the Ortygian shore;Like spirits that lieIn the azure skyWhen they love but live no more."

SHELLEY.

PERSEUS THE HERO

"We call such a man a hero in English to this day, and call it a 'heroic' thing to suffer pain and grief, that we may do good to our fellow-men."

CHARLES KINGSLEY.

In the pleasant land of Argos, now a place of unwholesome marshes, once upon a time there reigned a king called Acrisius, the father of one fair daughter. Danaë was her name, and she was very dear to the king until a day when he longed to know what lay hid for him in the lap of the gods, and consulted an oracle. With hanging head he returned from the temple, for the oracle had told him that when his daughter Danaë had borne a son, by the hand of that son death must surely come upon him. And because the fear of death was in him more strong than the love of his daughter, Acrisius resolved that by sacrificing her he would baffle the gods and frustrate Death itself. A great tower of brass was speedily built at his command, and in this prison Danaë was placed, to drag out her weary days.

But who can escape the designs of the gods? From Olympus great Zeus himself looked down and saw the air princess sighing away her youth. And, full of pity and of love, he himself entered the brazen tower in a golden shower, and Danaë became the bride of Zeus and happily passed with him the time of her imprisonment.

To her at length was born a son, a beautiful and kingly child, and great was the wrath of her father when he had tidings of the birth. Did the gods in the high heavens laugh at him? The laugh should yet be on his side. Down to the seashore he hurried Danaë and her newly-born babe, the little Perseus, put them in a great chest, and set them adrift to be a plaything for winds and waves and a prey for the cruel and hungry sea.

"When in the cunningly-wrought chest the raging blast and the stirred billow and terror fell upon her, with tearful cheeks she cast her arm around Perseus and spake, 'Alas, my child, what sorrow is mine! But thou slumberest, in baby-wise sleeping in this woeful ark; midst the darkness of the brazen rivet thou shinest and in the swart gloom sent forth; thou heedest not the deep foam of the passing wave above thy locks nor the voice of the blast as thou liest in thy purple covering, a sweet face. If terror had terrors for thee, and thou wert giving ear to my gentle words—I bid thee sleep, my babe, and may the sea sleep and our measureless woe; and may change of fortune come forth, Father Zeus, from thee. For that I make my prayer in boldness and beyond right, forgive me.'"

SIMONIDES OF KEOS.

For days and nights the mother and child were tossed on the billows, but yet no harm came near them, and one morning the chest grounded on the rocky beach of Seriphos, an island in the Ægean Sea. Here a fisherman came on this strange flotsam and jetsam of the waves and took the mother and child to Polydectes, the king, and the years that followed were peaceful years for Danaë and for Perseus. But as Perseus grew up, growing each day more goodly to look upon, more fearless, more ready to gaze with serene courage into the eyes of gods and of men, an evil thing befell his mother. She was but a girl when he was born, and as the years passed she grew ever more fair. And the crafty eyes of old Polydectes, the king, ever watched her more eagerly, always more hotly desired her for his wife. But Danaë, the beloved of Zeus himself, had no wish to wed the old king of the Cyclades, and proudly she scorned his suit. Behind her, as she knew well, was the stout arm of her son Perseus, and while Perseus was there, the king could do her no harm. But Perseus, unwitting of the danger his mother daily had to face, sailed the seas unfearingly, and felt that peace and safety surrounded him on every side. At Samos one day, while his ship was lading, Perseus lay down under the shade of a great tree, and soon his eyelids grew heavy with sleep, and there came to him, like butterflies that flit over the flowers in a sunlit garden, pleasant, light-winged dreams. But yet another dream followed close on the merry heels of those that went before. And before Perseus there stood one whose grey eyes were as the fathomless sea on the dawn of a summer day. Her long robes were blue as the hyacinths in spring, and the spear that she held in her hand was of a polished brightness, as the dart with which the gods smite the heart of a man, with joy inexpressible, with sorrow that is scarcely to be borne. To Perseus she spoke winged words.

"I am Pallas Athené," she said, "and to me the souls of men are known. Those whose fat hearts are as those of the beasts that perish do I know. They live at ease. No bitter sorrow is theirs, nor any fierce joy that lifts their feet free from the cumbering clay. But dear to my heart are the souls of those whose tears are tears of blood, whose joy is as the joy of the Immortals. Pain is theirs, and sorrow. Disappointment is theirs, and grief. Yet their love is as the love of those who dwell on Olympus. Patient they are and long-suffering, and ever they hope, ever do they trust. Ever they fight, fearless and unashamed, and when the sum of their days on earth is accomplished, wings, of whose existence they have never had knowledge, bear them upwards, out of the mist and din and strife of life, to the life that has no ending."

Then she laid her hand on the hand of Perseus. "Perseus," she said, "art thou of those whose dull souls forever dwell in pleasant ease, or wouldst thou be as one of the Immortals?"

And in his dream Perseus answered without hesitation:

"Rather let me die, a youth, living my life to the full, fighting ever, suffering ever," he said, "than live at ease like a beast that feeds on flowery pastures and knows no fiery gladness, no heart-bleeding pain."

Then Pallas Athené, laughing for joy, because she loved so well a hero's soul, showed him a picture that made even his brave heart sick for dread, and told him a terrible story.

In the dim, cold, far west, she said, there lived three sisters. One of them, Medusa, had been one of her priestesses, golden-haired and most beautiful, but when Athené found that she was as wicked as she was lovely, swiftly had she meted out a punishment. Every lock of her golden hair had been changed into a venomous snake. Her eyes, that had once been the cradles of love, were turned into love's stony tombs. Her rosy cheeks were now of Death's own livid hue. Her smile, which drew the hearts of lovers from their bosoms, had become a hideous thing. A grinning mask looked on the world, and to the world her gaping mouth and protruding tongue meant a horror before which the world stood terrified, dumb. There are some sadnesses too terrible for human hearts to bear, so it came to pass that in the dark cavern in which she dwelt, and in the shadowy woods around it, all living things that had met the awful gaze of her hopeless eyes were turned into stone. Then Pallas Athené showed Perseus, mirrored in a brazen shield, the face of one of the tragic things of the world. And as Perseus looked, his soul grew chill within him. But when Athené, in low voice, asked him:

"Perseus, wilt even end the sorrow of this piteous sinful one?" he answered, "Even that will I do—the gods helping me."

And Pallas Athené, smiling again in glad content, left him to dream, and Perseus awoke, in sudden fear, and found that in truth he had but dreamed, yet held his dream as a holy thing in the secret treasure-house of his heart.

Back to Seriphos he sailed, and found that his mother walked in fear of Polydectes the king. She told her son—a strong man now, though young in years—the story of his cruel persecution. Perseus saw red blood, and gladly would he have driven his keen blade far home in the heart of Polydectes. But his vengeance was to be a great vengeance, and the vengeance was delayed.

The king gave a feast, and on that day every one in the land brought offerings of their best and most costly to do him honour. Perseus alone came empty-handed, and as he stood in the king's court as though he were a beggar, the other youths mocked at him of whom they had ever been jealous.

"Thou sayest that thy father is one of the gods!" they said. "Where is thy godlike gift, O Perseus!"

And Polydectes, glad to humble the lad who was keeper of his mother's honour, echoed their foolish taunt.

"Where is the gift of the gods that the noble son of the gods has brought me?" he asked, and his fat cheeks and loose mouth quivered with ugly merriment.

Then Perseus, his head thrown back, gazed in the bold eyes of Polydectes.

Son of Zeus he was indeed, as he looked with royal scorn at those whom he despised.

"A godlike gift thou shalt have, in truth, O king," he said, and his voice rang out as a trumpet-call before the battle. "The gift of the gods shall be thine. The gods helping me, thou shalt have the head of Medusa."

A laugh, half-born, died in the throats of Polydectes and of those who listened, and Perseus strode out of the palace, a glow in his heart, for he knew that Pallas Athené had lit the fire that burned in him now, and that though he should shed the last drop of his life's blood to win what he sought, right would triumph, and wrong must be worsted.

Still quivering with anger, Perseus went down to the blue sea that gently whispered its secrets to the shore on which he stood.

"If Pallas Athené would but come," he thought—"if only my dreams might come true."

For, like many a boy before and since, Perseus had dreamed of gallant, fearless deeds. Like many a boy before and since, he had been the hero of a great adventure.

So he prayed, "Come to me! I pray you, Pallas Athené, come! and let me dream true."

His prayer was answered.

Into the sky there came a little silver cloud that grew and grew, and ever it grew nearer, and then, as in his dream, Pallas Athené came to him and smiled on him as the sun smiles on the water in spring. Nor was she alone. Beside her stood Hermes of the winged shoes, and Perseus knelt before the two in worship. Then, very gently, Pallas Athené gave him counsel, and more than counsel she gave.

In his hand she placed a polished shield, than which no mirror shone more brightly.

"Do not look at Medusa herself; look only on her image here reflected—then strike home hard and swiftly. And when her head is severed, wrap it in the goatskin on which the shield hangs. So wilt thou return in safety and in honour."

"But how, then, shall I cross the wet grey fields of this watery way?" asked Perseus. "Would that I were a white-winged bird that skims across the waves."

And, with the smile of a loving comrade, Hermes laid his hand on the shoulder of Perseus.

"My winged shoes shall be thine," he said, "and the white-winged sea-birds shalt thou leave far, far behind."

"Yet another gift is thine," said Athené. "Gird on, as gift from the gods, this sword that is immortal."

92

For a moment Perseus lingered. "May I not bid farewell to my mother?" he asked. "May I not offer burnt-offerings to thee and to Hermes, and to my father Zeus himself?"

But Athené said Nay, at his mother's weeping his heart might relent, and the offering that the Olympians desired was the head of Medusa.

Then, like a fearless young golden eagle, Perseus spread out his arms, and the winged shoes carried him across the seas to the cold northern lands whither Athené had directed him.

Each day his shoes took him a seven days' journey, and ever the air through which he passed grew more chill, till at length he reached the land of everlasting snow, where the black ice never knows the conquering warmth of spring, and where the white surf of the moaning waves freezes solid even as it touches the shore.

It was a dark grim place to which he came, and in a gloomy cavern by the sea lived the Graeæ, the three grey sisters that Athené had told him he must seek. Old and grey and horrible they were, with but one tooth amongst them, and but one eye. From hand to hand they passed the eye, and muttered and shivered in the blackness and the cold.

Boldly Perseus spoke to them and asked them to guide him to the place where Medusa and her sisters the Gorgons dwelt.

"No others know where they dwell," he said. "Tell me, I pray thee, the way that I may find them."

But the Grey Women were kin to the Gorgons, and hated all the children of men, and ugly was their evil mirth as they mocked at Perseus and refused to tell him where Medusa might be found.

But Perseus grew wily in his desire not to fail, and as the eye passed from one withered, clutching hand to another, he held out his own strong young palm, and in her blindness one of the three placed the eye within it.

Then the Grey Women gave a piteous cry, fierce and angry as the cry of old grey wolves that have been robbed of their prey, and gnashed upon him with their toothless jaws.

And Perseus said: "Wicked ye are and cruel at heart, and blind shall ye remain forever unless ye tell me where I may find the Gorgons. But tell me that, and I give back the eye."

Then they whimpered and begged of him, and when they found that all their beseeching was in vain, at length they told him.

"Go south," they said, "so far south that at length thou comest to the uttermost limits of the sea, to the place where the day and night meet. There is the Garden of the Hesperides, and of them must thou ask the way." And "Give us back our eye!" they wailed again most piteously, and Perseus gave back the eye into a greedy trembling old hand, and flew south like a swallow that is glad to leave the gloomy frozen lands behind.

To the garden of the Hesperides he came at last, and amongst the myrtles and roses and sunny fountains he came on the nymphs who there guard the golden fruit, and begged them to tell him whither he must wing his way in order to find the Gorgons. But the nymphs could not tell.

"We must ask Atlas," they said, "the giant who sits high up on the mountain and with his strong shoulders keeps the heavens and earth apart."

And with the nymphs Perseus went up the mountain and asked the patient giant to guide him to the place of his quest.

"Far away I can see them," said Atlas, "on an island in the great ocean. But unless thou wert to wear the helmet of Pluto himself, thy going must be in vain."

"What is this helmet?" asked Perseus, "and how can I gain it?"

"Didst thou wear the helmet of the ruler of Dark Places, thou wouldst be as invisible as a shadow in the blackness of night," answered Atlas; "but no mortal can obtain it, for only the Immortals can brave the terrors of the Shadowy Land and yet return; yet if thou wilt promise me one thing, the helmet shall be thine."

"What wouldst thou?" asked Perseus.

And Atlas said, "For many a long year have I borne this earth, and I grow aweary of my burden. When thou hast slain Medusa, let me gaze upon her face, that I may be turned into stone and suffer no more forever."

And Perseus promised, and at the bidding of Atlas one of the nymphs sped down to the land of the Shades, and for seven days Perseus and her sisters awaited her return. Her face was as the face of a white lily and her eyes were dark with sadness when she came, but with her she bore the helmet of Pluto, and when she and her sisters had kissed Perseus and bidden him a sorrowful farewell, he put on the helmet and vanished away.

Soon the gentle light of day had gone, and he found himself in a place where clammy fog blotted out all things, and where the sea was black as the water of that stream that runs through the Cocytus valley. And in that silent land where there is "neither night nor day, nor cloud nor breeze nor storm," he found the cave of horrors in which the Gorgons dwelt.

Two of them, like monstrous swine, lay asleep,

"But a third woman paced about the hall,And ever turned her head from wall to wall,And moaned aloud and shrieked in her despair,Because the golden tresses of her hairWere moved by writhing snakes from side to side,That in their writhing oftentimes would glideOn to her breast or shuddering shoulders white;Or, falling down, the hideous things would lightUpon her feet, and, crawling thence, would twineTheir slimy folds upon her ankles fine."

WILLIAM MORRIS.

In the shield of Pallas Athené the picture was mirrored, and as Perseus gazed on it his soul grew heavy for the beauty and the horror of Medusa. And "Oh that it had been her foul sisters that I must slay!" he thought at first, but then—"To slay her will be kind indeed," he said. "Her beauty has become corruption, and all the joy of life for her has passed into the agony of remembrance, the torture of unending remorse."

And when he saw her brazen claws that still were greedy and lustful to strike and to slay, his face grew stern, and he paused no longer, but with his sword he smote her neck with all his might and main. And to the rocky floor the body of Medusa fell with brazen clang, but her head he wrapped in the goatskin, while he turned his eyes away. Aloft then he sprang, and flew swifter than an arrow from the bow of Diana.

With hideous outcry the two other Gorgons found the body of Medusa, and, like foul vultures that hunt a little song-bird, they flew in pursuit of Perseus. For many a league they kept up the chase, and their howling was grim to hear. Across the seas they flew, and over the yellow sand of the Libyan desert, and as Perseus flew before them, some blood-drops fell from the severed head of Medusa, and from them bred the vipers that are found in the desert to this day. But bravely did the winged shoes of Hermes bear Perseus on, and by nightfall the Gorgon sisters had passed from sight, and Perseus found himself once more in the garden of the Hesperides. Ere he sought the nymphs, he knelt by the sea to cleanse from his hands Medusa's blood, and still does the seaweed that we find on sea-beaches after a storm bear the crimson stains.

And when Perseus had received glad welcome from the fair dwellers in the garden of the Hesperides, he sought Atlas, that to him he might fulfil his promise; and eagerly Atlas beheld him, for he was aweary of his long toil.

So Perseus uncovered the face of Medusa and held it up for the Titan to gaze upon.

And when Atlas looked upon her whose beauty had once been pure and living as that of a flower in spring, and saw only anguish and cruelty, foul wickedness, and hideous despair, his heart grew like stone within him. To stone, too, turned his great, patient face, and into stone grew his vast limbs and strong, crouching back. So did Atlas the Titan become Atlas the Mountain, and still his head, white-crowned with snow, and his great shoulder far up in misty clouds, would seem to hold apart the earth and the sky.

Then Perseus again took flight, and in his flight he passed over many lands and suffered weariness and want, and sometimes felt his faith growing low. Yet ever he sped on, hoping ever, enduring ever. In Egypt he had rest and was fed and honoured by the people of the land, who were fain to keep him to be one of their gods. And in a place called Chemmis they built a statue of him when he had gone, and for many hundreds of years it stood there. And the Egyptians said that ever and again Perseus returned, and that when he came the Nile rose high and the season was fruitful because he had blessed their land.

Far down below him as he flew one day he saw something white on a purple rock in the sea. It seemed too large to be a snowy-plumaged bird, and he darted swiftly downward that he might see more clearly. The spray lashed against the steep rocks of the desolate island, and showered itself upon a figure that at first he took to be a statue of white marble. The figure was but that of a girl, slight and very youthful, yet more fair even than any of the nymphs of the Hesperides. Invisible in his Helmet of Darkness, Perseus drew near, and saw that the fragile white figure was shaken by shivering sobs. The waves, every few moments, lapped up on her little cold white feet, and he saw that heavy chains held her imprisoned to that chilly rock in the sea. A great anger stirred the heart of Perseus, and swiftly he took the helmet from his head and stood beside her. The maid gave a cry of terror, but there was no evil thing in the face of Perseus. Naught but strength and kindness and purity shone out of his steady eyes.

Thus when, very gently, he asked her what was the meaning of her cruel imprisonment, she told him the piteous story, as a little child tells the story of its grief to the mother who comforts it. Her mother was queen of Ethiopia, she said, and very, very beautiful. But when the queen had boasted that no nymph who played amongst the snow-crested billows of the sea was as fair as she, a terrible punishment was sent to her. All along the coast of her father's kingdom a loathsome sea-monster came to hold its sway, and hideous were its ravages. Men and women, children and animals, all were equally desirable food for its insatiate maw, and the whole land of Ethiopia lay in mourning because of it. At last her father, the king, had consulted an oracle that he might find help to rid the land of the monster. And the oracle had told him that only when his fair daughter, Andromeda, had been sacrificed to the creature that scourged the sea-coast would the country go free. Thus had she been brought there by her parents that one life might be given for many, and that her mother's broken heart might expiate her sin of vanity. Even as Andromeda spoke, the sea was broken by the track of a creature that cleft the water as does the forerunning gale of a mighty storm. And Andromeda gave a piteous cry.

"Lo! he comes!" she cried. "Save me! ah, save me! I am so young to die."

Then Perseus darted high above her and for an instant hung poised like a hawk that is about to strike. Then, like the hawk that cannot miss its prey, swiftly did he swoop down and smote with his sword the devouring monster of the ocean. Not once, but again and again he smote, until all the water round the rock was churned into slime and blood-stained froth, and until his loathsome combatant floated on its back, mere carrion for the scavengers of the sea.

98

Then Perseus hewed off the chains that held Andromeda, and in his arms he held her tenderly as he flew with her to her father's land.

Who so grateful then as the king and queen of Ethiopia? and who so happy as Andromeda? for Perseus, her deliverer, dearest and greatest hero to her in all the world, not only had given her her freedom, but had given her his heart.

Willingly and joyfully her father agreed to give her to Perseus for his wife. No marriage feast so splendid had ever been held in Ethiopia in the memory of man, but as it went on, an angry man with a band of sullen-faced followers strode into the banqueting-hall. It was Phineus, he who had been betrothed to Andromeda, yet who had not dared to strike a blow for her rescue. Straight at Perseus they rushed, and fierce was the fight that then began. But of a sudden, from the goatskin where it lay hid, Perseus drew forth the head of Medusa, and Phineus and his warriors were turned into stone.

For seven days the marriage feast lasted, but on the eighth night Pallas Athené came to Perseus in a dream.

"Nobly and well hast thou played the hero, O son of Zeus!" she said; "but now that thy toil is near an end and thy sorrows have ended in joy, I come to claim the shoes of Hermes, the helmet of Pluto, the sword, and the shield that is mine own. Yet the head of the Gorgon must thou yet guard awhile, for I would have it laid in my temple at Seriphos that I may wear it on my shield for evermore."

As she ceased to speak, Perseus awoke, and lo, the shield and helmet and the sword and winged shoes were gone, so that he knew that his dream was no false vision.

Then did Perseus and Andromeda, in a red-prowed galley made by cunning craftsmen from Phœnicia, sail away westward, until at length they came to the blue water of the Ægean Sea, and saw rising out of the waves before them the rocks of Seriphos. And when the rowers rested on their long oars, and the red-prowed ship ground on the pebbles of the beach, Perseus and his bride sought Danaë, the fair mother of Perseus.

Black grew the brow of the son of Danaë when she told him what cruel things she had suffered in his absence from the hands of Polydectes the king. Straight to the palace Perseus strode, and there found the king and his friends at their revels. For seven years had Perseus been away, and now it was no longer a stripling who stood in the palace hall, but a man in stature and bearing like one of the gods. Polydectes alone knew him, and from his wine he looked up with mocking gaze.

"So thou hast returned? oh nameless son of a deathless god," he said. "Thou didst boast, but methinks thy boast was an empty one!"

But even as he spoke, the jeering smile froze on his face, and the faces of those who sat with him stiffened in horror.

"O king," Perseus said, "I swore that, the gods helping me, thou shouldst have the head of Medusa. The gods have helped me. Behold the Gorgon's head."

Wild horror in their eyes, Polydectes and his friends gazed on the unspeakable thing, and as they gazed they turned into stone—a ring of grey stones that still sit on a hillside of Seriphos.

With his wife and his mother, Perseus then sailed away, for he had a great longing to take Danaë back to the land of her birth and to see if her father, Acrisius, still lived and might not now repent of his cruelty to her and to his grandson. But there he found that the sins of Acrisius had been punished and that he had been driven from his throne and his own land by a usurper. Not for long did the sword of Perseus dwell in its scabbard, and speedily was the usurper cast forth, and all the men of Argos acclaimed Perseus as their glorious king. But Perseus would not be their king.

"I go to seek Acrisius," he said. "My mother's father is your king."

Again his galley sailed away, and at last, up the long Eubœan Sea they came to the town of Larissa, where the old king now dwelt.

A feast and sports were going on when they got there, and beside the king of the land sat Acrisius, an aged man, yet a kingly one indeed.

And Perseus thought, "If I, a stranger, take part in the sports and carry away prizes from the men of Larissa, surely the heart of Acrisius must soften towards me."

Thus did he take off his helmet and cuirass, and stood unclothed beside the youths of Larissa, and so godlike was he that they all said, amazed, "Surely this stranger comes from Olympus and is one of the Immortals."

In his hand he took a discus, and full five fathoms beyond those of the others he cast it, and a great shout arose from those who watched, and Acrisius cried out as loudly as all the rest.

"Further still!" they cried. "Further still canst thou hurl! thou art a hero indeed!"

And Perseus, putting forth all his strength, hurled once again, and the discus flew from his hand like a bolt from the hand of Zeus. The watchers held their breath and made ready for a shout of delight as they saw it speed on, further than mortal man had ever hurled before. But joy died in their hearts when a gust of wind caught the discus as it sped and hurled it against Acrisius, the king. And with a sigh like the sigh that passes through the leaves of a tree as the woodman fells it and it crashes to the earth, so did Acrisius fall and lie prone. To his side rushed Perseus, and lifted him tenderly in his arms. But the spirit of Acrisius had fled. And with a great cry of sorrow Perseus called to the people:

"Behold me! I am Perseus, grandson of the man I have slain! Who can avoid the decree of the gods?"

For many a year thereafter Perseus reigned as king, and to him and to his fair wife were born four sons and three daughters. Wisely and well he reigned, and when, at a good old age, Death took him and the wife of his heart, the gods, who had always held him dear, took him up among the stars to live for ever and ever. And there still, on clear and starry nights, we may see him holding the Gorgon's head. Near him are the father and mother of Andromeda—Cepheus and Cassiopeia, and close beside him stands Andromeda with her white arms spread out across the blue sky as in the days when she stood chained to the rock. And those who sail the watery ways look up for guidance to one whose voyaging is done and whose warfare is accomplished, and take their bearings from the constellation of Cassiopeia.

THEY WHIMPERED AND BEGGED OF HIM

NIOBE

"... Like Niobe, all tears."

SHAKESPEARE.

The quotation is an overworked quotation, like many another of those from *Hamlet*; yet, have half of those whose lips utter it more than the vaguest acquaintance with the story of Niobe and the cause of her tears? The noble group—attributed to Praxiteles—of Niobe and her last remaining child, in the Uffizi Palace at Florence, has been so often reproduced that it also has helped to make the anguished figure of the Theban queen a familiar one in pictorial tragedy, so that as long as the works of those Titans of art, Shakespeare and Praxiteles, endure, no other monument is wanted for the memory of Niobe.

Like many of the tales of mythology, her tragedy is a story of vengeance wreaked upon a mortal by an angry god. She was the daughter of Tantalus, and her husband was Amphion, King of Thebes, himself a son of Zeus. To her were born seven fair daughters and seven beautiful and gallant sons, and it was not because of her own beauty, nor her husband's fame, nor their proud descent and the greatness of their kingdom, that the Queen of Thebes was arrogant in her pride. Very sure she was that no woman had ever borne children like her own children, whose peers were not to be found on earth nor in heaven. Even in our own day there are mortal mothers who feel as Niobe felt.

But amongst the Immortals there was also a mother with children whom she counted as peerless. Latona, mother of Apollo and Diana, was magnificently certain that in all time, nor in eternity to come, could there be a son and daughter so perfect in beauty, in wisdom, and in power as the two that were her own. Loudly did she proclaim her proud belief, and when Niobe heard it she laughed in scorn.

103

"The goddess has a son and a daughter," she said. "Beautiful and wise and powerful they may be, but I have borne seven daughters and seven sons, and each son is more than the peer of Apollo, each daughter more than the equal of Diana, the moon-goddess!"

And to her boastful words Latona gave ear, and anger began to grow in her heart.

Each year the people of Thebes were wont to hold a great festival in honour of Latona and her son and daughter, and it was an evil day for Niobe when she came upon the adoring crowd that, laurel-crowned, bore frankincense to lay before the altars of the gods whose glories they had assembled together to celebrate.

"Oh foolish ones!" she said, and her voice was full of scorn, "am I not greater than Latona? I am the daughter of a goddess, my husband, the king, the son of a god. Am I not fair? am I not queenly as Latona herself? And, of a surety, I am richer by far than the goddess who has but one daughter and one son. Look on my seven noble sons! behold the beauty of my seven daughters, and see if they in beauty and all else do not equal the dwellers in Olympus!"

And when the people looked, and shouted aloud, for in truth Niobe and her children were like unto gods, their queen said, "Do not waste thy worship, my people. Rather make the prayers to thy king and to me and to my children who buttress us round and make our strength so great, that fearlessly we can despise the gods."

In her home on the Cynthian mountain top, Latona heard the arrogant words of the queen of Thebes, and even as a gust of wind blows smouldering ashes into a consuming fire, her growing anger flamed into rage. She called Apollo and Diana to her, and commanded them to avenge the blasphemous insult which had been given to them and to their mother. And the twin gods listened with burning hearts.

"Truly shalt thou be avenged!" cried Apollo. "The shameless one shall learn that not unscathed goes she who profanes the honour of the mother of the deathless gods!"

And with their silver bows in their hands, Apollo, the smiter from afar, and Diana, the virgin huntress, hasted to Thebes. There they found all the noble youths of the kingdom pursuing their sports. Some rode, some were having chariot-races, and excelling in all things were the seven sons of Niobe.

Apollo lost no time. A shaft from his quiver flew, as flies a bolt from the hand of Zeus, and the first-born of Niobe fell, like a young pine broken by the wind, on the floor of his winning chariot. His brother, who followed him, went on the heels of his comrade swiftly down to the Shades. Two of the other sons of Niobe were wrestling together, their great muscles moving under the skin of white satin that covered their perfect bodies, and as they gripped each other, yet another shaft was driven from the bow of Apollo, and both lads fell, joined by one arrow, on the earth, and there breathed their lives away.

Their elder brother ran to their aid, and to him, too, came death, swift and sure. The two youngest, even as they cried for mercy to an unknown god, were hurried after them by the unerring arrows of Apollo. The cries of those who watched this terrible slaying were not long in bringing Niobe to the place where her sons lay dead. Yet, even then, her pride was unconquered, and she defied the gods, and Latona, to whose jealousy she ascribed the fate of her "seven spears."

"Not yet hast thou conquered, Latona!" she cried. "My seven sons lie dead, yet to me still remain the seven perfect lovelinesses that I have borne. Try to match them, if thou canst, with the beauty of thy two! Still am I richer than thou, O cruel and envious mother of one daughter and one son!"

But even as she spoke, Diana had drawn her bow, and as the scythe of a mower quickly cuts down, one after the other, the tall white blossoms in the meadow, so did her arrows slay the daughters of Niobe. When one only remained, the pride of Niobe was broken. With her arms round the little slender frame of her golden-haired youngest born, she looked up to heaven, and cried upon all the gods for mercy.

"She is so little!" she wailed. "So young—so dear! Ah, spare me *one*," she said, "only one out of so many!"

But the gods laughed. Like a harsh note of music sounded the twang of Diana's bow. Pierced by a silver arrow, the little girl lay dead. The dignity of Latona was avenged.

Overwhelmed by despair, King Amphion killed himself, and Niobe was left alone to gaze on the ruin around her. For nine days she sat, a Greek Rachel, weeping for her children and refusing to be comforted, because they were not. On the tenth day, the sight was too much even for the superhuman hearts of the gods to endure. They turned the bodies into stone and themselves buried them. And when they looked on the face of Niobe and saw on it a bleeding anguish that no human hand could stay nor the word of any god comfort, the gods were merciful. Her grief was immortalised, for Niobe, at their will, became a stone, and was carried by a wailing tempest to the summit of Mount Sipylus, in Lydia, where a spring of Argos bore her name. Yet although a rock was Niobe, from her blind eyes of stone the tears still flowed, a clear stream of running water, symbol of a mother's anguish and never-ending grief.

HYACINTHUS

... "The sad deathOf Hyacinthus, when the cruel breathOf Zephyr slew him—Zephyr penitentWho now, ere Phœbus mounts the firmament,Fondles the flower amid the sobbing rain."

KEATS.

"Whom the gods love die young"—truly it would seem so, as we read the old tales of men and of women beloved of the gods. To those men who were deemed worthy of being companions of the gods, seemingly no good fortune came. Yet, after all, if even in a brief span of life they had tasted god-given happiness, was their fate one to be pitied? Rather let us keep our tears for those who, in a colourless grey world, have seen the dull days go past laden with trifling duties, unnecessary cares and ever-narrowing ideals, and have reached old age and the grave—no narrower than their lives— without ever having known a fulness of happiness, such as the Olympians knew, or ever having dared to reach upwards and to hold fellowship with the Immortals.

Hyacinthus was a Spartan youth, son of Clio, one of the Muses, and of the mortal with whom she had mated, and from mother, or father, or from the gods themselves, he had received the gift of beauty. It chanced one day that as Apollo drove his chariot on its all-conquering round, he saw the boy. Hyacinthus was as fair to look upon as the fairest of women, yet he was not only full of grace, but was muscular, and strong as a straight young pine on Mount Olympus that fears not the blind rage of the North Wind nor the angry tempests of the South.

When Apollo had spoken with him he found that the face of Hyacinthus did not belie the heart within him, and gladly the god felt that at last he had found the perfect companion, the ever courageous and joyous young mate, whose mood was always ready to meet his own. Did Apollo desire to hunt, with merry shout Hyacinthus called the hounds. Did the great god deign to fish,

Hyacinthus was ready to fetch the nets and to throw himself, whole-souled, into the great affair of chasing and of landing the silvery fishes. When Apollo wished to climb the mountains, to heights so lonely that not even the moving of an eagle's wing broke the everlasting stillness, Hyacinthus—his strong limbs too perfect for the chisel of any sculptor worthily to reproduce—was ready and eager for the climb. And when, on the mountain top, Apollo gazed in silence over illimitable space, and watched the silver car of his sister Diana rising slowly into the deep blue of the sky, silvering land and water as she passed, it was never Hyacinthus who was the first to speak—with words to break the spell of Nature's perfect beauty, shared in perfect companionship. There were times, too, when Apollo would play his lyre, and when naught but the music of his own making could fulfil his longing. And when those times came, Hyacinthus would lie at the feet of his friend—of the friend who was a god—and would listen, with eyes of rapturous joy, to the music that his master made. A very perfect friend was this friend of the sun-god.

Nor was it Apollo alone who desired the friendship of Hyacinthus. Zephyrus, god of the South Wind, had known him before Apollo crossed his path and had eagerly desired him for a friend. But who could stand against Apollo? Sulkily Zephyrus marked their ever-ripening friendship, and in his heart jealousy grew into hatred, and hatred whispered to him of revenge. Hyacinthus excelled at all sports, and when he played quoits it was sheer joy for Apollo, who loved all things beautiful, to watch him as he stood to throw the disc, his taut muscles making him look like Hermes, ready to spurn the cumbering earth from off his feet. Further even than the god, his friend, could Hyacinthus throw, and always his merry laugh when he succeeded made the god feel that nor man nor god could ever grow old. And so there came that day, fore-ordained by the Fates, when Apollo and Hyacinthus played a match together. Hyacinthus made a valiant throw, and Apollo took his place, and cast the discus high and far. Hyacinthus ran forward eager to measure the distance, shouting with excitement over a throw that had indeed been worthy of a god. Thus did Zephyrus gain his opportunity. Swiftly through the tree-tops ran the murmuring South Wind, and smote the discus of Apollo with a cruel hand. Against the forehead of Hyacinthus it dashed, smiting the locks that lay upon it, crashing through skin and flesh and bone, felling him to the earth. Apollo ran towards him and raised him in his arms. But the head of Hyacinthus fell over on the god's shoulder, like the head of a lily whose stem is broken. The red blood gushed to the ground, an unquenchable stream, and darkness fell on the eyes of Hyacinthus, and, with the flow of his life's blood, his gallant young soul passed away.

"Would that I could die for thee, Hyacinthus!" cried the god, his god's heart near breaking. "I have robbed thee of thy youth. Thine is the suffering, mine the crime. I shall sing thee ever—oh perfect friend! And evermore shalt thou live as a flower that will speak to the hearts of men of spring, of everlasting youth—of life that lives forever."

As he spoke, there sprang from the blood-drops at his feet a cluster of flowers, blue as the sky in spring, yet hanging their heads as if in sorrow.

And still, when winter is ended, and the song of birds tell us of the promise of spring, if we go to the woods, we find traces of the vow of the sun-god. The trees are budding in buds of rosy hue, the willow branches are decked with silvery catkins powdered with gold. The larches, like slender dryads, wear a feathery garb of tender green, and under the trees of the woods the primroses look up, like fallen stars. Along the woodland path we go, treading on fragrant pine-needles and on the beech leaves of last year that have not yet lost their radiant amber. And, at a turn of the way, the sun-god suddenly shines through the great dark branches of the giants of the forest, and before us lies a patch of exquisite blue, as though a god had robbed the sky and torn from it a precious fragment that seems alive and moving, between the sun and the shadow.

And, as we look, the sun caresses it, and the South Wind gently moves the little bell-shaped flowers of the wild hyacinth as it softly sweeps across them. So does Hyacinthus live on; so do Apollo and Zephyrus still love and mourn their friend.

DARKNESS FELL ON THE EYES OF HYACINTHUS

KING MIDAS OF THE GOLDEN TOUCH

In the plays of Shakespeare we have three distinct divisions—three separate volumes. One deals with Tragedy, another with Comedy, a third with History; and a mistake made by the young in their aspect of life is that they do the same thing, and keep tragedy and comedy severely apart, relegating them to separate volumes that, so they think, have nothing to do with each other. But those who have passed many milestones on the road know that *"History"* is the only right label for the Book of Life's many parts, and that the actors in the great play are in truth tragic comedians.

This is the story of Midas, one of the chief tragic comedians of mythology.

Once upon a time the kingdom of Phrygia lacked a king, and in much perplexity, the people sought help from an oracle. The answer was very definite:

"The first man who enters your city riding in a car shall be your king."

That day there came slowly jogging into the city in their heavy, wooden-wheeled wain, the peasant Gordias and his wife and son, whose destination was the marketplace, and whose business was to sell the produce of their little farm and vineyard—fowls, a goat or two, and a couple of skinsful of strong, purple-red wine. An eager crowd awaited their entry, and a loud shout of welcome greeted them. And their eyes grew round and their mouths fell open in amaze when they were hailed as King and Queen and Prince of Phrygia.

The gods had indeed bestowed upon Gordias, the low-born peasant, a surprising gift, but he showed his gratitude by dedicating his wagon to the deity of the oracle and tying it up in its place with the wiliest knot that his simple wisdom knew, pulled as tight as his brawny arms and strong rough hands could pull. Nor could anyone untie the famous Gordian knot, and therefore become, as the oracle promised, lord of all Asia, until centuries had passed, and Alexander the Great came to Phrygia and sliced through the knot with his all-conquering sword.

In time Midas, the son of Gordias, came to inherit the throne and crown of Phrygia. Like many another not born and bred to the purple, his honours sat heavily upon him. From the day that his father's wain had entered the city amidst the acclamations of the people, he had learned the value of power, and therefore, from his boyhood onward, power, always more power, was what he coveted. Also his peasant father had taught him that gold could buy power, and so Midas ever longed for more gold, that could buy him a place in the world that no descendant of a long race of kings should be able to contest. And from Olympus the gods looked down and smiled, and vowed that Midas should have the chance of realising his heart's desire.

Therefore one day when he and his court were sitting in the solemn state that Midas required, there rode into their midst, tipsily swaying on the back of a gentle full-fed old grey ass, ivy-crowned, jovial and foolish, the satyr Silenus, guardian of the young god Bacchus.

With all the deference due to the friend of a god Midas treated this disreputable old pedagogue, and for ten days and nights on end he feasted him royally. On the eleventh day Bacchus came in search of his preceptor, and in deep gratitude bade Midas demand of him what he would, because he had done Silenus honour when to dishonour him lay in his power.

Not even for a moment did Midas ponder.

"I would have gold," he said hastily—"much gold. I would have that touch by which all common and valueless things become golden treasures."

And Bacchus, knowing that here spoke the son of peasants who many times had gone empty to bed after a day of toilful striving on the rocky uplands of Phrygia, looked a little sadly in the eager face of Midas, and answered: "Be it as thou wilt. Thine shall be the golden touch."

Then Bacchus and Silenus went away, a rout of singing revellers at their heels, and Midas quickly put to proof the words of Bacchus.

An olive tree grew near where he stood, and from it he picked a little twig decked with leaves of softest grey, and lo, it grew heavy as he held it, and glittered like a piece of his crown. He stooped to touch the green turf on which some fragrant violets grew, and turf grew into cloth of gold, and violets lost their fragrance and became hard, solid, golden things. He touched an apple whose cheek grew rosy in the sun, and at once it became like the golden fruit in the Garden of the Hesperides. The stone pillars of his palace as he brushed past them on entering, blazed like a sunset sky. The gods had not deceived him. Midas had the Golden Touch. Joyously he strode into the palace and commanded a feast to be prepared—a feast worthy of an occasion so magnificent.

But when Midas, with the healthy appetite of the peasant-born, would have eaten largely of the savoury food that his cooks prepared, he found that his teeth only touched roast kid to turn it into a slab of gold, that garlic lost its flavour and became gritty as he chewed, that rice turned into golden grains, and curdled milk became a dower fit for a princess, entirely unnegotiable for the digestion of man. Baffled and miserable, Midas seized his cup of wine, but the red wine had become one with the golden vessel that held it; nor could he quench his thirst, for even the limpid water from the fountain was melted gold when it touched his dry lips. Only for a very few days was Midas able to bear the affliction of his wealth. There was nothing now for him to live for. He could buy the whole earth if he pleased, but even children shrank in terror from his touch, and hungry and thirsty and sick at heart he wearily dragged along his weighty robes of gold. Gold was power, he knew well, yet of what worth was gold while he starved? Gold could not buy him life and health and happiness.

In despair, at length he cried to the god who had given him the gift that he hated.

"Save me, O Bacchus!" he said. "A witless one am I, and the folly of my desire has been my undoing. Take away from me the accursed Golden Touch, and faithfully and well shall I serve thee forever."

Then Bacchus, very pitiful for him, told Midas to go to Sardis, the chief city of his worshippers, and to trace to its source the river upon which it was built. And in that pool, when he found it, he was to plunge his head, and so he would, for evermore, be freed from the Golden Touch.

It was a long journey that Midas then took, and a weary and a starving man was he when at length he reached the spring where the river Pactolus had its source. He crawled forward, and timidly plunged in his head and shoulders. Almost he expected to feel the harsh grit of golden water, but instead there was the joy he had known as a peasant boy when he laved his face and drank at a cool spring when his day's toil was ended. And when he raised his face from the pool, he knew that his hateful power had passed from him, but under the water he saw grains of gold glittering in the sand, and from that time forth the river Pactolus was noted for its gold.

One lesson the peasant king had learnt by paying in suffering for a mistake, but there was yet more suffering in store for the tragic comedian.

He had now no wish for golden riches, nor even for power. He wished to lead the simple life and to listen to the pipings of Pan along with the goat-herds on the mountains or the wild creatures in the woods. Thus it befell that he was present one day at a contest between Pan and Apollo himself. It was a day of merry-making for nymphs and fauns and dryads, and all those who lived in the lonely solitudes of Phrygia came to listen to the music of the god who ruled them. For as Pan sat in the shade of a forest one night and piped on his reeds until the very shadows danced, and the water of the stream by which he sat leapt high over the mossy stones it passed, and laughed aloud in its glee, the god had so gloried in his own power that he cried:

"Who speaks of Apollo and his lyre? Some of the gods may be well pleased with his music, and mayhap a bloodless man or two. But my music strikes to the heart of the earth itself. It stirs with rapture the very sap of the trees, and awakes to life and joy the innermost soul of all things mortal."

Apollo heard his boast, and heard it angrily.

"Oh, thou whose soul is the soul of the untilled ground!" he said, "wouldst thou place thy music, that is like the wind in the reeds, beside my music, which is as the music of the spheres?"

And Pan, splashing with his goat's feet amongst the water-lilies of the stream on the bank of which he sat, laughed loudly and cried:

"Yea, would I, Apollo! Willingly would I play thee a match—thou on thy golden lyre—I on my reeds from the river."

Thus did it come to pass that Apollo and Pan matched against each other their music, and King Midas was one of the judges.

First of all Pan took his fragile reeds, and as he played, the leaves on the trees shivered, and the sleeping lilies raised their heads, and the birds ceased their song to listen and then flew straight to their mates. And all the beauty of the world grew more beautiful, and all its terror grew yet more grim, and still Pan piped on, and laughed to see the nymphs and the fauns first dance in joyousness and then tremble in fear, and the buds to blossom, and the stags to bellow in their lordship of the hills. When he ceased, it was as though a tensely-drawn string had broken, and all the earth lay breathless and mute. And Pan turned proudly to the golden-haired god who had listened as he had spoken through the hearts of reeds to the hearts of men.

"Canst, then, make music like unto my music, Apollo?" he said.

Then Apollo, his purple robes barely hiding the perfection of his limbs, a wreath of laurel crowning his yellow curls, looked down at Pan from his godlike height and smiled in silence. For a moment his hand silently played over the golden strings of his lyre, and then his finger-tips gently touched them. And every creature there who had a soul, felt that that soul had wings, and the wings sped them straight to Olympus. Far away from all earth-bound creatures they flew, and dwelt in magnificent serenity amongst the Immortals. No longer was there strife, or any dispeace. No more was there fierce warring between the actual and the unknown. The green fields and thick woods had faded into nothingness, and their creatures, and the fair nymphs and dryads, and the wild fauns and centaurs longed and fought no more, and man had ceased to desire the impossible. Throbbing nature and passionately desiring life faded into dust before the melody that Apollo called forth, and when his strings had ceased to quiver and only the faintly remembered echo of his music remained, it was as though the earth had passed away and all things had become new.

For the space of many seconds all was silence.

Then, in low voice, Apollo asked:

"Ye who listen—who is the victor?"

And earth and sea and sky, and all the creatures of earth and sky, and of the deep, replied as one:

"The victory is thine, Divine Apollo."

Yet was there one dissentient voice.

Midas, sorely puzzled, utterly un-understanding, was relieved when the music of Apollo ceased. "If only Pan would play again," he murmured to himself. "I wish to live, and Pan's music gives me life. I love the woolly vine-buds and the fragrant pine-leaves, and the scent of the violets in the spring. The smell of the fresh-ploughed earth is dear to me, the breath of the kine that have grazed in the meadows of wild parsley and of asphodel. I want to drink red wine and to eat and love and fight and work and be joyous and sad, fierce and strong, and very weary, and to sleep the dead sleep of men who live only as weak mortals do."

Therefore he raised his voice, and called very loud: "Pan's music is sweeter and truer and greater than the music of Apollo. Pan is the victor, and I, King Midas, give him the victor's crown!"

With scorn ineffable the sun-god turned upon Midas, his peasant's face transfigured by his proud decision. For a little he gazed at him in silence, and his look might have turned a sunbeam to an icicle.

Then he spoke:

"The ears of an ass have heard my music," he said. "Henceforth shall Midas have ass's ears."

And when Midas, in terror, clapped his hands to his crisp black hair, he found growing far beyond it, the long, pointed ears of an ass. Perhaps what hurt him most, as he fled away, was the shout of merriment that came from Pan. And fauns and nymphs and satyrs echoed that shout most joyously.

Willingly would he have hidden in the woods, but there he found no hiding-place. The trees and shrubs and flowering things seemed to shake in cruel mockery. Back to his court he went and sent for the court hairdresser, that he might bribe him to devise a covering for these long, peaked, hairy symbols of his folly. Gladly the hairdresser accepted many and many oboli, many and many golden gifts, and all Phrygia wondered, while it copied, the strange headdress of the king.

But although much gold had bought his silence, the court barber was unquiet of heart. All day and all through the night he was tormented by his weighty secret. And then, at length, silence was to him a torture too great to be borne; he sought a lonely place, there dug a deep hole, and, kneeling by it, softly whispered to the damp earth: "King Midas has ass's ears."

Greatly relieved, he hastened home, and was well content until, on the spot where his secret lay buried, rushes grew up. And when the winds blew through them, the rushes whispered for all those who passed by to hear: "King Midas has ass's ears! King Midas has ass's ears!" Those who listen very carefully to what the green rushes in marshy places whisper as the wind passes through them, may hear the same thing to this day. And those who hear the whisper of the rushes may, perhaps, give a pitying thought to Midas—the tragic comedian of mythology.

CEYX AND HALCYONE

"St. Martin's summer, halcyon days."

King Henry VI, i. 2, 131.

"Halcyon days"—how often is the expression made use of, how seldom do its users realise from whence they have borrowed it.

"These were halcyon days," says the old man, and his memory wanders back to a time when for him

"All the world is young, lad,And all the trees are green;And every goose a swan, lad,And every lass a queen."

Yet the story of Halcyone is one best to be understood by the heavy-hearted woman who wanders along the bleak sea-beach and strains her weary eyes for the brown sail of the fishing-boat that will never more return.

Over the kingdom of Thessaly, in the days of long ago, there reigned a king whose name was Ceyx, son of Hesperus, the Day Star, and almost as radiant in grace and beauty as was his father. His wife was the fair Halcyone, daughter of Æolus, ruler of the winds, and most perfectly did this king and queen love one another. Their happiness was unmarred until there came a day when Ceyx had to mourn for the loss of a brother. Following close on the heels of this disaster came direful prodigies which led Ceyx to fear that in some way he must have incurred the hostility of the gods. To him there was no way in which to discover wherein lay his fault, and to make atonement for it, but by going to consult the oracle of Apollo at Claros, in Ionia. When he told Halcyone what he must do, she knew well that she must not try to turn him from his solemn purpose, yet there hung over her heart a black shadow of fear and of evil foreboding that no loving words of assurance could drive away. Most piteously she begged him to take her with him, but the king

119

knew too well the dangers of the treacherous Ægean Sea to risk on it the life of the woman that he loved so well.

"I promise," he said, "by the rays of my Father the Day Star, that if fate permits I will return before the moon shall have twice rounded her orb."

Down by the shore the sailors of King Ceyx awaited his coming, and when with passionately tender love he and Halcyone had taken farewell of each other, the rowers sat down on the benches and dipped their long oars into the water.

With rhythmic swing they drove the great ship over the grey sea, while Ceyx stood on deck and gazed back at his wife until his eyes could no longer distinguish her from the rocks on the shore, nor could she any longer see the white sails of the ship as it crested the restless waves. Heavier still was her heart when she turned away from the shore, and yet more heavy it grew as the day wore on and dark night descended. For the air was full of the clamorous wailings of the fierce winds whose joy it is to lash the waves into rage and to strew with dead men and broken timber the angry, surf-beaten shore.

"My King," she sighed to herself. "My King! my Own!" And through the weary hours she prayed to the gods to bring him safely back to her, and many times she offered fragrant incense to Juno, protectress of women, that she might have pity on a woman whose husband and true lover was out in the storm, a plaything for ruthless winds and waves.

A helpless plaything was the king of Thessaly. Long ere the dim evening light had made of the shore of his own land a faint, grey line, the white-maned horses of Poseidon, king of the seas, began to rear their heads, and as night fell, a black curtain, blotting out every landmark, and all home-like things, the East Wind rushed across the Ægean Sea, smiting the sea-horses into madness, seizing the sails with cruel grasp and casting them in tatters before it, snapping the mast as though it were but a dry reed by the river. Before so mighty a tempest no oars could be of any avail, and for a little time only the winds and waves gambolled like a half-sated wolf-pack over their helpless prey. With hungry roar the great weight of black water stove in the deck and swept the sailors out of the ship to choke them in its icy depths; and ever it would lift the wounded thing high up on its foaming white crests, as though to toss it to the dark sky, and ever again would suck it down into the blackness, while the shrieking winds drove it onward with howling taunts and mocking laughter. While life stayed in him, Ceyx thought only of Halcyone. He had no fear, only the fear of the grief his death must bring to her who loved him as he loved her, his peerless queen, his Halcyone. His prayers to the gods were prayers for her. For himself he asked one thing only—that the waves might bear his body to her sight, so that her gentle hands might lay him in his tomb. With shout of triumph that they had slain a king, winds and waves seized him even as he prayed, and the Day Star that was hidden behind the black pall of the sky knew that his son, a brave king and a faithful lover, had gone down to the Shades.

When Dawn, the rosy-fingered, had come to Thessaly, Halcyone, white-faced and tired-eyed, anxiously watched the sea, that still was tossing in half-savage mood. Eagerly she gazed at the place where last the white sail had been seen. Was it not possible that Ceyx, having weathered the gale, might for the present have foregone his voyage to Ionia, and was returning to her to bring peace to her heart? But the sea-beach was strewn with wrack and the winds still blew bits of tattered surf along the shore, and for her there was only the heavy labour of waiting, of waiting and of watching for the ship that never came. The incense from her altars blew out, in heavy sweetness, to meet the bitter-sweet tang of the seaweed that was carried in by the tide, for Halcyone prayed on, fearful, yet hoping that her prayers might still keep safe her man—her king—her lover. She busied herself in laying out the garments he would wear on his return, and in choosing the clothes in which she might be fairest in his eyes. This robe, as blue as the sky in spring—silver-bordered, as the sea in kind mood is bordered with a feathery silver fringe. She could recall just how Ceyx looked when first he saw her wear it. She could hear his very tones as he told her that of all queens she was the peeress, of all women the most beautiful, of all wives the most dear. Almost she forgot the horrors of the night, so certain did it seem that his dear voice must soon again tell her the words that have been love's litany since ever time began.

In the ears of Juno those petitions for him whose dead body was even then being tossed hither and thither by the restless waves, his murderers, came at last to be more than even she could bear. She gave command to her handmaiden Iris to go to the palace of Somnus, god of Sleep and brother of Death, and to bid him send to Halcyone a vision, in the form of Ceyx, to tell her that all her weary waiting was in vain.

In a valley among the black Cimmerian mountains the death-god Somnus had his abode. In her rainbow-hued robes, Iris darted through the sky at her mistress's bidding, tingeing, as she sped through them, the clouds that she passed. It was a silent valley that she reached at last. Here the sun never came, nor was there ever any sound to break the silence. From the ground the noiseless grey clouds, whose work it is to hide the sun and moon, rose softly and rolled away up to the mountain tops and down to the lowest valleys, to work the will of the gods. All around the cave lurked the long dark shadows that bring fear to the heart of children, and that, at nightfall, hasten the steps of the timid wayfarer. No noise was there, but from far down the valley there came a murmur so faint and so infinitely soothing that it was less a sound than of a lullaby remembered in dreams. For past the valley of Sleep flow the waters of Lethe, the river of Forgetfulness. Close up to the door of the cave where dwelt the twin brothers, Sleep and Death, blood-red poppies grew, and at the door itself stood shadowy forms, their fingers on their lips, enjoining silence on all those who would enter in, amaranth-crowned, and softly waving sheaves of poppies that bring dreams from which there is no awakening. There was there no gate with hinges to creak or bars to clang, and into the stilly darkness Iris walked unhindered. From outer cave to inner cave she went, and each cave she left behind was less dark than the one that she entered. In the innermost room of all, on an ebony couch draped with sable curtains, the god of sleep lay drowsing. His garments were black, strewn with golden stars. A wreath of half-opened poppies crowned his sleepy head, and he leaned on the strong shoulder of Morpheus, his favourite son. All round his bed hovered pleasant dreams, gently stooping over him to whisper their messages, like a field of wheat swayed by the breeze, or willows that bow their silver heads and murmur to each other the secrets that no one ever knows. Brushing the idle dreams aside, as a ray of sunshine brushes away the grey wisps of mist that hang to the hillside, Iris walked up to the couch where Somnus lay. The light from her rainbow-hued robe lit up the darkness of the cave, yet Somnus lazily only half-opened his eyes, moved his head so that it rested more easily, and in a sleepy voice asked of her what might be her errand. "Somnus," she said, "gentlest of gods, tranquilliser of minds and soother of careworn hearts, Juno sends you her commands that you despatch a dream to Halcyone in the city of Trachine, representing her lost husband and all the events of the wreck."

Her message delivered, Iris hastened away, for it seemed to her that already her eyelids grew heavy, and that there were creeping upon her limbs, throwing silver dust in her eyes, lulling into peaceful slumber her mind, those sprites born of the blood-red poppies that bring to weary mortals rest and sweet forgetfulness.

Only rousing himself sufficiently to give his orders, Somnus entrusted to Morpheus the task imposed upon him by Juno, and then, with a yawn, turned over on his downy pillow, and gave himself up to exquisite slumber.

When he had winged his way to Trachine, Morpheus took upon himself the form of Ceyx and sought the room where Halcyone slept. She had watched the far horizon many hours that day. For many an hour had she vainly burned incense to the gods. Tired in heart and soul, in body and in mind, she laid herself down on her couch at last, hoping for the gift of sleep. Not long had she slept, in the dead-still sleep that weariness and a stricken heart bring with

123

them, when Morpheus came and stood by her side. He was only a dream, yet his face was the face of Ceyx. Not the radiant, beautiful son of the Day Star was the Ceyx who stood by her now and gazed on her with piteous, pitying dead eyes. His clothing dripped sea-water; in his hair was tangled the weed of the sea, uprooted by the storm. Pale, pale was his face, and his white hands gripped the stones and sand that had failed him in his dying agony.

Halcyone whimpered in her sleep as she looked on him, and Morpheus stooped over her and spoke the words that he had been told to say.

"I am thy husband, Ceyx, Halcyone. No more do prayers and the blue-curling smoke of incense avail me. Dead am I, slain by the storm and the waves. On my dead, white face the skies look down and the restless sea tosses my chill body that still seeks thee, seeking a haven in thy dear arms, seeking rest on thy warm, loving heart."

With a cry Halcyone started up, but Morpheus had fled, and there were no wet footprints nor drops of sea-water on the floor, marking, as she had hoped, the way that her lord had taken. Not again did Sleep visit her that night.

A grey, cold morning dawned and found her on the seashore. As ever, her eyes sought the far horizon, but no white sail, a messenger of hope, was there to greet her. Yet surely she saw something—a black speck, like a ship driven on by the long oars of mariners who knew well the path to home through the watery ways. From far away in the grey it hasted towards her, and then there came to Halcyone the knowledge that no ship was this thing, but a lifeless body, swept onwards by the hurrying waves. Nearer and nearer it came, until at length she could recognise the form of this flotsam and jetsam of the sea. With heart that broke as she uttered the words, she stretched out her arms and cried aloud: "O Ceyx! my Beloved! is it thus that thou returnest to me?"

To break the fierce assaults of sea and of storm there had been built out from the shore a mole, and on to this barrier leapt the distraught Halcyone. She ran along it, and when the dead, white body of the man she loved was still out of reach, she prayed her last prayer—a wordless prayer of anguish to the gods.

"Only let me get near him," she breathed. "Grant only that I nestle close against his dear breast. Let me show him that, living or dead, I am his, and he mine forever."

And to Halcyone a great miracle was then vouchsafed, for from out of her snowy shoulders grew snow-white pinions, and with them she skimmed over the waves until she reached the rigid body of Ceyx, drifting, a helpless burden for the conquering waves, in with the swift-flowing tide. As she flew, she uttered cries of love and of longing, but only strange raucous cries came from the throat that had once only made music. And when she reached the body of Ceyx and would fain have kissed his marble lips, Halcyone found that no longer were her own lips like the petals of a fair red rose warmed by the sun. For the gods had heard her prayer, and her horny beak seemed to the watchers on the shore to be fiercely tearing at the face of him who had been king of Thessaly.

Yet the gods were not merciless—or, perhaps, the love of Halcyone was an all-conquering love. For as the soul of Halcyone had passed into the body of a white-winged sea-bird, so also passed the soul of her husband the king. And for evermore Halcyone and her mate, known as the Halcyon birds, defied the storm and tempest, and proudly breasted, side by side, the angriest waves of the raging seas.

To them, too, did the gods grant a boon: that, for seven days before the shortest day of the year, and for seven days after it, there should reign over the sea a great calm in which Halcyone, in her floating nest, should hatch her young. And to those days of calm and sunshine, the name of the Halcyon Days was given.

And still, as a storm approaches, the white-winged birds come flying inland with shrill cries of warning to the mariners whose ships they pass in their flight.

"Ceyx!" they cry. "Remember Ceyx!"

And hastily the fishermen fill their sails, and the smacks drive homeward to the haven where the blue smoke curls upwards from the chimneys of their homesteads, and where the red poppies are nodding sleepily amongst the yellow corn.

A GREY COLD MORNING FOUND HER ON THE SEASHORE

ARISTÆUS THE BEE-KEEPER

"... Every sound is sweet;Myriads of rivers hurrying thro' the lawn,The moan of doves in immemorial elms,And murmuring of innumerable bees."

TENNYSON.

In the fragrance of the blossom of the limes the bees are gleaning a luscious harvest. Their busy humming sounds like the surf on a reef heard from very far away, and would almost lull to sleep those who lazily, drowsily spend the sunny summer afternoon in the shadow of the trees. That line of bee-hives by the sweet-pea hedge shows where they store their treasure that men may rob them of it, but out on the uplands where the heather is purple, the wild bees hum in and out of the honey-laden bells and carry home their spoils to their own free fastnesses, from which none can drive them unless there comes a foray against them from the brown men of the moors.

How many of us who watch their ardent labours know the story of Aristæus—he who first brought the art of bee-keeping to perfection in his own dear land of Greece, and whose followers are those men in veils of blue and green, that motley throng who beat fire-irons and create a hideous clamour in order that the queen bee and her excited followers may be checked in their perilous voyagings and beguiled to swarm in the sanctuary of a hive.

Aristæus was a shepherd, the son of Cyrene, a water nymph, and to him there had come one day, as he listened to the wild bees humming amongst the wild thyme, the great thought that he might conquer these busy workers and make their toil his gain. He knew that hollow trees or a hole in a rock were used as the storage houses of their treasure, and so the wily shepherd lad provided for them the homes he knew that they would covet, and near them placed all the food that they most desired. Soon Aristæus became noted as a tamer of bees, and even in Olympus they spoke of his honey as a thing that was food for the gods. All might have gone well with Aristæus had there not come for him the fateful day when he saw the beautiful Eurydice and to her lost his heart. She fled before the fiery protestations of his love, and trod upon the serpent whose bite brought her down to the Shades. The gods were angry with Aristæus, and as punishment they slew his bees. His hives stood empty and silent, and no more did "the murmuring of innumerable bees" drowse the ears of the herds who watched their flocks cropping the red clover and the asphodel of the meadows.

Underneath the swift-flowing water of a deep river, the nymph who was the mother of Aristæus sat on her throne. Fishes darted round her white feet, and beside her sat her attendants, spinning the fine strong green cords that twine themselves round the throats of those who perish when their arms can no longer fight against the force of the rushing current. A nymph sang as she worked, an old, old song, that told one of the old, old tales of man's weakness and the power of the creatures of water, but above her song those who listened heard a man's voice, calling loudly and pitifully.

The voice was that of Aristæus, calling aloud for his mother. Then his mother gave command, and the waters of the river rolled asunder and let Aristæus pass down far below to where the fountains of the great rivers lie. A mighty roar of many waters dinned in his ears as the rivers started on the race that was to bring them all at last to their restless haven, the Ocean. To Cyrene he came at length, and to her told his sorrowful tale:

"To men who live their little lives and work and die as I myself— though son of a nymph and of a god—must do," he said, "I have brought two great gifts, oh my mother. I have taught them that from the grey olives they can reap a priceless harvest, and from me they have learned that the little brown bees that hum in and out of the flowers may be made slaves that bring to them the sweetest riches of which Nature may be robbed."

"This do I already know, my son," said Cyrene, and smiled upon Aristæus.

"Yet dost thou not know," said Aristæus, "the doom that has overtaken my army of busy workers. No longer does there come from my city of bees the boom of many wings and many busy little feet as they fly, swift and strong, hither and thither, to bring back to the hives their honeyed treasure. The comb is empty. The bees are all dead—or, if not dead, they have forsaken me forever."

Then spoke Cyrene. "Hast heard, my son," she said, "of Proteus? It is he who herds the flocks of the boundless sea. On days when the South Wind and the North Wind wrestle together, and when the Wind from the East smites the West Wind in shame before him, thou mayst see him raise his snowy head and long white beard above the grey-green waves of the sea, and lash the white-maned, unbridled, fierce sea-horses into fury before him. Proteus only—none but Proteus—can tell thee by what art thou canst win thy bees back once more."

Then Aristæus with eagerness questioned his mother how he might find Proteus and gain from him the knowledge that he sought, and Cyrene answered: "No matter how piteously thou dost entreat him, never, save by force, wilt thou gain his secret from Proteus. Only if thou canst chain him by guile as he sleeps and hold fast the chains, undaunted by the shapes into which he has the power to change himself, wilt thou win his knowledge from him."

Then Cyrene sprinkled her son with the nectar of the deathless gods, and in his heart there was born a noble courage and through him a new life seemed to run.

"Lead me now to Proteus, oh my mother!" he said, and Cyrene left her throne and led him to the cave where Proteus, herdsman of the seas, had his dwelling. Behind the seaweed-covered rocks Aristæus concealed himself, while the nymph used the fleecy clouds for her covering. And when Apollo drove his chariot across the high heavens at noon, and all land and all sea were hot as molten gold,

Proteus with his flocks returned to the shade of his great cave by the sobbing sea, and on its sandy floor he stretched himself, and soon lay, his limbs all lax and restful, in the exquisite joy of a dreamless sleep. From behind the rocks Aristæus watched him, and when, at length, he saw that Proteus slept too soundly to wake gently he stepped forward, and on the sleep-drowsed limbs of Proteus fixed the fetters that made him his captive. Then, in joy and pride at having been the undoing of the shepherd of the seas, Aristæus shouted aloud. And Proteus, awaking, swiftly turned himself into a wild boar with white tusks that lusted to thrust themselves into the thighs of Aristæus. But Aristæus, unflinching, kept his firm hold of the chain. Next did he become a tiger, tawny and velvet black, and fierce to devour. And still Aristæus held the chain, and never let his eye fall before the glare of the beast that sought to devour him. A scaly dragon came next, breathing out flames, and yet Aristæus held him. Then came a lion, its yellow pelt scented with the lust of killing, and while Aristæus yet strove against him there came to terrify his listening ears the sound of fire that lapped up and thirstily devoured all things that would stand against it. And ere the crackle of the flames and their great sigh of fierce desire had ceased, there came in his ears the sound of many waters, the booming rush of an angry river in furious flood, the irresistible command of the almighty waves of the sea. Yet still Aristæus held the chains, and at last Proteus took his own shape again, and with a sigh like the sigh of winds and waves on the desolate places where ships become wrecks, and men perish and there is never a human soul to save or to pity them, he spoke to Aristæus.

"Puny one!" he said, "and puny are thy wishes! Because thou didst by thy foolish wooing send the beautiful Eurydice swiftly down to the Shades and break the heart of Orpheus, whose music is the music of the Immortals, the bees that thou hast treasured have left their hives empty and silent. So little are the bees! so great, O Aristæus, the bliss or woe of Orpheus and Eurydice! Yet, because by guile thou hast won the power to gain from me the knowledge that thou dost seek, hearken to me now, Aristæus! Four bulls must thou find—four cows of equal beauty. Then must thou build in a leafy grove four altars, and to Orpheus and Eurydice pay such funeral honours as may allay their resentment. At the end of nine days, when thou hast fulfilled thy pious task, return and see what the gods have sent thee."

"This will I do most faithfully, O Proteus," said Aristæus, and gravely loosened the chains and returned to where his mother awaited him, and thence travelled to his own sunny land of Greece.

Most faithfully, as he had said, did Aristæus perform his vow. And when, on the ninth day, he returned to the grove of sacrifice, a sound greeted him which made his heart stop and then go on beating and throbbing as the heart of a man who has striven valiantly in a great fight and to whom the battle is assured.

For, from the carcase of one of the animals offered for sacrifice, and whose clean white bones now gleamed in the rays of the sun that forced its way through the thick shade of the grove of grey olives, there came the "murmuring of innumerable bees."

"Out of the eater came forth meat, out of the strong came forth sweetness."

And Aristæus, a Samson of the old Greek days, rejoiced exceedingly, knowing that his thoughtless sin was pardoned, and that for evermore to him belonged the pride of giving to all men the power of taming bees, the glory of mastering the little brown creatures that pillage from the fragrant, bright-hued flowers their most precious treasure.

PROSERPINE

"Sacred Goddess, Mother Earth,Thou from whose immortal bosom,Gods, and men, and beasts have birth,Leaf and blade, and bud and blossom,Breathe thine influence most divineOn thine own child, Proserpine.

If with mists of evening dewThou dost nourish those young flowersTill they grow, in scent and hue,Fairest children of the hours,Breathe thine influence most divineOn thine own child, Proserpine."

SHELLEY.

The story of Persephone—of Proserpine—is a story of spring. When the sun is warming the bare brown earth, and the pale primroses look up through the snowy blackthorns at a kind, blue sky, almost can we hear the soft wind murmur a name as it gently sways the daffodils and breathes through the honey sweetness of the gold-powdered catkins on the grey willows by the river—"Persephone! Persephone!"

Now once there was a time when there was no spring, neither summer nor autumn, nor chilly winter with its black frosts and cruel gales and brief, dark days. Always was there sunshine and warmth, ever were there flowers and corn and fruit, and nowhere did the flowers grow with more dazzling colours and more fragrant perfume than in the fair garden of Sicily.

To Demeter, the Earth Mother, was born a daughter more fair than any flower that grew, and ever more dear to her became her child, the lovely Proserpine. By the blue sea, in the Sicilian meadows, Proserpine and the fair nymphs who were her companions spent their happy days. Too short were the days for all their joy, and Demeter made the earth yet fairer than it was that she might bring more gladness to her daughter Proserpine. Each day the blossoms that the nymphs twined into garlands grew more perfect in form

133

and in hue, but from the anemones of royal purple and crimson, and the riotous red of geraniums, Proserpine turned one morning with a cry of gladness, for there stood before her beside a little stream, on one erect, slim stem, a wonderful narcissus, with a hundred blossoms. Her eager hand was stretched out to pluck it, when a sudden black cloud overshadowed the land, and the nymphs, with shrieks of fear, fled swiftly away. And as the cloud descended, there was heard a terrible sound, as of the rushing of many waters or the roll of the heavy wheels of the chariot of one who comes to slay. Then was the earth cleft open, and from it there arose the four coal-black horses of Pluto, neighing aloud in their eagerness, while the dark-browed god urged them on, standing erect in his car of gold.

"'The coal-black horses rise—they rise,O mother, mother!' low she cries—Persephone—Persephone! 'O light, light, light!' she cries, 'farewell;The coal-black horses wait for me.O shade of shades, where I must dwell,Demeter, mother, far from thee!'"

In cold, strong arms Pluto seized her—in that mighty grasp that will not be denied, and Proserpine wept childish tears as she shivered at his icy touch, and sobbed because she had dropped the flowers she had picked, and had never picked the flower she most desired. While still she saw the fair light of day, the little oddly-shaped rocky hills, the vineyards and olive groves and flowery meadows of Sicily, she did not lose hope. Surely the King of Terrors could not steal one so young, so happy, and so fair. She had only tasted the joy of living, and fain she would drink deeper in the coming years. Her mother must surely save her—her mother who had never yet failed her—her mother, and the gods.

But ruthless as the mower whose scythe cuts down the seeded grass and the half-opened flower and lays them in swathes on the meadow, Pluto drove on. His iron-coloured reins were loose on the black manes of his horses, and he urged them forward by name till the froth flew from their mouths like the foam that the furious surf of the sea drives before it in a storm. Across the bay and along the bank of the river Anapus they galloped, until, at the river head, they came to the pool of Cyane. He smote the water with his trident, and downward into the blackness of darkness his horses passed, and Proserpine knew no more the pleasant light of day.

"What ails her that she comes not home?Demeter seeks her far and wide,And gloomy-browed doth ceaseless roamFrom many a morn till eventide.'My life, immortal though it be,Is nought,' she cries, 'for want of thee,Persephone—Persephone!'"

So, to the great Earth Mother came the pangs that have drawn tears of blood from many a mortal mother's heart for a child borne off to the Shades.

"'My life is nought for want of thee,—Persephone! Persephone!'" ...

The cry is borne down through the ages, to echo and re-echo so long as mothers love and Death is still unchained.

Over land and sea, from where Dawn, the rosy-fingered, rises in the East, to where Apollo cools the fiery wheels of his chariot in the waters of far western seas, the goddess sought her daughter. With a black robe over her head and carrying a flaming torch in either hand, for nine dreary days she sought her loved one. And yet, for nine more weary days and nine sleepless nights the goddess, racked by human sorrow, sat in hopeless misery. The hot sun beat upon her by day. By night the silver rays from Diana's car smote her more gently, and the dew drenched her hair and her black garments and mingled with the saltness of her bitter tears. At the grey dawning of the tenth day her elder daughter, Hecate, stood beside her. Queen of ghosts and shades was she, and to her all dark places of the earth were known.

"Let us go to the Sun God," said Hecate. "Surely he hath seen the god who stole away the little Proserpine. Soon his chariot will drive across the heavens. Come, let us ask him to guide us to the place where she is hidden."

Thus did they come to the chariot of the glorious Apollo, and standing by the heads of his horses like two grey clouds that bar the passage of the sun, they begged him to tell them the name of him who had stolen fair Proserpine.

"No less a thief was he," said Apollo, "than Pluto, King of Darkness and robber of Life itself. Mourn not, Demeter. Thy daughter is safe in his keeping. The little nymph who played in the meadows is now Queen of the Shades. Nor does Pluto love her vainly. She is now in love with Death."

No comfort did the words of the Sun God bring to the longing soul of Demeter. And her wounded heart grew bitter. Because she suffered, others must suffer as well. Because she mourned, all the world must mourn. The fragrant flowers spoke to her only of Persephone, the purple grapes reminded her of a vintage when the white fingers of her child had plucked the fruit. The waving golden grain told her that Persephone was as an ear of wheat that is reaped before its time.

Then upon the earth did there come dearth and drought and barrenness.

"The wheatWas blighted in the ear, the purple grapesBlushed no more on the vines, and all the godsWere sorrowful ..."

Lewis Morris.

Gods and men alike suffered from the sorrow of Demeter. To her, in pity for the barren earth, Zeus sent an embassy, but in vain it came. Merciless was the great Earth Mother, who had been robbed of what she held most dear.

"Give me back my child!" she said. "Gladly I watch the sufferings of men, for no sorrow is as my sorrow. Give me back my child, and the earth shall grow fertile once more."

Unwillingly Zeus granted the request of Demeter.

"She shall come back," he said at last, "and with thee dwell on earth forever. Yet only on one condition do I grant thy fond request.

Persephone must eat no food through all the time of her sojourn in the realm of Pluto, else must thy beseeching be all in vain."

Then did Demeter gladly leave Olympus and hasten down to the darkness of the shadowy land that once again she might hold, in her strong mother's arms, her who had once been her little clinging child.

But in the dark kingdom of Pluto a strange thing had happened. No longer had the pale-faced god, with dark locks, and eyes like the sunless pools of a mountain stream, any terrors for Proserpine. He was strong, and cruel had she thought him, yet now she knew that the touch of his strong, cold hands was a touch of infinite tenderness. When, knowing the fiat of the ruler of Olympus, Pluto gave to his stolen bride a pomegranate, red in heart as the heart of a man, she had taken it from his hand, and, because he willed it, had eaten of the sweet seeds. Then, in truth, it was too late for Demeter to save her child. She "had eaten of Love's seed" and "changed into another."

"He takes the cleft pomegranate seeds:'Love, eat with me this parting day;'Then bids them fetch the coal-black steeds—'Demeter's daughter, wouldst away?'The gates of Hades set her free;'She will return full soon,' saith he—'My wife, my wife Persephone.'"

Ingelow.

Dark, dark was the kingdom of Pluto. Its rivers never mirrored a sunbeam, and ever moaned low as an earthly river moans before a coming flood, and the feet that trod the gloomy Cocytus valley were the feet of those who never again would tread on the soft grass and flowers of an earthly meadow. Yet when Demeter had braved all the shadows of Hades, only in part was her end accomplished. In part only was Proserpine now her child, for while half her heart was in the sunshine, rejoicing in the beauties of earth, the other half was with the god who had taken her down to the Land of Darkness and there had won her for his own. Back to the flowery island of Sicily her mother brought her, and the peach trees and the almonds blossomed snowily as she passed. The olives decked themselves with their soft grey leaves, the corn sprang up, green and lush and strong. The lemon and orange groves grew golden with luscious fruit, and all the land was carpeted with flowers. For six months of the year she stayed, and gods and men rejoiced at the bringing back of Proserpine. For six months she left her green and pleasant land for the dark kingdom of him whom she loved, and through those months the trees were bare, and the earth chill and brown, and under the earth the flowers hid themselves in fear and awaited the return of the fair daughter of Demeter.

And evermore has she come and gone, and seedtime and harvest have never failed, and the cold, sleeping world has awaked and rejoiced, and heralded with the song of birds, and the bursting of green buds and the blooming of flowers, the resurrection from the dead—the coming of spring.

"Time calls, and ChangeCommands both men and gods, and speeds us onWe know not whither; but the old earth smilesSpring after spring, and the seed bursts againOut of its prison mould, and the dead livesRenew themselves, and rise aloft and soarAnd are transformed, clothing themselves with change,Till the last change be done."

Lewis Morris.

LATONA AND THE RUSTICS

Through the tropic nights their sonorous, bell-like booming can be heard coming up from the marshes, and when they are unseen, the song of the bull-frogs would suggest creatures full of solemn dignity. The croak of their lesser brethren is less impressive, yet there is no escape from it on those evenings when the dragon-flies' iridescent wings are folded in sleep, and the birds in the branches are still, when the lilies on the pond have closed their golden hearts, and even the late-feeding trout have ceased to plop and to make eddies in the quiet water. "Krroak! krroak! krroak!" they go— "krroak! krroak! krroak!"

It is unceasing, unending. It goes on like the whirr of the wheels of a great clock that can never run down—a melancholy complaint against the hardships of destiny—a raucous protest against things as they are.

This is the story of the frogs that have helped to point the gibes of Aristophanes, the morals of Æsop, and which have always been, more or less, regarded as the low comedians of the animal world.

Latona, or Leto, was the goddess of dark nights, and upon her the mighty Zeus bestowed the doubtful favour of his errant love. Great was the wrath of Hera, his queen, when she found that she was no longer the dearest wife of her omnipotent lord, and with furious upbraidings she banished her rival to earth. And when Latona had reached the place of her exile she found that the vengeful goddess had sworn that she would place her everlasting ban upon anyone, mortal or immortal, who dared to show any kindness or pity to her whose only fault had been that Zeus loved her. From place to place she wandered, an outcast even among men, until, at length, she came to Lycia.

One evening, as the darkness of which she was goddess had just begun to fall, she reached a green and pleasant valley. The soft, cool grass was a delight to her tired feet, and when she saw the silvery gleam of water she rejoiced, for her throat was parched and her lips dry and she was very weary. By the side of this still pond, where the lilies floated, there grew lithe grey willows and fresh green osiers, and these were being cut by a crowd of chattering rustics.

Humbly, for many a rude word and harsh rebuff had the dictum of Hera brought her during her wanderings, Latona went to the edge of the pond, and, kneeling down, was most thankfully about to drink, when the peasants espied her. Roughly and rudely they told her to begone, nor dare to drink unbidden of the clear water beside which their willows grew. Very pitifully Latona looked up in their churlish faces, and her eyes were as the eyes of a doe that the hunters have pressed very hard.

"Surely, good people," she said, and her voice was sad and low, "water is free to all. Very far have I travelled, and I am aweary almost to death. Only grant that I dip my lips in the water for one deep draught. Of thy pity grant me this boon, for I perish of thirst."

Harsh and coarse were the mocking voices that made answer. Coarser still were the jests that they made. Then one, bolder than his fellows, spurned her kneeling figure with his foot, while another brushed before her and stepping into the pond, defiled its clarity by churning up the mud that lay below with his great splay feet.

Loudly the peasants laughed at this merry jest, and they quickly followed his lead, as brainless sheep will follow the one that scrambles through a gap. Soon they were all joyously stamping and dancing in what had so lately been a pellucid pool. The water-lilies and blue forget-me-nots were trodden down, the fish that had their homes under the mossy stones in terror fled away. Only the mud came up, filthy, defiling, and the rustics laughed in loud and foolish laughter to see the havoc they had wrought.

The goddess Latona rose from her knees. No longer did she seem a mere woman, very weary, hungry and athirst, travelled over far. In their surprised eyes she grew to a stature that was as that of the deathless gods. And her eyes were dark as an angry sea at even.

"Shameless ones!" she said, in a voice as the voice of a storm that sweeps destroyingly over forest and mountain. "Ah! shameless ones! Is it thus that thou wouldst defy one who has dwelt on Olympus? Behold from henceforth shalt thou have thy dwelling in the mud of the green-scummed pools, thy homes in the water that thy flat feet have defiled."

As she spoke, a change, strange and terrible, passed over the forms of the trampling peasants. Their stature shrank. They grew squat and fat. Their hands and feet were webbed, and their grinning mouths became great, sad, gaping openings by which to swallow worms and flies. Green and yellow and brown were their skins, and when they would fain have cried aloud for mercy, from their throats there would come only the *"Krroak! krroak! krroak!"* that we know so well.

And when, that night, the goddess of darkness was wrapped in peace in the black, silver star bespangled robe that none could take from her, there arose from the pond over which the grey willows hung, weeping, the clamour of a great lamentation. Yet no piteous words were there, only the incessant, harsh complaint of the frogs that we hear in the marshes.

From that time the world went well with Latona. Down to the seashore she came, and when she held out her arms in longing appeal to the Ægean islands that lay like purple flowers strewn, far apart, on a soft carpet of limpid blue, Zeus heard her prayer. He asked Poseidon to send a dolphin to carry the woman he loved to the floating island of Delos, and when she had been borne there in safety, he chained the island with chains of adamant to the golden-sanded floor of the sea.

And on this sanctuary there were born to Latona twin children, thereafter to be amongst the most famed of the deathless gods—the god and goddess, Apollo and Diana.

"... Those hinds that were transformed to frogsRailed at Latona's twin-born progeny,Which after held the sun and moon in fee."

MILTON.

Yet are there times, as we look at the squat, bronze bodies of the frogs—green-bronze, dark brown spotted, and all flecked with gold, the turned-down corners of their wistful mouths, their very exquisite black velvety eyes with golden rims—when the piteous croaks that come forth from their throats of pale daffodil colour do indeed awake a sympathy with their appeal against the inexorable decrees of destiny.

"We did not know! We did not understand! Pity us! Ah, pity us! *Krroak! krroak! krroak!*"

ECHO AND NARCISSUS

In the solitudes of the hills we find her, and yet we may come on her unawares in the din of a noisy city. She will answer us where the waves are lashing themselves against the rugged cliffs of our own British coast, or we may find her where the great yellow pillars of fallen temples lie hot in the sun close to the vivid blue water of the African sea. At nightfall, on the lonely northern moors, she mimics the cry of a wailing bird that calls for its mate, but it is she who prolongs the roll of the great organ in a vast cathedral, she who repeats the rattle and crack and boom of the guns, no matter in what land the war may be raging. In the desolate Australian bush she makes the crash of the falling limb of a dead gum tree go on and on, and tortures the human being who is lost, hopelessly lost, and facing a cruel death, by repeating his despairing calls for help. Through the night, in old country-houses, she sports at will and gives new life to sad old tales of the restless dead who restlessly walk. But she echoes the children's voices as they play by the seashore or pick primroses in the woods in spring, and when they greet her with laughter, she laughs in merry response. They may fear her when the sun has gone down, and when they are left all alone they begin to dread her mockery. Yet the nymph who sought for love and failed to gain what she sought must surely find some comfort on those bright days of summer and of spring when she gives the little children happiness and they give her their love.

When all the world was young, and nymphs and fauns and dryads dwelt in the forests, there was no nymph more lovely and more gay than she whose name was Echo. Diana would smile on her for her fleetness of foot when she followed her in the chase, and those whom she met in the leafy pathways of the dim, green woods, would pass on smiling at the remembrance of her merry chatter and her tricksy humour.

It was an evil day for Echo when she crossed the path of Hera, queen of the gods. The jealous goddess sought her errant husband, who was amusing himself with some nymphs, and Echo, full of mischievous glee, kept her in talk until the nymphs had fled to safety. Hera was furious indeed when she found out that a frolicsome nymph had dared to play on her such a trick, and ruthlessly she spoke fair Echo's doom.

"Henceforth," she said, "the tongue with which thou hast cheated me shall be in bonds. No longer wilt thou have the power to speak in greeting. To the tongues of others shall thy tongue be slave, and from this day until time shall cease thou shalt speak only to repeat the last words that have fallen on thine ears."

A maimed nymph indeed was Echo then, yet whole in all that matters most, in that her merry heart was still her own. But only for a little while did this endure.

Narcissus, the beautiful son of a nymph and a river god, was hunting in a lonely forest one day when Echo saw him pass. To her he seemed more fair than god or man, and once she had seen him she knew that she must gain his love or die. From that day on, she haunted him like his shadow, gliding from tree to tree, nestling down amongst thick fern and undergrowth, motionless as one who stalks a wild thing, watching him afar off while he rested, gladdening her eyes with his beauty. So did she feed her hungering heart, and sought to find contentment by looking on his face each day.

To her at length came a perfect moment when Narcissus was separated from his companions in the chase and, stopping suddenly where the evening sun chequered the pathway of the forest with black and gold, heard the nymph's soft footfall on the rustling leaves.

"Who's here?" he called.

"*Here!*" answered Echo.

Narcissus, peering amongst the trees' long shadows and seeing no one, called "Come!"

And *"Come!"* called the glad voice of Echo, while the nymph, with fast-beating heart, felt that her day of happiness had come indeed.

"Why do you shun me?" then called Narcissus.

"Why do you shun me?" Echo repeated.

"Let us join one another," said the lad, and the simple words seemed turned into song when Echo said them over.

"Let us join one another!" she said, and not Eos herself, as with rosy fingers she turns aside the dark clouds of night, could be fairer than was the nymph as she pushed aside the leaves of the trackless wood, and ran forward with white arms outstretched to him who was lord of her life.

With cold eyes and colder heart the one she loved beheld her.

"Away!" he cried, shrinking back as if from something that he hated. *"Away!* I would rather die than that you should have me!"

"Have me!" cried Echo pitifully, but she pled in vain. Narcissus had no love to give her, and his scorn filled her with shame. Thenceforth in the forest revels she never more was seen, and the nymphs danced gaily as ever, with never a care for her who had faded and gone away as completely as though she were a blossom in the passing of spring. In the solitude of mountain cliffs and caves and rocky places, and in the loneliest depths of the forest, Echo hid her grief, and when the winds blew through the dark branches of the trees at night, moaning and sighing, they could hear far below them the voice of Echo repeating their lamentations. For her, long nights followed hopeless days, and nights and days only told her that her love was all in vain. Then came a night when the winds no longer saw the figure of the nymph, white and frail as a broken flower, crouching close to the rocks they passed over. Grief had slain the body of Echo. Only her voice was left to repeat their mocking laughter, their wistful sighs—only her voice that lives on still though all the old gods are gone, and but few there are who know her story.

Heartwhole and happy, Narcissus, slayer of happiness, went on his way, and other nymphs besides fair Echo suffered from loving him in vain. One nymph, less gentle than Echo, poured the tale of her love that was scorned into the sympathetic ears of the goddess of Love, and implored her to punish Narcissus.

Hot and tired from the chase, Narcissus sought one day a lonely pool in the woods, there to rest and to quench his thirst.

"In some delicious ramble, he had foundA little space, with boughs all woven round;And in the midst of all, a clearer poolThan e'er reflected in its pleasant coolThe blue sky here, and there, serenely peepingThrough tendril wreaths fantastically creeping."

As he stooped down to drink, a face looked at his through the crystal clear water, and a pair of beautiful eyes met his own. His surprise and joy at the sight of what he felt sure must be the most beautiful creature on earth, was evidently shared by the nymph of the pool, who gazed fearlessly up at him.

Round her head she had a nimbus of curls than which that of Adonis—nay, of the sun-god himself, was not more perfect, while her eyes were like the brown pools of water in a rippling mountain stream, flecked with sunshine, yet with depths untold. When Narcissus smiled at her in rapture, her red lips also parted in a smile. He stretched out his arms towards her, and her arms were stretched to him. Almost trembling in his delight, he slowly stooped to kiss her. Nearer she drew to him, nearer still, but when his mouth would have given itself to that other mouth that was formed like the bow of Eros—a thing to slay hearts—only the chilly water of the pool touched his lips, and the thing of his delight vanished away. In passionate disappointment Narcissus waited for her to return, and as soon as the water of the pool grew still, once more he saw her exquisite face gazing wistfully up into his. Passionately he pled with the beautiful creature—spoke of his love— besought her to have pity on him, but although the face in the pool reflected his every look of adoration and of longing, time and again he vainly tried to clasp in his arms what was but the mirrored likeness of himself.

In full measure had the avenging goddess meted out to Narcissus the restless longing of unsatisfied love. By day and by night he haunted the forest pool, and ere long the face that looked back at his was pale as a lily in the dawn. When the moonbeams came straying down through the branches and all the night was still, they found him kneeling by the pool, and the white face that the water mirrored had the eyes of one of the things of the woods to which a huntsman has given a mortal wound. Mortally wounded he truly was, slain, like many another since his day, by a hopeless love for what was in truth but an image, and that an image of his own creation. Even when his shade passed across the dark Stygian river, it stooped over the side of the boat that it might try to catch a glimpse of the beloved one in the inky waters.

Echo and the other nymphs were avenged, yet when they looked on the beautiful dead Narcissus, they were filled with sorrow, and when they filled the air with their lamentations, most piteously did the voice of Echo repeat each mournful cry. Even the gods were pitiful, and when the nymphs would have burned the body on a funeral pyre which their own fair hands had built for him, they sought it in vain. For the Olympians had turned Narcissus into a white flower, the flower that still bears his name and keeps his memory sweet.

"A lonely flower he spied,A meek and forlorn flower, with naught of pride,Drooping its beauty o'er the watery clearness,To woo its own sad image into nearness;Deaf to light Zephyrus it would not move,But still would seem to droop, to pine, to love."

KEATS.

SHE HAUNTED HIM LIKE HIS SHADOW

ICARUS

Fourteen years only have passed since our twentieth century began. In those fourteen years how many a father's and mother's heart has bled for the death of gallant sons, greatly-promising, greatly-daring, who have sought to rule the skies? With wings not well enough tried, they have soared dauntlessly aloft, only to add more names to the tragic list of those whose lives have been sacrificed in order that the groping hands of science may become sure, so that in time the sons of men may sail through the heavens as fearlessly as their fathers sailed through the seas.

High overhead we watch the monoplane, the great, swooping thing, like a monster black-winged bird, and our minds travel back to the story of Icarus, who died so many years ago that there are those who say that his story is but a foolish fable, an idle myth.

Dædalus, grandson of a king of Athens, was the greatest artificer of his day. Not only as an architect was he great, but as a sculptor he had the creative power, not only to make men and women and animals that looked alive, but to cause them to move and to be, to all appearances, endowed with life. To him the artificers who followed him owed the invention of the axe, the wedge, the wimble, and the carpenter's level, and his restless mind was ever busy with new inventions. To his nephew, Talus, or Perdrix, he taught all that he himself knew of all the mechanical arts. Soon it seemed that the nephew, though he might not excel his uncle, equalled Dædalus in his inventive power. As he walked by the seashore, the lad picked up the spine of a fish, and, having pondered its possibilities, he took it home, imitated it in iron, and so invented the saw. A still greater invention followed this. While those who had always thought that there could be none greater than Dædalus were still acclaiming the lad, there came to him the idea of putting two pieces of iron together, connecting them at one end with a rivet, and sharpening both ends, and a pair of compasses was made. Louder still were the acclamations of the people. Surely greater than Dædalus was here. Too much was this for the artist's jealous spirit.

One day they stood together on the top of the Acropolis, and Dædalus, murder that comes from jealousy in his heart, threw his nephew down. Down, down he fell, knowing well that he was going to meet a cruel death, but Pallas Athené, protectress of all clever craftsmen, came to his rescue. By her Perdrix was turned into the bird that still bears his name, and Dædalus beheld Perdrix, the partridge, rapidly winging his way to the far-off fields. Since then, no partridge has ever built or roosted in a high place, but has nestled in the hedge-roots and amongst the standing corn, and as we mark it we can see that its flight is always low.

For his crime Dædalus was banished from Athens, and in the court of Minos, king of Crete, he found a refuge. He put all his mighty powers at the service of Minos, and for him designed an intricate labyrinth which, like the river Meander, had neither beginning nor ending, but ever returned on itself in hopeless intricacy. Soon he stood high in the favour of the king, but, ever greedy for power, he incurred, by one of his daring inventions, the wrath of Minos. The angry monarch threw him into prison, and imprisoned along with him his son, Icarus. But prison bars and locks did not exist that were strong enough to baffle this master craftsman, and from the tower in which they were shut, Dædalus and his son were not long in making their escape. To escape from Crete was a less easy matter. There were many places in that wild island where it was easy for the father and son to hide, but the subjects of Minos were mostly mariners, and Dædalus knew well that all along the shore they kept watch lest he should make him a boat, hoist on it one of the sails of which he was part inventor, and speed away to safety like a sea-bird driven before the gale. Then did there come to Dædalus, the pioneer of inventions, the great idea that by his skill he might make a way for himself and his son through another element than water. And he laughed aloud in his hiding place amongst the cypresses on the hillside at the thought of how he would baffle the simple sailormen who watched each creek and

150

beach down on the shore. Mockingly, too, did he think of King Minos, who had dared to pit his power against the wits and skill of Dædalus, the mighty craftsman.

Many a Cretan bird was sacrificed before the task which the inventor had set himself was accomplished. In a shady forest on the mountains he fashioned light wooden frames and decked them with feathers, until at length they looked like the pinions of a great eagle, or of a swan that flaps its majestic way from lake to river. Each feather was bound on with wax, and the mechanism of the wings was so perfect a reproduction of that of the wings from which the feathers had been plucked, that on the first day that he fastened them to his back and spread them out, Dædalus found that he could fly even as the bird flew. Two pairs he made; having tested one pair, a second pair was made for Icarus, and, circling round him like a mother bird that teaches her nestlings how to fly, Dædalus, his heart big with the pride of invention, showed Icarus how he might best soar upwards to the sun or dive down to the blue sea far below, and how he might conquer the winds and the air currents of the sky and make them his servants.

That was a joyous day for father and son, for the father had never before drunk deeper of the intoxicating wine of the gods—Success— and for the lad it was all pure joy. Never before had he known freedom and power so utterly glorious. As a little child he had watched the birds fly far away over the blue hills to where the sun was setting, and had longed for wings that he might follow them in their flight. At times, in his dreams, he had known the power, and in his dreaming fancy had risen from the cumbering earth and soared high above the trees and fields on strong pinions that bore him away to the fair land of heart's desire—to the Islands of the Blessed. But when Sleep left him and the dreams silently slipped out before the coming of the light of day, and the boy sprang from his couch and eagerly spread his arms as, in his dreams, he had done, he could no longer fly. Disappointment and unsatisfied longing ever came with his waking hours. Now all that had come to an end, and

Dædalus was glad and proud as well to watch his son's joy and his fearless daring. One word of counsel only did he give him.

"Beware, dear son of my heart," he said, "lest in thy new-found power thou seekest to soar even to the gates of Olympus. For as surely as the scorching rays from the burnished wheels of the chariot of Apollo smite thy wings, the wax that binds on thy feathers will melt, and then will come upon thee and on me woe unutterable."

In his dreams that night Icarus flew, and when he awoke, fearing to find only the haunting remembrance of a dream, he found his father standing by the side of his bed of soft leaves under the shadowy cypresses, ready to bind on his willing shoulders the great pinions that he had made.

Gentle Dawn, the rosy-fingered, was slowly making her way up from the East when Dædalus and Icarus began their flight. Slowly they went at first, and the goat-herds who tended their flocks on the slopes of Mount Ida looked up in fear when they saw the dark shadows of their wings and marked the monster birds making their way out to sea. From the river beds the waterfowl arose from the reeds, and with great outcry flew with all their swiftness to escape them. And down by the seashore the mariners' hearts sank within them as they watched, believing that a sight so strange must be a portent of disaster. Homewards they went in haste to offer sacrifices on the altars of Poseidon, ruler of the deep.

Samos and Delos were passed on the left and Lebynthos on the right, long ere the sun-god had started on his daily course, and as the mighty wings of Icarus cleft the cold air, the boy's slim body grew chilled, and he longed for the sun's rays to turn the waters of the Ægean Sea over which he flew from green-grey into limpid sapphire and emerald and burning gold. Towards Sicily he and his father bent their course, and when they saw the beautiful island afar off lying like a gem in the sea, Apollo made the waves in which it lay, for it a fitting setting. With a cry of joy Icarus marked the sun's rays paint the chill water, and Apollo looked down at the great white-winged bird, a snowy swan with the face and form of a beautiful boy, who sped exulting onwards, while a clumsier thing, with wings of darker hue, followed less quickly, in the same line of flight. As the god looked, the warmth that radiated from his chariot touched the icy limbs of Icarus as with the caressing touch of gentle, life-giving hands. Not long before, his flight had lagged a little, but now it seemed as if new life was his. Like a bird that wheels and soars and dives as if for lightness of heart, so did Icarus, until each feather of his plumage had a sheen of silver and of gold. Down, down, he darted, so near the water that almost the white-tipped waves caught at his wings as he skimmed over them. Then up, up, up he soared, ever higher, higher still, and when he saw the radiant sun-god smiling down on him, the warning of Dædalus was forgotten. As he had excelled other lads in foot races, now did Icarus wish to excel the birds themselves. Dædalus he left far behind, and still upwards he mounted. So strong he felt, so fearless was he, that to him it seemed that he could storm Olympus, that he could call to Apollo as he swept past him in his flight, and dare him to race for a wager from the Ægean Sea to where the sun-god's horses took their nightly rest by the trackless seas of the unknown West.

In terror his father watched him, and as he called to him in a voice of anguished warning that was drowned by the whistling rush of the air currents through the wings of Icarus and the moist whisper of the clouds as through them he cleft a way for himself, there befell the dreaded thing. It seemed as though the strong wings had begun to lose their power. Like a wounded bird Icarus fluttered, lunged sidewise from the straight, clean line of his flight, recovered himself, and fluttered again. And then, like the bird into whose soft breast the sure hand of a mighty archer has driven an arrow, downwards he fell, turning over and yet turning again, downwards, ever downwards, until he fell with a plunge into the sea that still was radiant in shining emerald and translucent blue.

Then did the car of Apollo drive on. His rays had slain one who was too greatly daring, and now they fondled the little white feathers that had fallen from the broken wings and floated on the water like the petals of a torn flower.

On the dead, still face of Icarus they shone, and they spangled as if with diamonds the wet plumage that still, widespread, bore him up on the waves.

Stricken at heart was Dædalus, but there was no time to lament his son's untimely end, for even now the black-prowed ships of Minos might be in pursuit. Onward he flew to safety, and in Sicily built a temple to Apollo, and there hung up his wings as a propitiatory offering to the god who had slain his son.

And when grey night came down on that part of the sea that bears the name of Icarus to this day, still there floated the body of the boy whose dreams had come true. For only a little while had he known the exquisite realisation of dreamed-of potentialities, for only a few hours tasted the sweetness of perfect pleasure, and then, by an over-daring flight, had lost it all for ever.

The sorrowing Nereids sang a dirge over him as he was swayed gently hither and thither by the tide, and when the silver stars came out from the dark firmament of heaven and were reflected in the blackness of the sea at night, it was as though a velvet pall, silver-decked in his honour, was spread around the slim white body with its outstretched snowy wings.

So much had he dared—so little accomplished.

Is it not the oft-told tale of those who have followed Icarus? Yet who can say that gallant youth has lived in vain when, as Icarus did, he has breasted the very skies, has flown with fearless heart and soul to the provinces of the deathless gods?—when, even for the space of a few of the heart-beats of Time, he has tasted supreme power—the ecstasy of illimitable happiness?

CLYTIE

The sunbeams are basking on the high walls of the old garden—smiling on the fruit that grows red and golden in their warmth. The bees are humming round the bed of purple heliotrope, and drowsily murmuring in the shelter of the soft petals of the blush roses whose sweetness brings back the fragrance of days that are gone. On the old grey sundial the white-winged pigeons sleepily croon as they preen their snowy plumage, and the Madonna lilies hang their heads like a procession of white-robed nuns who dare not look up from telling their beads until the triumphal procession of an all-conquering warrior has gone by. What can they think of that long line of tall yellow flowers by the garden wall, who turn their faces sunwards with an arrogant assurance, and give stare for stare to golden-haired Apollo as he drives his blazing car triumphant through the high heavens?

"Sunflowers" is the name by which we know those flamboyant blossoms which somehow fail so wholly to suggest the story of Clytie, the nymph whose destruction came from a faithful, unrequited love. She was a water-nymph, a timid, gentle being who frequented lonely streams, and bathed where the blue dragon-flies dart across the white water-lilies in pellucid lakes. In the shade of the tall poplar trees and the silvery willows she took her midday rest, and feared the hours when the flowers drooped their heads and the rippling water lost its coolness before the fierce glare of the sun.

But there came a day when, into the dark pool by which she sat, Apollo the Conqueror looked down and mirrored his face. And nevermore did she hide from the golden-haired god who, from the moment when she had seen in the water the picture of his radiant beauty, became the lord and master of her heart and soul. All night she awaited his coming, and the Dawn saw her looking eastward for the first golden gleams from the wheels of his chariot. All day she followed him with her longing gaze, nor did she ever cease to feast her eyes upon his beauty until the last reflection of his radiance had faded from the western sky.

Such devotion might have touched the heart of the sun-god, but he had no wish to own a love for which he had not sought. The nymph's adoration irked him, nor did pity come as Love's pale substitute when he marked how, day by day, her face grew whiter and more white, and her lovely form wasted away. For nine days, without food or drink, she kept her shamed vigil. Only one word of love did she crave. Unexacting in the humility of her devotion, she would gratefully have nourished her hungry heart upon one kindly glance. But Apollo, full of scorn and anger, lashed up his fiery steeds as he each day drove past her, nor deigned for her a glance more gentle than that which he threw on the satyrs as they hid in the dense green foliage of the shadowy woods.

Half-mocking, Diana said, "In truth the fair nymph who throws her heart's treasures at the feet of my golden-locked brother that he may trample on them, is coming to look like a faded flower!" And, as she spoke, the hearts of the other immortal dwellers in Olympus were stirred with pity.

"A flower she shall be!" they said, "and for all time shall she live, in life that is renewed each year when the earth stirs with the quickening of spring. The long summer days shall she spend forever in fearless worship of the god of her love!"

And, as they willed, the nymph passed out of her human form, and took the form of a flower, and evermore—the emblem of constancy—does she gaze with fearless ardour on the face of her love.

"The heart that has truly loved never forgets,But as truly loves on to the close;As the sunflower turns on her god when he setsThe same look that she turned when he rose."

Some there are who say that not into the bold-faced sunflower did her metamorphosis take place, but into that purple heliotrope that gives an exquisite offering of fragrance to the sun-god when his warm rays touch it. And in the old walled garden, while the bees drowsily hum, and the white pigeons croon, and the dashing sunflower gives Apollo gaze for gaze, and the scent of the mignonette mingles with that of clove pinks and blush roses, the fragrance of the heliotrope is, above all, worthy incense to be offered upon his altar by the devout lover of a god.

THE CRANES OF IBYCUS

"For murder, though it have no tongue, will speakWith most miraculous organ."

SHAKESPEARE.

Ibycus, the poet friend of Apollo, was a happy man as he journeyed on foot through the country where the wild flowers grew thick and the trees were laden with blossom towards the city of Corinth. His tuneful voice sang snatches of song of his own making, and ever and again he would try how his words and music sounded on his lyre. He was light of heart, because ever had he thought of good, and not evil, and had always sung only of great and noble deeds and of those things that helped his fellow-men. And now he went to Corinth for the great chariot-races, and for the great contest of musicians where every true poet and musician in Greece was sure to be found.

It was the time of the return to earth of Adonis and of Proserpine, and as he was reverently about to enter the sacred grove of Poseidon, where the trees grew thick, and saw, crowning the height before him, the glittering towers of Corinth, he heard, overhead, the harsh cries of some other returned exiles. Ibycus smiled, as he looked up and beheld the great flock of grey birds, with their long legs and strong, outstretched wings, come back from their winter sojourn on the golden sands of Egypt, to dance and beck and bow to each other by the marshes of his homeland.

"Welcome back, little brothers!" he cried. "May you and I both meet with naught but kindness from the people of this land!"

And when the cranes again harshly cried, as if in answer to his greeting, the poet walked gaily on, further into the shadow of that dark wood out of which he was never to pass as living man. Joyous, and fearing no evil, he had been struck and cast to the ground by cruel and murderous hands ere ever he knew that two robbers

159

were hidden in a narrow pass where the brushwood grew thick. With all his strength he fought, but his arms were those of a musician and not of a warrior, and very soon he was overpowered by those who assailed him. He cried in vain to gods and to men for help, and in his final agony he heard once more the harsh voices of the migratory birds and the rush of their speeding wings. From the ground, where he bled to death, he looked up to them.

"Take up my cause, dear cranes!" he said, "since no voice but yours answers my cry!"

And the cranes screamed hoarsely and mournfully as if in farewell, as they flapped their way towards Corinth and left the poet lying dead.

When his body was found, robbed and terribly wounded, from all over Greece, where he was known and loved, there uprose a great clamour of lamentation.

"Is it thus I find you restored to me?" said he who had expected him in Corinth as his honoured guest; "I who hoped to place the victor's laurels on your head when you triumphed in the temple of song!"

And all those whom the loving personality of Ibycus and the charm of his music had made his friends were alert and eager to avenge so foul a murder. But none knew how the wicked deed had come to pass—none, save the cranes.

Then came the day to which Ibycus had looked forward with such joy, when thousands upon thousands of his countrymen sat in the theatre at Cyprus and watched a play that stirred their hearts within them.

The theatre had for roof the blue vault of heaven; the sun served for footlights and for the lights above the heads of those who acted. The three Furies—the Eumenides—with their hard and cruel faces and snaky locks, and with blood dripping from their eyes, were represented by actors so great that the hearts of their beholders

160

trembled within them. In their dread hands lay the punishment of murder, of inhospitality, of ingratitude, and of all the cruellest and basest of crimes. Theirs was the duty of hurrying the doomed spirits entrusted to their merciless care over the Phlegethon, the river of fire that flows round Hades, and through the brazen gates that led to Torment, and their robes were robes worn

"With all the pomp of horror, dy'd in gore."

VIRGIL.

In solemn cadence, while the thousands of beholders watched and listened enthralled, the Furies walked round the theatre and sang their song of terror:

"Woe! woe! to him whose hands are soiled with blood! The darkness shall not hide him, nor shall his dread secret lie hidden even in the bowels of the earth! He shall not seek by flight to escape us, for vengeance is ours, and swifter than a hawk that strikes its quarry shall we strike. Unwearying we pursue, nor are our swift feet and our avenging arms made slow by pity. Woe! woe! to the shedder of innocent blood, for nor peace nor rest is his until we have hurried his tormented soul down to torture that shall endure everlastingly!"

As the listeners heard the dirge of doom, there were none who did not think of Ibycus, the gentle-hearted poet, so much beloved and so foully done to death, and in the tensity of the moment when the voices ceased, a great thrill passed over the multitudes as a voice, shrill with amazed horror, burst from one of the uppermost benches:

"See there! see there! behold, comrade, the cranes of Ibycus!"

Every eye looked upwards, and, harshly crying, there passed overhead the flock of cranes to whom the poet had entrusted his dying message. Then, like an electric shock, there came to all those who beheld the knowledge that he who had cried aloud was the murderer of Ibycus.

"Seize him! seize him!" cried in unison the voices of thousands. "Seize the man, and him to whom he spoke!"

Frantically the trembling wretch tried to deny his words, but it was too late. The roar of the multitudes was as that of an angry sea that hungers for its prey and will not be denied. He who had spoken and him to whom he spoke were seized by a score of eager hands.

In white-faced terror, because the Furies had hunted them down, they made confession of their crime and were put to death. And the flock of grey-plumaged, rosy-headed cranes winged their way on to the marshes, there to beck and bow to each other, and to dance in the golden sunset, well content because their message was delivered, and Ibycus, the poet-musician who had given them welcome, was avenged.

SYRINX

"Is it because the wild-wood passion still lingers in our hearts, because still in our minds the voice of Syrinx lingers in melancholy music, the music of regret and longing, that for most of us there is so potent a spell in running waters?"

Fiona Macleod.

As the evening shadows lengthen, and the night wind softly steals through the trees, touching with restless fingers the still waters of the little lochans that would fain have rest, there can be heard a long, long whisper, like a sigh. There is no softer, sadder note to be heard in all Pan's great orchestra, nor can one marvel that it should be so, for the whisper comes from the reeds who gently sway their heads while the wind passes over them as they grow by lonely lake or river.

This is the story of Syrinx, the reed, as Ovid has told it to us.

In Arcadia there dwelt a nymph whose name was Syrinx. So fair she was that for her dear sake fauns and satyrs forgot to gambol, and sat in the green woods in thoughtful stillness, that they might see her as she passed. But for none of them had Syrinx a word of kindness. She had no wish for love.

"But as for Love, truly I know him not,I have passionately turned my lips therefrom,And from that fate the careless gods allot."

Lady Margaret Sackville.

To one only of the gods did she give her loyal allegiance. She worshipped Diana, and with her followed the chase. As she lightly sped through the forest she might have been Diana herself, and there were those who said they would not know nymph from goddess, but that the goddess carried a silver bow, while that of Syrinx was made of horn. Fearless, and without a care or sorrow, Syrinx passed her happy days. Not for all the gold of Midas would

163

she have changed places with those love-lorn nymphs who sighed their hearts out for love of a god or of a man. Heartwhole, fancy free, gay and happy and lithe and strong, as a young boy whose joy it is to run and to excel in the chase, was Syrinx, whose white arms against the greenwood trees dazzled the eyes of the watching fauns when she drew back her bow to speed an arrow at the stag she had hunted since early dawn. Each morning that she awoke was the morning of a day of joy; each night that she lay down to rest, it was to sleep as a child who smiles in his sleep at the remembrance of a perfect day.

But to Syrinx, who knew no fear, Fear came at last. She was returning one evening from the shadowy hills, untired by the chase that had lasted for many an hour, when, face to face, she met with one whom hitherto she had only seen from afar. Of him the other nymphs spoke often. Who was so great as Pan?—Pan, who ruled the woods. None could stand against Pan. Those who defied him must ever come under his power in the end. He was Fear; he was Youth; he was Joy; he was Love; he was Beast; he was Power; he was Man; he was God. He was Life itself. So did they talk, and Syrinx listened with a smile. Not Pan himself could bring Fear to her.

Yet when he met her in the silent loneliness of a great forest and stood in her path and gazed on her with eyes of joyous amazement that one so fair should be in his kingdom without his having had knowledge of it, Syrinx felt something come to her heart that never before had assailed it.

Pan's head was crowned with sharp pine-leaves. His face was young and beautiful, and yet older than the mountains and the seas. Sadness and joy were in his eyes at the same time, and at the same moment there looked out from them unutterable tenderness and merciless cruelty. For only a little space of time did he stand and hold her eyes with his own, and then in low caressing voice he spoke, and his words were like the song of a bird to his mate, like the call of the earth to the sun in spring, like the lap of the waves when they tell the rocks of their eternal longing. Of love he spoke, of love that demanded love, and of the nymph's most perfect beauty. Yet as he spoke, the unknown thing came and smote with icy hands the heart of Syrinx.

"Ah! I have Fear! I have Fear!" she cried, and more cruel grew the cruelty in the eyes of Pan, but his words were still the words of passionate tenderness. Like a bird that trembles, helpless, before the serpent that would slay it, so did Syrinx the huntress stand, and her face in the shade of the forest was like a white lily in the night. But when the god would have drawn her close to him and kissed her red lips, Fear leapt to Terror, and Terror winged her feet. Never in the chase with Diana had she run as now she ran. But like a rushing storm did Pan pursue her, and when he laughed she knew that what the nymphs had said was true—he was Power—he was Fear—he was Beast—he was Life itself. The darkness of the forest swiftly grew more dark. The climbing trails of ivy and the fragrant creeping plants caught her flying feet and made her stumble. Branches and twigs grew alive and snatched at her and baulked her as she passed. Trees blocked her path. All Nature had grown cruel, and everywhere there seemed to her to be a murmur of mocking laughter, laughter from the creatures of Pan, echoing the merciless merriment of their lord and master. Nearer he came, ever nearer. Almost she could feel his breath on her neck; but even as he stretched out his arms to seize the nymph whose breath came with sobs like that of a young doe spent by the chase, they reached the brink of the river Ladon. And to her "watery sisters" the nymphs of the river, Syrinx breathed a desperate prayer for pity and for help, then stumbled forward, a quarry run to the death.

With an exultant shout, Pan grasped her as she fell. And lo, in his arms he held no exquisite body with fiercely beating heart, but a clump of slender reeds. Baffled he stood for a little space, and, as he stood, the savagery of the beast faded from his eyes that were fathomless as dark mountain tarns where the sun-rays seldom come, and there came into them a man's unutterable woe. At the reeds by the river he gazed, and sighed a great sigh, the sigh that comes from the heart of a god who thinks of the pain of the world. Like a gentle zephyr the sigh breathed through the reeds, and from the reeds there came a sound as of the sobbing sorrow of the world's desire. Then Pan drew his sharp knife, and with it he cut seven of the reeds that grew by the murmuring river.

"Thus shalt thou still be mine, my Syrinx," he said.

Deftly he bound them together, cut them into unequal lengths, and fashioned for himself an instrument, that to this day is called the Syrinx, or Pan's Pipes.

So did the god make music.

And all that night he sat by the swift-flowing river, and the music from his pipe of reeds was so sweet and yet so passing sad, that it seemed as though the very heart of the earth itself were telling of its sadness. Thus Syrinx still lives—still dies:

"A note of music by its own breath slain, Blown tenderly from the frail heart of a reed,"

and as the evening light comes down on silent places and the trembling shadows fall on the water, we can hear her mournful whisper through the swaying reeds, brown and silvery-golden, that grow by lonely lochan and lake and river.

THE DEATH OF ADONIS

"The fairest youth that ever maiden's dream conceived."

LEWIS MORRIS.

The ideally beautiful woman, a subject throughout the centuries for all the greatest powers of sculptor's and painter's art, is Venus, or Aphrodite, goddess of beauty and of love. And he who shares with her an unending supremacy of perfection of form is not one of the gods, her equals, but a mortal lad, who was the son of a king.

As Aphrodite sported one day with Eros, the little god of love, by accident she wounded herself with one of his arrows. And straightway there came into her heart a strange longing and an ache such as the mortal victims of the bow of Eros knew well. While still the ache remained, she heard, in a forest of Cyprus, the baying of hounds and the shouts of those who urged them on in the chase. For her the chase possessed no charms, and she stood aside while the quarry burst through the branches and thick undergrowth of the wood, and the hounds followed in hot pursuit. But she drew her breath sharply, and her eyes opened wide in amazed gladness, when she looked on the perfect beauty of the fleet-footed hunter, who was only a little less swift than the shining spear that sped from his hand with the sureness of a bolt from the hand of Zeus. And she knew that this must be none other than Adonis, son of the king of Paphos, of whose matchless beauty she had heard not only the dwellers on earth, but the Olympians themselves speak in wonder. While gods and men were ready to pay homage to his marvellous loveliness, to Adonis himself it counted for nothing. But in the vigour of his perfect frame he rejoiced; in his fleetness of foot, in the power of that arm that Michael Angelo has modelled, in the quickness and sureness of his aim, for the boy was a mighty hunter with a passion for the chase.

Aphrodite felt that her heart was no longer her own, and knew that the wound that the arrow of Eros had dealt would never heal until she knew that Adonis loved her. No longer was she to be found by the Cytherian shores or in those places once held by her most dear, and the other gods smiled when they beheld her vying with Diana in the chase and following Adonis as he pursued the roe, the wolf, and the wild boar through the dark forest and up the mountain side. The pride of the goddess of love must often have hung its head. For her love was a thing that Adonis could not understand. He held her "Something better than his dog, a little dearer than his horse," and wondered at her whim to follow his hounds through brake and marsh and lonely forest. His reckless courage was her pride and her torture. Because he was to her so infinitely dear, his path seemed ever bestrewn with dangers. But when she spoke to him with anxious warning and begged him to beware of the fierce beasts that might one day turn on him and bring him death, the boy laughed mockingly and with scorn.

There came at last a day when she asked him what he did on the morrow, and Adonis told her with sparkling eyes that had no heed for her beauty, that he had word of a wild boar, larger, older, more fierce than any he had ever slain, and which, before the chariot of Diana next passed over the land of Cyprus, would be lying dead with a spear-wound through it.

With terrible foreboding, Aphrodite tried to dissuade him from his venture.

"O, be advised: thou know'st not what it isWith javelin's point a churlish swine to gore,Whose tushes never sheathed he whetteth still,Like to a mortal butcher, bent to kill.

Alas, he naught esteems that face of thine,To which love's eyes pay tributary gazes;Nor thy soft hands, sweet lips, and crystal eyne,Whose full perfection all the world amazes;But having thee at vantage—wondrous dread!—Would root these beauties as he roots the mead."

SHAKESPEARE.

To all her warnings, Adonis would but give smiles. Ill would it become him to slink abashed away before the fierceness of an old monster of the woods, and, laughing in the pride of a whole-hearted boy at a woman's idle fears, he sped homewards with his hounds.

With the gnawing dread of a mortal woman in her soul, Aphrodite spent the next hours. Early she sought the forest that she might again plead with Adonis, and maybe persuade him, for love of her, to give up the perilous chase because she loved him so.

But even as the rosy gates of the Dawn were opening, Adonis had begun his hunt, and from afar off the goddess could hear the baying of his hounds. Yet surely their clamour was not that of hounds in full cry, nor was it the triumphant noise that they so fiercely make as they pull down their vanquished quarry, but rather was it baying, mournful as that of the hounds of Hecate. Swift as a great bird, Aphrodite reached the spot from whence came the sound that made her tremble.

Amidst the trampled brake, where many a hound lay stiff and dead, while others, disembowelled by the tusks of the boar, howled aloud in mortal agony, lay Adonis. As he lay, he "knew the strange, slow chill which, stealing, tells the young that it is death."

And as, *in extremis*, he thought of past things, manhood came to Adonis and he knew something of the meaning of the love of Aphrodite—a love stronger than life, than time, than death itself. His hounds and his spear seemed but playthings now. Only the eternities remained—bright Life, and black-robed Death.

Very still he lay, as though he slept; marble-white, and beautiful as a statue wrought by the hand of a god. But from the cruel wound in the white thigh, ripped open by the boar's profaning tusk, the red blood dripped, in rhythmic flow, crimsoning the green moss under him. With a moan of unutterable anguish, Aphrodite threw herself beside him, and pillowed his dear head in her tender arms. Then, for a little while, life's embers flickered up, his cold lips tried to form themselves into a smile of understanding and held themselves up to hers. And, while they kissed, the soul of Adonis passed away.

"A cruel, cruel wound on his thigh hath Adonis, but a deeper wound in her heart doth Cytherea bear. About him his dear hounds are loudly baying, and the nymphs of the wild woods wail him; but Aphrodite with unbound locks through the glades goes wandering—wretched, with hair unbraided, with feet unsandalled, and the thorns as she passes wound her and pluck the blossom of her sacred blood. Shrill she wails as down the woodland she is borne…. And the rivers bewail the sorrows of Aphrodite, and the wells are weeping Adonis on the mountains. The flowers flush red for anguish, and Cytherea through all the mountain-knees, through every dell doth utter piteous dirge:

"'*Woe, woe for Cytherea, he hath perished, the lovely Adonis!*'"

BION.

Passionately the god besought Zeus to give her back her lost love, and when there was no answer to her prayers, she cried in bitterness: "Yet shall I keep a memorial of Adonis that shall be to all everlasting!" And, as she spoke, her tears and his blood, mingling together, were turned into flowers.

"A tear the Paphian sheds for each blood-drop of Adonis, and tears and blood on the earth are turned to flowers. The blood brings forth the roses, the tears, the wind-flower."

Yet, even then, the grief of Aphrodite knew no abatement. And when Zeus, wearied with her crying, heard her, to his amazement, beg to be allowed to go down to the Shades that she might there endure eternal twilight with the one of her heart, his soul was softened.

"Never can it be that the Queen of Love and of Beauty leaves Olympus and the pleasant earth to tread for evermore the dark Cocytus valley," he said. "Nay, rather shall I permit the beauteous youth of thy love to return for half of each year from the Underworld that thou and he may together know the joy of a love that hath reached fruition."

Thus did it come to pass that when dark winter's gloom was past, Adonis returned to the earth and to the arms of her who loved him.

"But even in death, so strong is love, I could not wholly die; and year by year, When the bright springtime comes, and the earth lives, Love opens these dread gates, and calls me forthAcross the gulf. Not here, indeed, she comes, Being a goddess and in heaven, but smoothsMy path to the old earth, where still I knowOnce more the sweet lost days, and once againBlossom on that soft breast, and am againA youth, and rapt in love; and yet not allAs careless as of yore; but seem to knowThe early spring of passion, tamed by timeAnd suffering, to a calmer, fuller flow, Less fitful, but more strong."

Lewis Morris.

And when the time of the singing of birds has come, and the flowers have thrown off their white snow pall, and the brown earth grows radiant in its adornments of green blade and of fragrant blossom, we know that Adonis has returned from his exile, and trace his footprints by the fragile flower that is his very own, the white flower with the golden heart, that trembles in the wind as once the white hands of a grief-stricken goddess shook for sorrow.

"The flower of Death" is the name that the Chinese give to the wind-flower—the wood-anemone. Yet surely the flower that was born of tears and of blood tells us of a life that is beyond the grave—of a love which is unending.

The cruel tusk of a rough, remorseless winter still yearly slays the "lovely Adonis" and drives him down to the Shades. Yet we know that Spring, with its*Sursum Corda*, will return as long as the earth shall endure; even as the sun must rise each day so long as time shall last, to make

"Le ciel tout en fleur semble une immense roseQu'un Adonis céleste
a teinte de son sang."

DE HEREDIA.

PAN

"What was he doing, the great god Pan,Down in the reeds by the river?Spreading ruin and scattering ban,Splashing and paddling with hoofs of a goat,And breaking the golden lilies afloatWith the dragon-fly on the river.

He tore out a reed, the great god Pan,From the deep cool bed of the river:The limpid water turbidly ran,And the broken lilies a-dying lay,And the dragon-fly had fled away,Ere he brought it out of the river.

'This is the way,' laughed the great god Pan(Laughed while he sat by the river),'The only way, since gods beganTo make sweet music, they could succeed.'Then, dropping his mouth to a hole in the reed,He blew in power by the river.

Sweet, sweet, sweet, O Pan!Piercing sweet by the river!Blinding sweet, O great god Pan!The sun on the hill forgot to die,And the lilies revived, and the dragon-flyCame back to dream on the river.

Yet half a beast is the great god Pan,To laugh as he sits by the river,Making a poet out of a man:The true gods sigh for the cost and pain,For the reed which grows nevermore againAs a reed with the reeds in the river."

E. B. BROWNING.

Were we to take the whole of that immense construction of fable that was once the religion of Greece, and treat it as a vast play in which there were many thousands of actors, we should find that one of these actors appeared again and again. In one scene, then in another, in connection with one character, then with another, unexpectedly slipping out from the shadows of the trees from the first act even to the last, we should see Pan—so young and yet so old, so heedlessly gay, yet so infinitely sad.

If, rather, we were to regard the mythology of Greece as a colossal and wonderful piece of music, where the thunders of Jupiter and the harsh hoof-beats of the fierce black steeds of Pluto, the king whose coming none can stay, made way for the limpid melodies of Orpheus and the rustling whisper of the footfall of nymphs and of fauns on the leaves, through it all we should have an ever-recurring *motif*–the clear, magical fluting of the pipes of Pan.

We have the stories of Pan and of Echo, of Pan and of Midas, of Pan and Syrinx, of Pan and Selene, of Pan and Pitys, of Pan and Pomona. Pan it was who taught Apollo how to make music. It was Pan who spoke what he deemed to be comfort to the distraught Psyche; Pan who gave Diana her hounds. The other gods had their own special parts in the great play that at one time would have Olympus for stage, at another the earth. Pan was Nature incarnate. He was the Earth itself.

Many are the stories of his genealogy, but the one that is given in one of the Homeric hymns is that Hermes, the swift-footed young god, wedded Dryope, the beautiful daughter of a shepherd in Arcadia, and to them was born, under the greenwood tree, the infant, Pan. When Dryope first looked on her child, she was smitten with horror, and fled away from him. The deserted baby roared lustily, and when his father, Hermes, examined him he found a rosy-cheeked thing with prick ears and tiny horns that grew amongst his thick curls, and with the dappled furry chest of a faun, while instead of dimpled baby legs he had the strong, hairy hind legs of a goat. He was a fearless creature, and merry withal, and when Hermes had wrapped him up in a hare skin, he sped to Olympus and showed his fellow-gods the son that had been born to him and the beautiful nymph of the forest. Baby though he was, Pan made the Olympians laugh. He had only made a woman, his own mother, cry; all others rejoiced at the new creature that had come to increase their merriment. And Bacchus, who loved him most of all, and felt that here was a babe after his own heart, bestowed on him the name by which he was forever known–Pan, meaning *All*.

Thus Pan grew up, the earthly equal of the Olympians, and, as he grew, he took to himself the lordship of woods and of solitary places. He was king of huntsmen and of fishermen, lord of flocks and herds and of all the wild creatures of the forest. All living, soulless things owned him their master; even the wild bees claimed him as their overlord. He was ever merry, and when a riot of music and of laughter slew the stillness of the shadowy woods, it was Pan who led the dancing throng of white-limbed nymphs and gambolling satyrs, for whom he made melody from the pipes for whose creation a maid had perished.

Round his horns and thick curls he presently came to wear a crown of sharp pine-leaves, remembrance of another fair nymph whose destruction he had brought about.

Pitys listened to the music of Pan, and followed him even as the children followed the Pied Piper of later story. And ever his playing lured her further on and into more dangerous and desolate places, until at length she stood on the edge of a high cliff whose pitiless front rushed sheer down to cruel rocks far below. There Pan's music ceased, and Pitys knew all the joy and the sorrow of the world as the god held out his arms to embrace her. But neither Pan nor Pitys had remembrance of Boreas, the merciless north wind, whose love the nymph had flouted.

Ere Pan could touch her, a blast, fierce and strong as death, had seized the nymph's fragile body, and as a wind of March tears from the tree the first white blossom that has dared to brave the ruthless gales, and casts it, torn and dying, to the earth, so did Boreas grip the slender Pitys and dash her life out on the rocks far down below. From her body sprang the pine tree, slender, erect, clinging for dear life to the sides of precipices, and by the prickly wreath he always wore, Pan showed that he held her in fond remembrance.

Joy, and youth, and force, and spring, was Pan to all the creatures whose overlord he was. Pan meant the richness of the sap in the trees, the lushness of grass and of the green stems of the blue hyacinths and the golden daffodils; the throbbing of growth in the woodland and in the meadows; the trilling of birds that seek for their mates and find them; the coo of the doves on their nests of young; the arrogant virility of bulls and of stags whose lowing and belling wake the silence of the hills; the lightness of heart that made the nymphs dance and sing, the fauns leap high, and shout aloud for very joy of living. All of these things was Pan to those of his own kingdom.

Yet to the human men and women who had also listened to his playing, Pan did not mean only joyousness. He was to them a force that many times became a terror because of its sheer irresistibleness.

While the sun shone and the herdsmen could see the nodding white cotton-grass, the asphodel, and the golden kingcups that hid the black death-traps of the pitiless marshes, they had no fear of Pan. Nor in the daytime, when in the woods the sunbeams played amongst the trees and the birds sang of Spring and of love, and the syrinx sent an echo from far away that made the little silver birches give a whispering laugh of gladness and the pines cease to sigh, did man or maid have any fear. Yet when darkness fell on the land, terror would come with it, and, deep in their hearts, they would know that the terror was Pan. Blindly, madly, they would flee from something that they could not see, something they could barely hear, and many times rush to their own destruction. And there would be no sweet sound of music then, only mocking laughter. *Panic* was the name given to this fear—the name by which it still is known. And, to this day, panic yet comes, and not only by night, but only in very lonely places. There are those who have known it, and for shame have scarce dared to own it, in highland glens, in the loneliness of an island in the western sea, in a green valley amongst the "solemn, kindly, round-backed hills" of the Scottish Border, in the remoteness of the Australian bush. They have no reasons to give—or their reasons are far-fetched. Only, to them as to Mowgli, *Fear* came, and the fear seemed to them to come from a malignant something from which they must make all haste to flee, did they value safety of mind and of body. Was it for this reason that the Roman legionaries on the Great Wall so often reared altars in that lonely land of moor and mountain where so many of them fought and died—

"To Pan, and to the Sylvan deities"?

For surely Pan was there, where the curlew cried and the pewit mourned, and sometimes the waiting soldiers must almost have imagined his mocking laughter borne in the winds that swept across the bleak hills of their exiled solitude.

He who was surely one of the bravest of mankind, one who always, in his own words, "clung to his paddle," writes of such a fear when he escaped death by drowning from the Oise in flood.

"The devouring element in the universe had leaped out against me, in this green valley quickened by a running stream. The bells were all very pretty in their way, but I had heard some of the hollow notes of Pan's music. Would the wicked river drag me down by the heels, indeed? and look so beautiful all the time? Nature's good humour was only skin-deep, after all."

And of the reeds he writes: "Pan once played upon their forefathers; and so, by the hands of his river, he still plays upon these later generations down all the valley of the Oise; and plays the same air, both sweet and shrill, to tell us of the beauty and the terror of the world."

"The Beauty and the terror of the world"—was not this what Pan stood for to the Greeks of long ago?

The gladness of living, the terror of living—the exquisite joy and the infinite pain—that has been the possession of Pan—for we have not yet found a more fitting title—since ever time began. And because Pan is as he is, from him has evolved a higher Pantheism. We have done away with his goat's feet and his horns, although these were handed on from him to Satan when Christianity broke down the altars of Paganism.

"Nature, which is the Time-vesture of God and reveals Him to the wise, hides Him from the foolish," writes Carlyle. Pan is Nature, and Nature is not the ugly thing that the Calvinists would once have had us believe it to be. Nature is capable of being made the garment of God.

"In Being's floods, in Action's storm,I walk and work, above, beneath,Work and weave in endless motion!Birth and Death,An infinite ocean;A seizing and givingThe fire of Living;'Tis thus at the roaring loom of Time I ply,And weave for God the Garment thou seest Him by."

So speaks the *Erdgeist* in Goethe's *Faust*, and yet another of the greatest of the poets writes:

"The sun, the moon, the stars, the seas, the hills and the plains—Are not these, O Soul, the Vision of Him who reigns?

And the ear of man cannot hear, and the eye of man cannot see;But if we could see and hear, this Vision—were it not He?"

TENNYSON.

Carlyle says that "The whole universe is the Garment of God," and he who lives very close to Nature must, at least once in a lifetime, come, in the solitude of the lonely mountain tops, upon that bush that burns and is not yet consumed, and out of the midst of which speaks the voice of the Eternal.

The immortal soul—the human body—united, yet ever in conflict—that is Pan. The sighing and longing for things that must endure everlastingly—the riotous enjoyment of the beauty of life—the perfect appreciation of the things that are. Life is so real, so strong, so full of joyousness and of beauty,—and on the other side of a dark stream, cold, menacing, cruel, stands Death. Yet Life and Death make up the sum of existence, and until we, who live our paltry little lives here on earth in the hope of a Beyond, can realise what is the true air that is played on those pipes of Pan, there is no hope for us of even a vague comprehension of the illimitable Immortality.

It is a very old tale that tells us of the passing of Pan. In the reign of Tiberius, on that day when, on the hill of Calvary, at Jerusalem in Syria, Jesus Christ died as a malefactor, on the cross—"And it was about the sixth hour, and there was a darkness all over the earth"— Thamus, an Egyptian pilot, was guiding a ship near the islands of Paxæ in the Ionian Sea; and to him came a great voice, saying, "Go! make everywhere the proclamation, *Great Pan is dead!*"

And from the poop of his ship, when, in great heaviness of heart, because for him the joy of the world seemed to have passed away, Thamus had reached Palodes, he shouted aloud the words that he had been told. Then, from all the earth there arose a sound of great lamentation, and the sea and the trees, the hills, and all the creatures of Pan sighed in sobbing unison an echo of the pilot's words—"*Pan is dead—Pan is dead.*"

"The lonely mountains o'erAnd the resounding shore,A voice of weeping heard, and loud lament;From haunted spring and daleEdg'd with poplar pale,The parting genius is with sighing sent;With flow'r-inwoven tresses torn,The Nymphs in twilight shade of tangled thickets mourn."

MILTON.

Pan was dead, and the gods died with him.

"Gods of Hellas, gods of Hellas,Can ye listen in your silence?Can your mystic voices tell usWhere ye hide? In floating islands,With a wind that evermoreKeeps you out of sight of shore?Pan, Pan is dead.

Gods! we vainly do adjure you,—Ye return nor voice nor sign!Not a votary could secure youEven a grave for your Divine!Not a grave to show thereby,'Here these grey old gods do lie,'Pan, Pan is dead."

E. B. BROWNING.

Pan is dead. In the old Hellenistic sense Pan is gone forever. Yet until Nature has ceased to be, the thing we call Pan must remain a living entity. Some there be who call his music, when he makes all humanity dance to his piping, "*Joie de vivre,*" and De Musset speaks of "*Le vin de la jeunesse*" which ferments "*dans les veines de Dieu.*" It is Pan who inspires Seumas, the old islander, of whom Fiona Macleod writes, and who, looking towards the sea at sunrise, says, "Every morning like this I take my hat off to the beauty of the world."

Half of the flesh and half of the spirit is Pan. There are some who have never come into contact with him, who know him only as the emblem of Paganism, a cruel thing, more beast than man, trampling, with goat's feet, on the gentlest flowers of spring. They know not the meaning of "the Green Fire of Life," nor have they ever known Pan's moods of tender sadness. Never to them has come in the forest, where the great grey trunks of the beeches rise from a carpet of primroses and blue hyacinths, and the slender silver beeches are the guardian angels of the starry wood-anemones, and the sunbeams slant through the oak and beech leaves of tender green and play on the dead amber leaves of a year that is gone, the whisper of little feet that cannot be seen, the piercing sweet music from very far away, that fills the heart with gladness and yet with a strange pain—the ache of the *Weltschmerz*—the echo of the pipes of Pan.

"... Oftenest in the dark woods I hear him singDim, half-remembered things, where the old mosses clingTo the old trees, and the faint wandering eddies bringThe phantom echoes of a phantom spring."

FIONA MACLEOD.

LORELEI

"Ich weiss nicht, was soll es bedeuten,Dass ich so traurig bin;Ein Märchen aus alten Zeiten,Das kommt mir nicht aus dem Sinn.

Die schönste Jungfrau sitzetDort oben wunderbar,Ihr gold'nes Geschmeide blitzet,Sie kämmt ihr gold'nes Haar.

Sie kämmt es mit gold'nem Kamme,Und singt ein Lied dabei;Das hat eine wundersame,Gewaltige Melodei."

HEINE.

In every land, North and South, East and West, from sea to sea, myth and legend hand down to us as cruel and malignant creatures, who ceaselessly seek to slay man's body and to destroy his soul, the half-human children of the restless sea and of the fiercely running streams.

In Scotland and in Australia, in every part of Europe, we have tales of horrible formless things which frequent lonely rivers and lochs and marshes, and to meet which must mean Death. And equal in malignity with them, and infinitely more dangerous, are the beautiful beings who would seem to claim descent from Lilith, the soulless wife of Adam.

Such were the sirens who would have compassed the destruction of Odysseus. Such are the mermaids, to wed with one of whom must bring unutterable woe upon any of the sons of men. In lonely far-off places by the sea there still are tales of exquisite melodies heard in the gloaming, or at night when the moon makes a silver pathway across the water; still are there stories of women whose home is in the depths of the ocean, and who come to charm away men's souls by their beauty and by their pitiful longing for human love.

Those who have looked on the yellow-green waters of the Seine, or who have seen the more turbid, more powerful Thames sweeping her serious, majestic way down towards the open ocean, at Westminster, or at London Bridge, can perhaps realise something of that inwardness of things that made the people of the past, and that makes the mentally uncontrolled people of the present, feel a fateful power calling upon them to listen to the insistence of the exacting waters, and to surrender their lives and their souls forever to a thing that called and which would brook no denial. In the Morgue, or in a mortuary by the river-side, their poor bodies have lain when the rivers have worked their will with them, and "Suicide," "Death by drowning," or "By Misadventure" have been the verdicts given. We live in a too practical, too utterly common-sensical age to conceive a poor woman with nothing on earth left to live for, being lured down to the Shades by a creature of the water, or a man who longs for death seeing a beautiful daughter of a river-god beckoning to him to come where he will find peace everlasting.

Yet ever we war with the sea. All of us know her seductive charm, but all of us fear her. The boundary line between our fear of the fierce, remorseless, ever-seeking, cruel waves that lap up life swiftly as a thirsty beast laps water, and the old belief in cruel sea-creatures that sought constantly for the human things that were to be their prey, is a very narrow one. And once we have seen the sea in a rage, flinging herself in terrible anger against the poor, frail toy that the hands of men have made and that was intended to rule and to resist her, foaming and frothing over the decks of the thing that carries human lives, we can understand much of the old pagan belief. If one has watched a river in spate, red as with blood, rushing triumphantly over all resistance, smashing down the trees that baulk it, sweeping away each poor, helpless thing, brute or human, that it encounters, dealing out ruin and death, and proceeding superbly on to carry its trophies of disaster to the bosom of the Ocean Mother, very easy is it to see from whence came those old tales of cruelty, of irresistible strength, of desire.

Many are the tales of sea-maidens who have stolen men's lives from them and sent their bodies to move up and down amidst the wrack, like broken toys with which a child has grown tired of playing and cast away in weariness. In an eighth-century chronicle concerning St. Fechin, we read of evil powers whose rage is "seen in that watery fury and their hellish hate and turbulence in the beating of the sea against the rocks." "The bitter gifts of our lord Poseidon" is the name given to them by one of the earliest poets of Greece and a poet of our own time—poet of the sea, of running water, and of lonely places—quotes from the saying of a fisherman of the isle of Ulva words that show why simple minds have so many times materialised the restless, devouring element into the form of a woman who is very beautiful, but whose tender mercies are very cruel. "She is like a woman of the old tales whose beauty is dreadful," said Seumas, the islander, "and who breaks your heart at last whether she smiles or frowns. But she doesn't care about that, or whether you are hurt or not. It's because she has no heart, being all a wild water."

Treacherous, beautiful, remorseless, that is how men regard the sea and the rushing rivers, of whom the sirens and mermaids of old tradition have come to stand as symbols. Treacherous and pitiless, yet with a fascination that can draw even the moon and the stars to her breast:

"Once I sat upon a promontory,And heard a mermaid, on a dolphin's back,Uttering such dulcet and harmonious breath,That the rude sea grew civil at her song;And certain stars shot madly from their spheres,To hear the sea-maid's music."

SHAKESPEARE.

Very many are the stories of the women of the sea and of the rivers, but that one who must forever hold her own, because Heine has immortalised her in song, is the river maiden of the Rhine—the Lorelei.

Near St. Goar, there rises out of the waters of the Rhine a perpendicular rock, some four hundred feet high. Many a boatman in bygone days there met his death, and the echo which it possesses is still a mournful one. Those who know the great river, under which lies hid the treasure of the Nibelungs, with its "gleaming towns by the river-side and the green vineyards combed along the hills," and who have felt the romance of the rugged crags, crowned by ruined castles, that stand like fantastic and very ancient sentries to guard its channel, can well understand how easy of belief was the legend of the Lorelei.

Down the green waters came the boatman's frail craft, ever drawing nearer to the perilous rock. All his care and all his skill were required to avert a very visible danger. But high above him, from the rock round which the swirling eddies splashed and foamed, there came a voice.

"Her voice was like the voice the starsHad when they sang together."

And when the boatman looked up at the sound of such sweet music, he beheld a maiden more fair than any he had ever dreamed of. On the rock she sat, combing her long golden hair with a comb of red gold. Her limbs were white as foam and her eyes green like the emerald green of the rushing river. And her red lips smiled on him and her arms were held out to him in welcome, and the sound of her song thrilled through the heart of him who listened, and her eyes drew his soul to her arms.

Forgotten was all peril. The rushing stream seized the little boat and did with it as it willed. And while the boatman still gazed upwards, intoxicated by her matchless beauty and the magic of her voice, his boat was swept against the rock, and, with the jar and crash, knowledge came back to him, and he heard, with broken heart, the mocking laughter of the Lorelei as he was dragged down as if by a thousand icy hands, and, with a choking sigh, surrendered his life to the pitiless river.

To one man only was it granted to see the siren so near that he could hold her little, cold, white hands, and feel the wondrous golden hair sweep across his eyes. This was a young fisherman, who met her by the river and listened to the entrancing songs that she sang for him alone. Each evening she would tell him where to cast his nets on the morrow, and he prospered greatly and was a marvel to all others who fished in the waters of the Rhine. But there came an evening when he was seen joyously hastening down the river bank in response to the voice of the Lorelei, that surely never had sounded so honey-sweet before, and he came back nevermore. They said that the Lorelei had dragged him down to her coral caves that he might live with her there forever, and, if it were not so, the rushing water could never whisper her secret and theirs, of a lifeless plaything that they swept seawards, and that wore a look of horror and of great wonder in its dead, wide-open eyes.

It is "ein Märchen aus alten Zeiten"—a legend of long ago.

But it is a very much older *Märchen* that tells us of the warning of Circe to Odysseus:

"To the Sirens first shalt thou come, who bewitch all men, whosoever shall come to them. Whoso draws nigh them unwittingly and hears the sound of the Siren's voice, never doth he see wife or babes stand by him on his return, nor have they joy at his coming; but the Sirens enchant him with their clear song."

And until there shall be no more sea and the rivers have ceased to run, the enchantment that comes from the call of the water to the hearts of men must go on. Day by day the toll of lives is paid, and still the cruel daughters of the deep remain unsatisfied. We can hear their hungry whimper from the rushing river through the night, and the waves of the sea that thunders along the coast would seem to voice the insistence of their desire. And we who listen to their ceaseless, restless moan can say with Heine:

"*Ich weiss nicht, was soll es bedeuten,Dass ich so traurig bin.*"

For the sadness of heart, the melancholy that their music brings us is a mystery which none on this earth may ever unravel.

FREYA, QUEEN OF THE NORTHERN GODS

"Friday's bairn is loving and giving," says the old rhyme that sets forth the special qualities of the children born on each day of the week, and to the superstitious who regard Friday as a day of evil omen, it seems strange that Friday's bairn should be so blessed. But they forget that before Christianity swept paganism before it, and taught those who worshipped the northern gods the story of that first black "Good Friday," the tragedy in which all humanity was involved, Friday was the day of Freya, "The Beloved," gentle protectress, and most generous giver of all joys, delights, and pleasures. From her, in mediæval times, the high-born women who acted as dispensers to their lords first took the title *Frouwa* (=Frau), and when, in its transition stage, the old heathenism had evolved into a religion of strong nature worship, overshadowed by fatalism, only thinly veneered by Christianity, the minds of the Christian converts of Scandinavia, like those of puzzled children, transferred to the Virgin Mary the attributes that had formerly been those of their "Lady"—Freya, the goddess of Love.

Long before the Madonna was worshipped, Freya gave her name to plants, to flowers, and even to insects, and the child who says to the beautiful little insect, that he finds on a leaf, "Ladybird, ladybird, fly away home," is commemorating the name of the Lady, Freya, to whom his ancestors offered their prayers.

In her home in the Hall of Mists, Freya (or Frigga), wife of Odin the All Father, sat with her golden distaff spinning the clouds. Orion's Belt was known as "Frigga's spindle" by the Norsemen, and the men on the earth, as they watched the great cumulous masses of snowy-white, golden or silver edged, the fleecy cloudlets of grey, soft as the feathers on the breast of a dove, or the angry banks of black and purple, portending a storm, had constant proof of the diligence of their goddess. She was the protectress of those who sailed the seas, and the care of children as they came into the world was also hers. Hers, too, was the happy task of bringing together after death, lovers whom Death had parted, and to her belonged the glorious task of going down to the fields of battle where the slain lay strewn like leaves in autumn and leading to Valhalla the half of the warriors who, as heroes, had died. Her vision enabled her to look over all the earth, and she could see into the Future, but she held her knowledge as a profound secret that none could prevail upon her to betray.

"Of me the gods are sprung;And all that is to come I know, but lockIn my own breast, and have to none reveal'd."

MATTHEW ARNOLD.

Thus she came to be pictured crowned with heron plumes, the symbol of silence—the silence of the lonely marshes where the heron stands in mutest contemplation—a tall, very stately, very queenly, wholly beautiful woman, with a bunch of keys at her girdle—symbol of her protection of the Northern housewife—sometimes clad in snow-white robes, sometimes in robes of sombre black. And because her care was for the anxious, weary housewife, for the mother and her new-born babe, for the storm-tossed mariner, fighting the billows of a hungry sea, for those whose true and pure love had suffered the crucifixion of death, and for the glorious dead on the field of battle, it is very easy to see Freya as her worshippers saw her—an ideal of perfect womanhood.

But the gods of the Norsemen were never wholly gods. Always they, like the gods of Greece, endeared themselves to humanity by possessing some little, or big, human weakness. And Freya is none the less lovable to the descendants of her worshippers because she possessed the so-called "feminine weakness" of love of dress. Jewels, too, she loved, and knowing the wondrous skill of the dwarfs in fashioning exquisite ornaments, she broke off a piece of gold from the statue of Odin, her husband, and gave it to them to make into a necklace—the marvellous jewelled necklace Brisingamen, that in time to come was possessed by Beowulf. It was so exquisite a thing that it made her beauty twice more perfect, and Odin loved her doubly much because of it. But when he discovered that his statue had been tampered with, his wrath was very great, and furiously he summoned the dwarfs—they who dealt always with fine metal—and demanded of them which of them had done him this grievous wrong. But the dwarfs loved Freya, and from them he got no answer.

Then he placed the statue above the temple gate, and laboured with guile to devise runes that might give it the power of speech, so that it might shout aloud the name of the impious robber as the robber went by. Freya, no longer an omnipotent goddess, but a frightened wife, trembled before his wrath, and begged the dwarfs to help her. And when one of them—the most hideous of all—promised that he would prevent the statue from speaking if Freya would but deign to smile upon him, the queen of the gods, who had no dread of ugly things, and whose heart was full of love and of pity, smiled her gentle smile on the piteous little creature who had never known looks of anything but horror and disgust from any of the deathless gods. It was for him a wondrous moment, and the payment was worth Death itself. That night a deep sleep fell on the guards of Odin's statue, and, while they slept, the statue was pulled down from its pedestal and smashed into pieces. The dwarf had fulfilled his part of the bargain.

When Odin next morning discovered the sacrilege, great was his anger, and when no inquiry could find for him the criminal, he quitted Asgard in furious wrath. For seven months he stayed away, and in that time the Ice Giants invaded his realm, and all the land was covered with a pall of snow, viciously pinched by black frosts, chilled by clinging, deadening, impenetrable mists. But at the end of seven dreary months Odin returned, and with him came the blessings of light and of sunshine, and the Ice Giants in terror fled away.

Well was it for woman or for warrior to gain the favour of Freya, the Beloved, who knew how to rule even Odin, the All Father, himself. The Winilers who were warring with the Vandals once sought her aid, and gained her promise of help. From Hlidskialf, the mighty watch-tower, highest point in Asgard, from whence Odin and his queen could look down and behold what was happening all the world over, amongst gods and men, dwarfs, elves, and giants, and all creatures of their kingdom, Freya watched the Vandals and the Winilers making ready for the battle which was to decide forever which people should rule the other.

Night was descending, but in the evening light the two gods beheld the glitter of spears, the gleam of brass helmets and of swords, and heard from afar the hoarse shouts of the warriors as they made ready for the great fight on the morrow. Knowing well that her lord favoured the Vandals, Freya asked him to tell her which army was to gain the victory. "The army upon which my eyes shall first rest when I awake at the dawning," said Odin, full well knowing that his couch was so placed that he could not fail to see the Vandals when he woke. Well pleased with his own astuteness, he then retired to rest, and soon sleep lay heavy on his eyelids. But, while he slept, Freya gently moved the couch upon which he lay, so that he must open his eyes not on the army who had won his favour, but on the army that owned hers. To the Winilers, she gave command to dress up their women as men, and let them meet the gaze of Odin in the dawning, in full battle array.

"Take thou thy women-folk,Maidens and wives;Over your anklesLace on the white war-hose;Over your bosomsLink up the hard mail-nets;Over your lipsPlait long tresses with cunning;—So war beasts full-beardedKing Odin shall deem you,When off the grey sea-beachAt sunrise ye greet him."

CHARLES KINGSLEY.

When the sun sent its first pale green light next morning over grey sky and sea, Odin awoke, and gazed from his watch-tower at the army on the beach. And, with great amazement, "What Longbeards are those?" he cried.

"They are Winilers!" said Freya, in joyous triumph, "but you have given them a new name. Now must you also give them a gift! Let it be the victory, I pray you, dear lord of mine."

And Odin, seeing himself outwitted and knowing that honour bade him follow the Northern custom and give the people he had named a gift, bestowed on the Longbeards and their men the victory that Freya craved. Nor was the gift of Odin one for that day alone, for to him the *Langobarden* attributed the many victories that led them at last to find a home in the sunny land of Italy, where beautiful Lombardy still commemorates by its name the stratagem of Freya, the queen.

With the coming of Christianity, Freya, the Beloved, was cast out along with all the other old forgotten gods. The people who had loved and worshipped her were taught that she was an evil thing and that to worship her was sin. Thus she was banished to the lonely peaks of the mountains of Norway and of Sweden and to the Brocken in Germany, no longer a goddess to be loved, but transformed into a malignant power, full of horror and of wickedness. On Walpurgis Night she led the witches' revels on the Brocken, and the cats who were said to draw her car while still she was regarded as a beneficent protectress of the weak and needy, ceased to be the gentle creatures of Freya the Good, and came under the ban of religion as the satanic companions of witches by habit and repute.

One gentle thing only was her memory allowed to keep. When, not as an omnipotent goddess but as a heart-broken mother, she wept the death of her dearly-loved son, Baldur the Beautiful, the tears that she shed were turned, as they fell, into pure gold that is found in the beds of lonely mountain streams. And we who claim descent from the peoples who worshipped her—

"Saxon and Norman and Dane are we"—

can surely cleanse her memory from all the ugly impurities of superstition and remember only the pure gold of the fact that our warrior ancestors did not only pray to a fierce and mighty god of battles, but to a woman who was "loving and giving"—the little child's deification of the mother whom it loves and who holds it very dear.

FREYA SAT SPINNING THE CLOUDS

THE DEATH OF BALDUR

"I heard a voice, that cried,'Baldur the BeautifulIs dead, is dead!'And through the misty airPassed like the mournful cryOf sunward sailing cranes."

LONGFELLOW.

Among the gods of Greece we find gods and goddesses who do unworthy deeds, but none to act the permanent part of villain of the play. In the mythology of the Norsemen we have a god who is wholly treacherous and evil, ever the villain of the piece, cunning, malicious, vindictive, and cruel—the god Loki. And as his foil, and his victim, we have Baldur, best of all gods, most beautiful, most greatly beloved. Baldur was the Galahad of the court of Odin the king, his father.

"My strength is of the strength of ten,Because my heart is pure."

No impure thing was to be found in his dwelling; none could impugn his courage, yet ever he counselled peace, ever was gentle and infinitely wise, and his beauty was as the beauty of the whitest of all the flowers of the Northland, called after him *Baldrsbrá*. The god of the Norsemen was essentially a god of battles, and we are told by great authorities that Baldur was originally a hero who fought on the earth, and who, in time, came to be deified. Even if it be so, it is good to think that a race of warriors could worship one whose chief qualities were wisdom, purity, and love.

In perfect happiness, loving and beloved, Baldur lived in Asgard with his wife Nanna, until a night when his sleep was assailed by horrible dreams of evil omen. In the morning he told the gods that he had dreamed that Death, a thing till then unknown in Asgard, had come and cruelly taken his life away. Solemnly the gods debated how this ill happening might be averted, and Freya, his mother, fear for her best beloved hanging heavy over her heart, took upon herself the task of laying under oath fire and water, iron and all other metals, trees and shrubs, birds, beasts and creeping things, to do no harm to Baldur. With eager haste she went from place to place, nor did she fail to exact the oath from anything in all nature, animate or inanimate, save one only.

"A twig of mistletoe, tender and fair, grew high above the field," and such a little thing it was, with its dainty green leaves and waxen white berries, nestling for protection under the strong arm of a great oak, that the goddess passed it by. Assuredly no scathe could come to Baldur the Beautiful from a creature so insignificant, and Freya returned to Asgard well pleased with her quest.

Then indeed was there joy and laughter amongst the gods, for each one tried how he might slay Baldur, but neither sword nor stone, hammer nor battle-axe could work him any ill.

Odin alone remained unsatisfied. Mounted on his eight-footed grey steed, Sleipnir, he galloped off in haste to consult the giant prophetess Angrbotha, who was dead and had to be followed to Niflheim, the chilly underworld that lies far north from the world of men, and where the sun never comes. Hel, the daughter of Loki and of Angrbotha, was queen of this dark domain.

"There, in a bitterly cold place, she received the souls of all who died of sickness or old age; care was her bed, hunger her dish, starvation her knife. Her walls were high and strong, and her bolts and bars huge; 'Half blue was her skin, and half the colour of human flesh. A goddess easy to know, and in all things very stern and grim.'"

DASENT.

In her kingdom no soul that passed away in glorious battle was received, nor any that fought out the last of life in a fierce combat with the angry waves of the sea. Only those who died ingloriously were her guests.

When he had reached the realm of Hel, Odin found that a feast was being prepared, and the couches were spread, as for an honoured guest, with rich tapestry and with gold. For many a year had Angrbotha rested there in peace, and it was only by chanting a magic spell and tracing those runes which have power to raise the dead that Odin awoke her. When she raised herself, terrible and angry from her tomb, he did not tell her that he was the mighty father of gods and men. He only asked her for whom the great feast was prepared, and why Hel was spreading her couches so gorgeously. And to the father of Baldur she revealed the secret of the future, that Baldur was the expected guest, and that by his blind brother Hodur his soul was to be hastened to the Shades.

"Who, then, would avenge him?" asked the father, great wrath in his heart. And the prophetess replied that his death should be avenged by Vali, his youngest brother, who should not wash his hands nor comb his hair until he had brought the slayer of Baldur to the funeral pyre. But yet another question Odin would fain have answered.

"*Who,*" he asked, "*would refuse to weep at Baldur's death?*"

Thereat the prophetess, knowing that her questioner could be none other than Odin, for to no mortal man could be known so much of the future, refused for evermore to speak, and returned to the silence of her tomb. And Odin was forced to mount his steed and to return to his own land of warmth and pleasure.

On his return he found that all was well with Baldur. Thus he tried to still his anxious heart and to forget the feast in the chill regions of Niflheim, spread for the son who was to him the dearest, and to laugh with those who tried in vain to bring scathe to Baldur.

Only one among those who looked at those sports and grew merry, as he whom they loved stood like a great cliff against which the devouring waves of the fierce North Sea beat and foam and crash in vain, had malice in his heart as he beheld the wonder. In the evil heart of Loki there came a desire to overthrow the god who was beloved by all gods and by all men. He hated him because he was pure, and the mind of Loki was as a stream into which all the filth of the world is discharged. He hated him because Baldur was truth and loyalty, and he, Loki, was treachery and dishonour. He hated him because to Loki there came never a thought that was not full of meanness and greed and cruelty and vice, and Baldur was indeed one *sans peur et sans reproche*.

Thus Loki, taking upon himself the form of a woman, went to Fensalir, the palace, all silver and gold, where dwelt Freya, the mother of Baldur.

The goddess sat, in happy majesty, spinning the clouds, and when Loki, apparently a gentle old woman, passed by where she sat, and then paused and asked, as if amazed, what were the shouts of merriment that she heard, the smiling goddess replied:

"All things on earth have sworn to me never to injure Baldur, and all the gods use their weapons against him in vain. Baldur is safe for evermore."

"All things?" queried Loki.

And Freya answered, "All things but the mistletoe. No harm can come to him from a thing so weak that it only lives by the lives of others."

Then the vicious heart of Loki grew joyous. Quickly he went to where the mistletoe grew, cut a slender green branch, shaped it into a point, and sought the blind god Hodur.

Hodur stood aside, while the other gods merrily pursued their sport.

"Why dost thou not take aim at Baldur with a weapon that fails and so join in the laughter?" asked Loki.

And Hodur sadly made answer:

"Well dost thou know that darkness is my lot, nor have I ought to cast at my brother."

196

Then Loki placed in his hand the shaft of mistletoe and guided his aim, and well and surely Hodur cast the dart. He waited, then, for the merry laughter that followed ever on the onslaught of those against him whom none could do harm. But a great and terrible cry smote his ears. *"Baldur the Beautiful is dead! is dead!"*

On the ground lay Baldur, a white flower cut down by the scythe of the mower. And all through the realm of the gods, and all through the land of the Northmen there arose a cry of bitter lamentation.

"That was the greatest woe that ever befell gods and men," says the story.

The sound of terrible mourning in place of laughter brought Freya to where

"on the floor lay Baldur dead; and round lay thickly strewn swords, axes, darts, and spears, which all the gods in sport had lightly thrown at Baldur, whom no weapon pierced or clove; but in his breast stood fixed the fatal bough of mistletoe."

MATTHEW ARNOLD.

When she saw what had befallen him, Freya's grief was a grief that refused to be comforted, but when the gods, overwhelmed with sorrow, knew not what course to take, she quickly commanded that one should ride to Niflheim and offer Hel a ransom if she would permit Baldur to return to Asgard.

Hermoder the Nimble, another of the sons of Odin, undertook the mission, and, mounted on his father's eight-footed steed, he speedily reached the ice-cold domain of Hel.

There he found Baldur, sitting on the noblest seat of those who feasted, ruling among the people of the Underworld. With burning words Hermoder pled with Hel that she would permit Baldur to return to the world of gods and the world of men, by both of whom he was so dearly beloved. Said Hel:

"Come then! if Baldur was so dear beloved,And this is true, and such a loss is Heaven's—Hear, how to Heaven may Baldur be restored.Show me through all the world the signs of grief!Fails but one thing to grieve, here Baldur stops!Let all that lives and moves upon the earthWeep him, and all that is without life weep;Let Gods, men, brutes, beweep him; plants and stones,So shall I know the loss was dear indeed,And bend my heart, and give him back to Heaven."

MATTHEW ARNOLD.

Gladly Hermoder made answer:

"All things shall weep for Baldur!"

Swiftly he made his perilous return journey, and at once, when the gods heard what Hel had said, messengers were despatched all over the earth to beg all things, living and dead, to weep for Baldur, and so dear to all nature was the beautiful god, that the messengers everywhere left behind them a track of the tears that they caused to be shed.

Meantime, in Asgard, preparations were made for Baldur's pyre. The longest of the pines in the forest were cut down by the gods, and piled up in a mighty pyre on the deck of his great ship *Ringhorn*, the largest in the world.

"Seventy ells and four extendedOn the grass the vessel's keel;High above it, gilt and splendid,Rose the figure-head ferociousWith its crest of steel."

LONGFELLOW.

Down to the seashore they bore the body, and laid it on the pyre with rich gifts all round it, and the pine trunks of the Northern forests that formed the pyre, they covered with gorgeous tapestries and fragrant flowers. And when they had laid him there, with all love and gentleness, and his fair young wife, Nanna, looked on his beautiful still face, sorrow smote her heart so that it was broken, and she fell down dead. Tenderly they laid her beside him, and by him, too, they laid the bodies of his horse and his hounds, which they slew to bear their master company in the land whither his soul had fled; and around the pyre they twined thorns, the emblem of sleep.

Yet even then they looked for his speedy return, radiant and glad to come home to a sunlit land of happiness. And when the messengers who were to have brought tidings of his freedom were seen drawing near, eagerly they crowded to hear the glad words, *"All creatures weep, and Baldur shall return!"*

But with them they brought not hope, but despair. All things, living and dead, had wept, save one only. A giantess who sat in a dark cave had laughed them to scorn. With devilish merriment she mocked:

"Neither in life, nor yet in death,Gave he me gladness.Let Hel keep her prey."

Then all knew that yet a second time had Baldur been betrayed, and that the giantess was none other than Loki, and Loki, realising the fierce wrath of Odin and of the other gods, fled before them, yet could not escape his doom. And grief unspeakable was that of gods and of men when they knew that in the chill realm of the inglorious dead Baldur must remain until the twilight of the gods had come, until old things had passed away, and all things had become new.

Not only the gods, but the giants of the storm and frost, and the frost elves came to behold the last of him whom they loved. Then the pyre was set alight, and the great vessel was launched, and glided out to sea with its sails of flame.

"They launched the burning ship!It floated far awayOver the misty sea,Till like the sun it seemed,Sinking beneath the waves,Baldur returned no more!"

Yet, ere he parted from his dead son, Odin stooped over him and whispered a word in his ear. And there are those who say that as the gods in infinite sorrow stood on the beach staring out to sea, darkness fell, and only a fiery track on the waves showed whither he had gone whose passing had robbed Asgard and the Earth of their most beautiful thing, heavy as the weight of chill Death's remorseless hand would have been their hearts, but for the knowledge of that word. They knew that with the death of Baldur the twilight of the gods had begun, and that by much strife and infinite suffering down through the ages the work of their purification and hallowing must be wrought. But when all were fit to receive him, and peace and happiness reigned again on earth and in heaven, Baldur would come back. For the word was *Resurrection*.

"So perish the old Gods!But out of the sea of timeRises a new land of song,Fairer than the old."

LONGFELLOW.

"Heartily know,When half-gods go,The gods arrive."

EMERSON.

"BALDUR THE BEAUTIFUL IS DEAD"

BEOWULF

"He was of mankindIn might the strongest."

Longfellow's Translation.

Whether those who read it be scholars who would argue about the origin and date of the poem, ingenious theorists who would fain use all the fragmentary tales and rhymes of the nursery as parts of a vast jig-saw puzzle of nature myths, or merely simple folk who read a tale for a tale's sake, every reader of the poem of Beowulf must own that it is one of the finest stories ever written.

It is "the most ancient heroic poem in the Germanic language," and was brought to Britain by the "Wingèd Hats" who sailed across the grey North Sea to conquer and to help to weld that great amalgam of peoples into what is now the British Race.

But once it had arrived in England, the legend was put into a dress that the British-born could more readily appreciate. In all probability the scene of the story was a corner of that island of Saeland upon which Copenhagen now stands, but he who wrote down the poem for his countrymen and who wrote it in the pure literary Anglo-Saxon of Wessex, painted the scenery from the places that he and his readers knew best. And if you should walk along the breezy, magnificent, rugged Yorkshire coast for twelve miles, from Whitby northward to the top of Bowlby Cliff, you would find it quite easy to believe that it was there amongst the high sea-cliffs that Beowulf and his hearth-sharers once lived, and there, on the highest ness of our eastern coast, under a great barrow, that Beowulf was buried. *Beowulfesby—Bowlby* seems a quite easy transition. But the people of our island race have undoubtedly a gift for seizing the imports of other lands and hall-marking them as their own, and, in all probability, the Beowulf of the heroic poem was one who lived and died in the land of Scandinavia.

In Denmark, so goes the story, when the people were longing for a king, to their shores there drifted, on a day when the white birds were screaming over the sea-tangle and wreckage that a stormy sea, now sinking to rest, was sweeping up on the shore, a little boat in which, on a sheaf of ripe wheat and surrounded by priceless weapons and jewels, there lay a most beautiful babe, who smiled in his sleep. That he was the son of Odin they had no doubt, and they made him their king, and served him faithfully and loyally for the rest of his life.

A worthy and a noble king was King Scyld Scefing, a ruler on land and on the sea, of which even as an infant he had had no fear. But when many years had come and gone, and when Scyld Scefing felt that death drew near, he called his nobles to him and told them in what manner he fain would pass. So they did as he said, and in a ship they built a funeral pyre, and round it placed much gold and jewels, and on it laid a sheaf of wheat. Then with very great pain and labour, for he was old and Death's hand lay heavy upon him, the king climbed into the ship and stretched out his limbs on the pyre, and said farewell to all his faithful people. And the ship drifted out with the tide, and the hearts of the watchers were heavy as they saw the sails of the vessel that bore him vanish into the grey, and knew that their king had gone back to the place from whence he came, and that they should look on his face no more.

Behind him Scyld left descendants, and one after the other reigned over Denmark. It was in the reign of his great-grandson, Hrothgar, that there took place those things that are told in the story of Beowulf.

A mighty king and warrior was Hrothgar, and far across the northern seas his fame spread wide, so that all the warriors of the land that he ruled were proud to serve under him in peace, and in war to die for him. During his long life he and his men never went forth in their black-prowed ships without returning with the joyous shouts of the victor, with for cargo the rich spoil they had won from their enemies. As he grew old, Hrothgar determined to raise for himself a mighty monument to the magnificence of his reign, and so there was builded for him a vast hall with majestic towers and lofty pinnacles—the finest banqueting-hall that his skilled artificers could dream of. And when at length the hall was completed, Hrothgar gave a feast to all his thanes, and for days and for nights on end the great rafters of Heorot—as his palace was named—echoed the shouts and laughter of the mighty warriors, and the music of the minstrels and the songs that they sang. A proud man was Hrothgar on the night that the banquet was ended amidst the acclamations of his people, and a proud and happy man he lay down to rest, while his bodyguard of mighty warriors stretched themselves on the rush-strewn floor of the great room where they had feasted, and deeply slumbered there.

Now, in the dark fens of that land there dwelt a monster—fierce, noisome, and cruel, a thing that loved evil and hated all that was joyous and good. To its ears came the ring of the laughter and the shouts of King Hrothgar's revellers, and the sweet song of the gleemen and the melody of harps filled it with fierce hatred. From its wallow in the marshes, where the pestilent grey fog hung round its dwelling, the monster, known to all men as the Grendel, came forth, to kill and to devour. Through the dark night, across the lonely moorland, it made its way, and the birds of the moor flew screaming in terror before it, and the wild creatures of the desolate country over which it padded clapped down in their coverts and trembled as it passed. It came at length to the great hall where

"A fair troop of warrior thanes guarding it found he;Heedlessly sleeping, they recked not of sorrow."

Never a thought did they give to the Grendel,—

"A haunter of marshes, a holder of moors,... SecretThe land he inhabits; dark, wolf-haunted waysOf the windy hillside, by the treacherous tarn;Or where, covered up in its mist, the hill streamDownward flows."

Soundly slept Hrothgar, nor opened eye until, in the bright light of the morning, he was roused by terrified servants, forgetful of his august royalty, impelled by terror, crying aloud their terrible tale. They had come, they said, to lay on the floor of the banqueting-hall, sweet, fresh rushes from the meadows, and to clear away all trace of the feasting overnight. But the two-and-thirty knights who, in full armour, had lain down to sleep were all gone, and on the floor was the spoor of something foul and noisome, and on the walls and on the trampled rushes were great and terrible smears of human blood.

They tracked the Grendel back to the marsh from whence he had come, and shuddered at the sight of bestial footprints that left blood-stains behind.

Terrible indeed was the grief of Hrothgar, but still more terrible was his anger. He offered a royal reward to any man who would slay the Grendel, and full gladly ten of his warriors pledged themselves to sleep that night in the great hall and to slay the Grendel ere morning came.

But dawn showed once more a piteous sight. Again there were only trampled and blood-stained rushes, with the loathsome smell of unclean flesh. Again the foul tracks of the monster were found where it had padded softly back to its noisome fens.

There were many brave men in the kingdom of Hrothgar the Dane, and yet again did they strive to maintain the dignity of the great hall, Heorot, and to uphold the honour of their king. But through twelve dismal years the Grendel took its toll of the bravest in the realm, and to sleep in the place that Hrothgar had built as monument to his magnificent supremacy, ever meant, for the sleeper, shameful death. Well content was the Grendel, that grew fat and lusty amongst the grey mists of the black marshes, unknowing that in the land of the Goths there was growing to manhood one whose feet already should be echoing along that path from which Death was to come.

In the realm of the Goths, Hygelac was king, and no greater hero lived in his kingdom than Beowulf, his own sister's son. From the age of seven Beowulf was brought up at the court of his uncle.

A great, fair, blue-eyed lad was Beowulf, lazy, and very slow to wrath. When he had at last become a yellow-haired giant, of wondrous good-temper, and leisurely in movement, the other young warriors of Gothland had mocked at him as at one who was only a very huge, very amiable child. But, like others of the same descent, Beowulf's anger, if slow to kindle, was a terrible fire once it began to flame. A few of those flares-up had shown the folk of his uncle's kingdom that no mean nor evil deed might lightly be done, nor evil word spoken in the presence of Beowulf. In battle against the Swedes, no sword had hewn down more men than the sword of Beowulf. And when the champion swimmer of the land of the Goths challenged the young giant Beowulf to swim a match with him, for five whole days they swam together. A tempest driving down from the twilight land of the ice and snow parted them then, and he who had been champion was driven ashore and thankfully struggled on to the beach of his own dear country once again. But the foaming seas cast Beowulf on some jagged cliffs, and would fain have battered his body into broken fragments against them, and as he fought and struggled to resist their raging cruelty, mermaids and nixies and many monsters of the deep joined forces with the waves and strove to wrest his life from him. And while with one hand he held on to a sharp rock, with the other he dealt with his sword stark blows on those children of the deep who would fain have devoured him. Their bodies, deep-gashed and dead, floated down to the coast of Gothland, and the king and all those who looked for the corpse of Beowulf saw them, amazed. Then at length came Beowulf himself, and with great gladness was he welcomed, and the king, his uncle, gave him his treasured sword, Nägeling, in token of his valour.

In the court of Hrothgar, the number of brave warriors ever grew smaller. One man only had witnessed the terrible slaughter of one of those black nights and yet had kept his life. He was a bard—a scald—and from the land where he had seen such grim horror, he fled to the land of the Goths, and there, in the court of the king, he sang the gloomy tale of the never-ending slaughter of noble warriors by the foul Grendel of the fens and moors.

Beowulf listened, enthralled, to his song. But those who knew him saw his eyes gleam as the good steel blade of a sword gleams when it is drawn for battle, and when he asked his uncle to allow him to go to the land of the Danes and slay this filthy thing, his uncle smiled, with no surprise, and was very well content.

So it came to pass that Beowulf, in his black-prowed ship, with fourteen trusty followers, set sail from Gothland for the kingdom of Hrothgar.

The warden of the Danish coast was riding his rounds one morning when he beheld from the white cliffs a strange war-vessel making for the shore. Skilfully the men on board her ran her through the surf, and beached her in a little creek between the cliffs, and made her fast to a rock by stout cables. Only for a little time the valiant warden watched them from afar, and then, one man against fifteen, he rode quickly down and challenged the warriors.

"What are ye warlike men wielding bright weapons,Wearing grey corselets and boar-adorned helmets,Who o'er the water-paths come with your foaming keelPloughing the ocean surge? I was appointedWarden of Denmark's shores; watch hold I by the waveThat on this Danish coast no deadly enemyLeading troops over sea should land to injure.None have here landed yet more frankly comingThan this fair company: and yet ye answer notThe password of warriors, and customs of kinsmen.Ne'er have mine eyes beheld a mightier warrior,An earl more lordly than is he the chief of you;He is no common man; if looks belie him not,He is a hero bold, worthily weaponed.Anon must I know of you kindred and country,Lest ye of spies should go free on our Danish soil.Now ye men from afar, sailing the surging sea,Have heard my earnest thought: best is a quick reply,That I may swiftly know whence ye have hither come."

Then Beowulf, with fearless eyes, gazed in the face of the warden and told him simply and unboastfully who he was, from whence he came, and what was his errand. He had come as the nation's deliverer, to slay the thing that

"Cometh in dark of night, sateth his secret hate, Worketh through fearsome awe, slaughter and shame."

With joy the warden heard his noble words.

"My men shall beach your ship," he said, "and make her fast with a barrier of oars against the greedy tide. Come with me to the king."

It was a gallant band that strode into Heorot, where sat the old king, gloom overshadowing his soul. And fit leader for a band of heroes was Beowulf, a giant figure in ring-mail, spear and shield gleaming in his hand, and by his side the mighty sword, Nägeling. To Hrothgar, as to the warden, Beowulf told the reason of his coming, and hope began again to live in the heart of the king.

That night the warriors from the land of the Goths were feasted in the great banqueting-hall where, for twelve unhappy years, voices had never rung out so bravely and so merrily. The queen herself poured out the mead with which the king and the men from Gothland pledged each other, and with her own hand she passed the goblet to each one. When, last of it all, it came to the guest of honour, Beowulf took the cup of mead from the fair queen and solemnly pledged himself to save the land from the evil thing that devoured it like a pestilence, or to die in his endeavour.

"Needs must I now perform knightly deeds in this hall, Or here must meet my doom in darksome night."

When darkness fell the feast came to an end, and all left the hall save Beowulf and his fourteen followers. In their armour, with swords girt on their sides, the fourteen heroes lay down to rest, but Beowulf laid aside all his arms and gave his sword to a thane to bear away. For, said he,

"I have heardThat that foul miscreant's dark and stubborn fleshRecks not the force of arms ...Hand to hand ... Beowulf will grapple with the mighty foe."

From his fastnesses in the fens, the Grendel had heard the shouts of revelry, and as the Goths closed their eyes to sleep, knowing they might open them again only to grapple with hideous death, yet unafraid because of their sure belief that "What is to be goes ever as it must," the monster roused himself. Through the dank, chill, clinging mists he came, and his breath made the poisonous miasma of the marshes more deadly as he padded over the shivering reeds and trembling rushes, across the bleak moorland and the high cliffs where the fresh tang of the grey sea was defiled by the hideous stench of a foul beast of prey. There was fresh food for him to-night, he knew, some blood more potent than any that for twelve years had come his bestial way. And he hastened on with greedy eagerness, nightmare incarnate. He found the great door of the banqueting-hall bolted and barred, but one angry wrench set at naught the little precautionary measures of mere men.

The dawn was breaking dim and grey and very chill when Beowulf heard the stealthy tread without, and the quick-following crash of the bolts and bars that gave so readily. He made no movement, but only waited. In an instant the dawn was blotted out by a vast black shadow, and swifter than any great bear could strike, a scaly hand had struck one of the friends of Beowulf. In an instant the man was torn from limb to limb, and in a wild disgust and hatred Beowulf heard the lapping of blood, the scrunching of bones and chewing of warm flesh as the monster ravenously devoured him. Again the loathsome hand was stretched out to seize and to devour. But in the darkness two hands, like hands of iron, gripped the outstretched arm, and the Grendel knew that he had met his match at last. The warriors of Beowulf awoke to find a struggle going on such as their eyes never before beheld, for it was a fight to the death between man and monster. Vainly they tried to aid their leader, but their weapons only glanced harmlessly off the Grendel's scaly hide. Up and down the hall the combatants wrestled, until the

210

walls shook and the great building itself rocked to its foundations. Ever and again it seemed as though no human power could prevail against teeth and claws and demonic fury, and as tables and benches crashed to the ground and broke under the tramping feet of the Grendel, it appeared an impossible thing that Beowulf should overcome. Yet ever tighter and more tight grew the iron grip of Beowulf. His fingers seemed turned to iron. His hatred and loathing made his grasp crash through scales, into flesh, and crush the marrow out of the bone it found there. And when at length the Grendel could no more, and with a terrible cry wrenched himself free, and fled, wailing, back to the fenland, still in his grasp Beowulf held the limb. The Grendel had freed himself by tearing the whole arm out of its socket, and, for once, the trail of blood across the moors was that of the monster and not of its victims.

Great indeed was the rejoicing of Hrothgar and of his people when, in the morning, instead of crimson-stained rushes and the track of vermin claws imbrued in human blood, they found all but one of the men from Gothland alive, and looked upon the hideous trophy that told them that their enemy could only have gone to find a shameful death in the marshes. They cleansed out the great hall, hung it with lordly trappings, and made it once more fit habitation for the lordliest in the land. That night a feast was held in it, such as had never before been held all through the magnificent reign of Hrothgar. The best of the scalds sung songs in honour of the triumph of Beowulf, and the queen herself pledged the hero in a cup of mead and gave to him the beautiful most richly jewelled collar Brisingamen, of exquisite ancient workmanship, that once was owned by Freya, queen of the gods, and a great ring of the purest red gold. To Beowulf, too, the king gave a banner, all broidered in gold, a sword of the finest, with helmet and corselet, and eight fleet steeds, and on the back of the one that he deemed the best Hrothgar had placed his own saddle, cunningly wrought, and decked with golden ornaments. To each of the warriors of Beowulf there were also given rich gifts. And ere the queen, with her maidens, left the hall that night she said to Beowulf:

"Enjoy thy reward, O dear Beowulf, while enjoy it thou canst. Live noble and blessed! Keep well thy great fame, and to my dear sons, in time to come, should ever they be in need, be a kind protector!"

With happy hearts in very weary bodies, Beowulf and his men left the hall when the feast was ended, and they slept through the night in another lodging as those sleep who have faced death through a very long night, and to whom joy has come in the morning.

But the Danish knights, careless in the knowledge that the Grendel must even now be in his dying agonies, and that once more Hereot was for them a safe and noble sleeping-place, lay themselves down to sleep in the hall, their shields at their heads, and, fastened high up on the roof above them, the hideous trophy of Beowulf.

Next morning as the grey dawn broke over the northern sea, it saw a sight that made it more chill than death. Across the moorland went a thing—half wolf, half woman—the mother of Grendel. The creature she had borne had come home to die, and to her belonged his avenging. Softly she went to Hereot. Softly she opened the unguarded door. Gladly, in her savage jaws, she seized Aschere, the thane who was to Hrothgar most dear, and from the roof she plucked her desired treasure—the arm of Grendel, her son. Then she trotted off to her far-off, filthy den, leaving behind her the noise of lamentation.

Terrible was the grief of Hrothgar over the death of Aschere, dearest of friends and sharer of his councils. And to his lamentations Beowulf listened, sad at heart, humble, yet with a heart that burned for vengeance. The hideous creature of the night was the mother of Grendel, as all knew well. On her Beowulf would be avenged, for Aschere's sake, for the king's, and for the sake of his own honour. Then once again did he pledge himself to do all that man's strength could do to rid the land of an evil thing. Well did he know how dangerous was the task before him, and he gave directions for the disposal of all that he valued should he never return from his quest. To the King, who feared greatly that he was going forth on a forlorn hope, he said:

"Grieve not!... Each man must undergo death at the end of life.Let him win, while he may, warlike fame in the world!That is best after death for the slain warrior."

His own men, and Hrothgar, and a great company of Danes went with him when he set out to trace the blood-stained tracks of the Grendel's mother. Near the edge of a gloomy mere they found the head of Aschere. And when they looked at the fiord itself, it seemed to be blood-stained—stained with blood that ever welled upwards, and in which revelled with a fierce sort of joy—the rapture of bestial cruelty—water-monsters without number.

Beowulf, his face white and grim like that of an image of Thor cast in silver, watched a little while, then drew his bow and drove a bolt into the heart of one of them, and when they had drawn the slain carcase to shore, the thanes of Hrothgar marvelled at the horror of it.

Then Beowulf took leave of Hrothgar and told him that if in two days he did not return, certain it would be that he would return no more. The hearts of all who said farewell to him were heavy, but Beowulf laughed, and bade them be of good cheer. Then into the black waters he dived, sword in hand, clad in ring-armour, and the dark pool closed over him as the river of Death closes over the head of a man when his day is done. To him it seemed as if the space of a day had passed ere he reached the bottom, and in his passing he encountered many dread dangers from tusk and horn of a myriad evil creatures of the water who sought to destroy him. Then at length he reached the bottom of that sinister mere, and there was clasped in the murderous grip of the Wolf-Woman who strove to crush his life out against her loathsome breast. Again and again, when her hideous embrace failed to slay him, she stabbed him with her knife. Yet ever did he escape. His good armour resisted the power of her arm, and his own great muscles thrust her from him. Yet his own sword failed him when he would have smitten her, and the hero would have been in evil case had he not spied, hanging on the wall of that most foul den,

"A glorious sword,An old brand gigantic, trusty in point and edge,An heirloom of heroes."

Swiftly he seized it, and with it he dealt the Wolf-Woman a blow that shore her head from her body. Through the foul blood that flowed from her and that mingled with the black water of the mere, Beowulf saw a very terrible horror—the body of the Grendel, lying moaning out the last of his life. Again his strong arm descended, and, his left hand gripping the coiled locks of the Evil Thing, he sprang upwards through the water, that lost its blackness and its clouded crimson as he went ever higher and more high. In his hand he still bore the sword that had saved him, but the poisonous blood of the dying monsters had made the water of such fiery heat that the blade melted as he rose, and only the hilt, with strange runes engraved upon it, remained in his hand.

Where he left them, his followers, and the Danes who went with them, remained, watching, waiting, ever growing more hopeless as night turned into day, and day faded into night, and they saw the black waters of the lonely fen bubbling up, terrible and blood-stained. But when the waters cleared, hope returned to their hearts, and when, at length, Beowulf uprose from the water of the mere and they saw that in his hand he bore the head of the Grendel, there was no lonely scaur, nor cliff, nor rock of the land of the Danes that did not echo the glad cry of *"Beowulf! Beowulf!"*

Well-nigh overwhelmed by gifts from those whom he had preserved was the hero, Beowulf. But in modest, wise words he spoke to the King:

"Well hast thou treated us.If on this earth I can do more to win thy love,O prince of warriors, than I have wrought as yet,Here stand I ready now weapons to wield for thee.If I shall ever hear o'er the encircling floodThat any neighbouring foes threaten thy nation's fall,As Grendel grim before, swift will I bring to theeThousands of noble thanes, heroes to help thee."

Then, in their ship, that the Warden of the Coast once had challenged, Beowulf and his warriors set sail for their own dear land.

Gaily the vessel danced over the waves, heavy though it was with treasure, nobly gained. And when Beowulf had come in safety to his homeland and had told his kinsman the tale of the slaying of the Grendel and of the Wolf-Woman, he gave the finest of his steeds to the King, and to the Queen the jewelled collar, Brisingamen, that the Queen of the Goths had bestowed on him. And the heart of his uncle was glad and proud indeed, and there was much royal banqueting in the hero's honour. Of him, too, the scalds made up songs, and there was no hero in all that northern land whose fame was as great as was the fame of Beowulf.

"The Must Be often helps an undoomed man when he is brave" was the precept on which he ruled his life, and he never failed the King whose chief champion and warrior he was. When, in an expedition against the Frieslanders, King Hygelac fell a victim to the cunning of his foes, the sword of Beowulf fought nobly for him to the end, and the hero was a grievously wounded man when he brought back to Gothland the body of the dead King. The Goths would fain have made him their King, in Hygelac's stead, but Beowulf was too loyal a soul to supplant his uncle's own son. On his shield he laid the infant prince, Hardred, and held him up for the people to see. And when he had proclaimed the child King and vowed to serve him faithfully all the days of his life, there was no man there who did not loyally echo the promise of their hero, Beowulf.

When Hardred, a grown man, was treacherously slain by a son of Othere, he who discovered the North Cape, Beowulf once again was chosen King, and for forty years he reigned wisely and well. The fame of his arms kept war away from the land, and his wisdom as a statesman brought great prosperity and happiness to his people. He had never known fear, and so for him there was nothing to dread when the weakness of age fell upon him and when he knew that his remaining years could be but few:

"Seeing that Death, a necessary end,Will come when it will come."

Through all those years of peace, the thing that was to bring death to him had lurked, unknown, unimagined, in a cave in the lonely mountains.

Many centuries before the birth of Beowulf, a family of mighty warriors had won by their swords a priceless treasure of weapons and of armour, of richly chased goblets and cups, of magnificent ornaments and precious jewels, and of gold "beyond the dreams of avarice." In a great cave among the rocks it was hoarded by the last of their line, and on his death none knew where it was hidden. Upon it one day there stumbled a fiery dragon—a Firedrake—and for three hundred years the monster gloated, unchallenged, over the magnificent possession. But at the end of that time, a bondsman, who fled before his master's vengeance and sought sanctuary in the mountains, came on an opening in the rocks, and, creeping in, found the Firedrake asleep upon a mass of red gold and of sparkling gems that dazzled his eyes even in the darkness. For a moment he stood, trembling, then, sure of his master's forgiveness if he brought him as gift a golden cup all studded with jewels, he seized one and fled with it ere the monster could awake. With its awakening, terror fell upon the land. Hither and thither it flew, searching for him who had robbed it, and as it flew, it sent flames on the earth and left behind it a black trail of ruin and of death.

When news of its destroyings came to the ears of the father of his people, Beowulf knew that to him belonged the task of saving the land for them and for all those to come after them. But he was an old man, and strength had gone from him, nor was he able now to wrestle with the Firedrake as once he had wrestled with the Grendel and the Wolf-Woman, but had to trust to his arms. He had an iron shield made to withstand the Firedrake's flaming breath, and, with a band of eleven picked followers, and taking the bondsman as guide, Beowulf went out to fight his last fight. As they drew near the place, he bade his followers stay where they were, "For I alone," he said, "will win the gold and save my people, or Death shall take me."

From the entrance to the cave there poured forth a sickening cloud of steam and smoke, suffocating and blinding, and so hot that he could not go forward. But with a loud voice the old warrior shouted an arrogant challenge of defiance to his enemy, and the Firedrake rushed forth from its lair, roaring with the roar of an unquenchable fire whose fury will destroy a city. From its wings of flame and from its eyes heat poured forth scorchingly, and its great mouth belched forth devouring flames as it cast itself on Beowulf.

The hero's sword flashed, and smote a stark blow upon its scaly head. But Beowulf could not deal death strokes as once he had done, and only for a moment was his adversary stunned. In hideous rage the monster coiled its snaky folds around him, and the heat from his body made the iron shield redden as though the blacksmith in his smithy were welding it, and each ring of the armour that Beowulf wore seared right into his flesh. His breast swelled with the agony, and his great heart must have come near bursting for pain and for sorrow. For he saw that panic had come on his followers and that they were fleeing, leaving him to his fate. Yet not all of them were faithless. Wiglaf, young and daring, a dear kinsman of Beowulf, from whom he had received many a kindness, calling shame on the dastards who fled, rushed forward, sword in hand, and with no protection but that of his shield of linden wood. Like a leaf scorched in a furnace the shield curled up, but new strength came to Beowulf with the knowledge that Wiglaf had not failed him in his need. Together the two heroes made a gallant stand, although blood flowed in a swift red stream from a wound that the monster had made in Beowulf's neck with its venomous fangs, and ran down his corselet. A stroke which left the Firedrake unharmed shivered the sword that had seen many fights, but Wiglaf smote a shrewd blow ere his lord could be destroyed, and Beowulf swiftly drew his broad knife and, with an effort so great that all the life that was left in him seemed to go with it, he shore the Firedrake asunder.

Then Beowulf knew that his end drew very near, and when he had thanked Wiglaf for his loyal help, he bade him enter the cave and bring forth the treasure that he might please his dying eyes by looking on the riches that he had won for his people. And Wiglaf hastened into the cave, for he knew that he raced with Death, and brought forth armfuls of weapons, of magnificent ornaments, of goblets and of cups, of bars of red gold. Handfuls of sparkling jewels, too, he brought, and each time he came and went, seizing without choosing, whatever lay nearest, it seemed as though the Firedrake's hoard were endless. A magical golden standard and armour and swords that the dwarfs had made brought a smile of joy into the dying King's eyes. And when the ten shamed warriors, seeing that the fight was at an end, came to where their mighty ruler lay, they found him lying near the vile carcase of the monster he had slain, and surrounded by a dazzlement of treasure uncountable. To them, and to Wiglaf, Beowulf spoke his valediction, urging on them to maintain the honour of the land of the Goths, and then he said:

"I thank God eternal, the great King of Glory,For the vast treasures which I here gaze upon,That I ere my death-day might for my peopleWin so great wealth— Since I have given my life,Thou must now look to the needs of the nation;Here dwell I no longer, for Destiny calleth me!Bid thou my warriors after my funeral pyreBuild me a burial-cairn high on the sea-cliffs head;It shall for memory tower up to Hronesness,So that the sea-farers Beowulf's BarrowHenceforth shall name it, they who drive far and wideOver the mighty flood their foaming Reels.Thou art the last of all the kindred of Wagmund!Wyrd has swept all my kin, all the brave chiefs away!Now must I follow them!"

Such was the passing of Beowulf, greatest of Northern heroes, and under a mighty barrow on a cliff very high above the sea, they buried him, and with him a great fortune from the treasure he had won. Then with heavy hearts, "round about the mound rode his hearth-sharers, who sang that he was of kings, of men, the mildest, kindest, to his people sweetest, and the readiest in search of praise":

"Gentlest, most gracious, most keen to win glory."

And if, in time, the great deeds of a mighty king of the Goths have become more like fairy tale than solid history, this at least we know, that whether it is in Saeland or on the Yorkshire coast—where

"High on the sea-cliff ledgesThe white gulls are trooping and crying"

—the barrow of Beowulf covers a very valiant hero, a very perfect gentleman.

A STROKE SHIVERED THE SWORD

ROLAND THE PALADIN

"Roland, the flower of chivalry,Expired at Roncevall."

Thomas Campbell.

"Hero-worship endures for ever while man endures."

Carlyle.

"Roland, the gode knight."

Turpin's *History of Charlemagne.*

The old chroniclers tell us that on that momentous morning when William the Conqueror led his army to victory at Hastings, a Norman knight named Taillefer (and a figure of iron surely was his) spurred his horse to the front. In face of the enemy who hated all things that had to do with France, he lifted up his voice and chanted aloud the exploits of Charlemagne and of Roland. As he sang, he threw his sword in the air and always caught it in his right hand as it fell, and, proudly, the whole army, moving at once, joined with him in the *Chanson de Roland*, and shouted, as chorus, "God be our help! God be our help!"

"Taillefer ... chantoit de RollantEt d'Olivier, et de VassauxQui mourent en Rainschevaux."

Wace, *Roman de Rose.*

Fifteen thousand of those who sang fell on that bloody day, and one wonders how many of those who went down to the Shades owed half their desperate courage to the remembrance of the magnificent deeds of the hero of whom they sang, ere ever sword met sword, or spear met the sullen impact of the stark frame of a Briton born, fighting for his own.

The story of Roland, so we are told, is only a splendid coating of paint put on a very slender bit of drawing. A contemporary chronicle tells of the battle of Roncesvalles, and says: "In which battle was slain Roland, prefect of the marches of Brittany." Merely a Breton squire, we are told to believe—a very gallant country gentleman whose name would not have been preserved in priestly archives had he not won for himself, by his fine courage, such an unfading laurel crown. But because we are so sure that "it is the memory that the soldier leaves after him, like the long trail of light that follows the sunken sun," and because so often oral tradition is less misleading than the written word, we gladly and undoubtingly give Roland high place in the Valhalla of heroes of all races and of every time.

777 or 778 A.D. is the date fixed for the great fight at Roncesvalles, where Roland won death and glory. Charlemagne, King of the Franks, and Head of the Holy Roman Empire, was returning victoriously from a seven years' campaign against the Saracens in Spain.

"No fortress stands before him unsubdued,Nor wall, nor city left to be destroyed,"

save one—the city of Saragossa, the stronghold of King Marsile or Marsiglio. Here amongst the mountains the King and his people still held to their idols, worshipped "Mahommed, Apollo, and Termagaunt," and looked forward with horror to a day when the mighty Charlemagne might, by the power of the sword, thrust upon them the worship of the crucified Christ. Ere Charlemagne had returned to his own land, Marsile held a council with his peers. To believe that the great conqueror would rest content with Saragossa still unconquered was too much to hope for. Surely he would return to force his religion upon them. What, then, was it best to do? A very wily emir was Blancandrin, brave in war, and wise in counsel, and on his advice Marsile sent ambassadors to Charlemagne to ask of him upon what conditions he would be allowed to retain his kingdom in peace and to continue to worship the gods of his fathers. Mounted on white mules, with silver saddles, and with reins of gold, and bearing olive branches in their hands, Blancandrin and the ten messengers sent by Marsile arrived at Cordova, where Charlemagne rested with his army. Fifteen thousand tried veterans were with him there, and his "Douzeperes"—his Twelve Peers—who were to him what the Knights of the Round Table were to King Arthur of Britain. He held his court in an orchard, and under a great pine tree from which the wild honeysuckle hung like a fragrant canopy, the mighty king and emperor sat on a throne of gold.

The messengers of Marsile saw a man of much more than ordinary stature and with the commanding presence of one who might indeed conquer kingdoms, but his sword was laid aside and he watched contentedly the contests between the older of his knights who played chess under the shade of the fruit trees, and the fencing bouts of the younger warriors. Very dear to him were all his Douzeperes, yet dearest of all was his own nephew, Roland. In him he saw his own youth again, his own imperiousness, his reckless gallantry, his utter fearlessness—all those qualities which endeared him to the hearts of other men. Roland was his sister's son, and it was an evil day for the fair Bertha when she told her brother that, in spite of his anger and scorn, she had disobeyed his commands and had wed the man she loved, Milon, a poor young knight.

No longer would Charlemagne recognise her as sister, and in obscurity and poverty Roland was born. He was still a very tiny lad when his father, in attempting to ford a flooded river, was swept down-stream and drowned, and Bertha had no one left to fend for her and for her child. Soon they had no food left, and the little Roland watched with amazed eyes his famished mother growing so weak that she could not rise from the bed where she lay, nor answer him when he pulled her by the hand and tried to make her come with him to seek his father and to find something to eat. And when he saw that it was hopeless, the child knew that he must take his father's place and get food for the mother who lay so pale, and so very still. Into a great hall where Charlemagne and his lords were banqueting Roland strayed. Here was food in plenty! Savoury smelling, delicious to his little empty stomach were the daintily cooked meats which the Emperor and his court ate from off their silver platters. Only one plateful of food such as this must, of a surety, make his dear mother strong and well once more. Not for a moment did Roland hesitate. Even as a tiny sparrow darts into a lion's cage and picks up a scrap almost out of the monarch's hungry jaws, so acted Roland. A plateful of food stood beside the King. At this Roland sprang, seized it with both hands, and joyfully ran off with his prey. When the serving men would have caught him, Charlemagne, laughing, bade them desist.

"A hungry one this," he said, "and very bold."

So the meal went on, and when Roland had fed his mother with some pieces of the rich food and had seen her gradually revive, yet another thought came to his baby mind.

"My father gave her wine," he thought. "They were drinking wine in that great hall. It will make her white cheeks red again."

Thus he ran back, as fast as his legs could carry him, and Charlemagne smiled yet more when he saw the beautiful child, who knew no fear, return to the place where he had thieved. Right up to the King's chair he came, solemnly measured with his eye the cups of wine that the great company quaffed, saw that the cup of Charlemagne was the most beautiful and the fullest of the purple-red wine, stretched out a daring little hand, grasped the cup, and prepared to go off again, like a marauding bright-eyed bird. Then the King seized in his own hand the hand that held the cup.

"No! no! bold thief," he said, "I cannot have my golden cup stolen from me, be it done by ever so sturdy a robber. Tell me, who sent thee out to steal?"

And Roland, an erect, gallant, little figure, his hand still in the iron grip of the King, fearlessly and proudly gazed back into the eyes of Charlemagne.

"No one sent me," he said. "My mother lay very cold and still and would not speak, and she had said my father would come back no more, so there was none but me to seek her food. Give me the wine, I say! for she is so cold and so very, very white"—and the child struggled to free his hand that still held the cup.

"Who art thou, then?" asked Charlemagne.

"My name is Roland—let me go, I pray thee," and again he tried to drag himself free. And Charlemagne mockingly said:

"Roland, I fear thy father and mother have taught thee to be a clever thief."

Then anger blazed in Roland's eyes.

"My mother is a lady of high degree!" he cried, "and I am her page, her cupbearer, her knight! I do not speak false words!"—and he would have struck the King for very rage.

Then Charlemagne turned to his lords and asked—"Who is this child?"

And one made answer: "He is the son of thy sister Bertha, and of Milon the knight, who was drowned these three weeks agone."

Then the heart of Charlemagne grew heavy with remorse when he found that his sister had so nearly died of want, and from that day she never knew aught but kindness and tenderness from him, while Roland was dear to him as his own child.

He was a Douzepere now, and when the envoys from Saragossa had delivered their message to Charlemagne, he was one of those who helped to do them honour at a great feast that was held for them in a pavilion raised in the orchard.

Early in the morning Charlemagne heard mass, and then, on his golden throne under the great pine, he sat and took counsel with his Douzeperes. Not one of them trusted Marsile, but Ganelon, who had married the widowed Bertha and who had a jealous hatred for his step-son—so beloved by his mother, so loved and honoured by the King—was ever ready to oppose the counsel of Roland. Thus did he persuade Charlemagne to send a messenger to Marsile, commanding him to deliver up the keys of Saragossa, in all haste to become a Christian, and in person to come and, with all humility, pay homage as vassal to Charlemagne.

Then arose the question as to which of the peers should bear the arrogant message. Roland, ever greedy for the post of danger, impetuously asked that he might be chosen. But Charlemagne would have neither him nor his dear friend and fellow-knight, Oliver—he who was the Jonathan of Roland's David—nor would he have Naismes de Bavière, nor Turpin, "the chivalrous and undaunted Bishop of Rheims." He could not afford to risk their lives, and Marsile was known to be treacherous. Then he said to his peers:

"Choose ye for me whom I shall send. Let it be one who is wise; brave, yet not over-rash, and who will defend mine honour valiantly."

Then Roland, who never knew an ungenerous thought, quickly said: "Then, indeed, it must be Ganelon who goes, for if he goes, or if he stays, you have none better than he."

And all the other peers applauded the choice, and Charlemagne said to Ganelon:

"Come hither, Ganelon, and receive my staff and glove, which the voice of all the Franks have given to thee."

But the honour which all the others coveted was not held to be an honour by Ganelon. In furious rage he turned upon Roland:

"You and your friends have sent me to my death!" he cried. "But if by a miracle I should return, look you to yourself, Roland, for assuredly I shall be revenged!"

And Roland grew red, then very white, and said:

"I had taken thee for another man, Ganelon. Gladly will I take thy place. Wilt give me the honour to bear thy staff and glove to Saragossa, sire?" And eagerly he looked Charlemagne in the face— eager as, when a child, he had craved the cup of wine for his mother's sake.

But Charlemagne, with darkened brow, shook his head.

"Ganelon must go," he said, "for so have I commanded. Go! for the honour of Jesus Christ, and for your Emperor."

Thus, sullenly and unwillingly, and with burning hatred against Roland in his heart, Ganelon accompanied the Saracens back to Saragossa. A hate so bitter was not easy to hide, and as he rode beside him the wily Blancandrin was not long in laying a probing finger on this festering sore. Soon he saw that Ganelon would pay even the price of his honour to revenge himself upon Roland and on the other Douzeperes whose lives were more precious than his in the eyes of Charlemagne. Yet, when Saragossa was reached, like a brave man and a true did Ganelon deliver the insulting message that his own brain had conceived and that the Emperor, with magnificent arrogance, had bidden him deliver. And this he did, although he knew his life hung but by a thread while Marsile and the Saracen lords listened to his words. But Marsile kept his anger under, thinking with comfort of what Blancandrin had told him of his discovery by the way. And very soon he had shown Ganelon how he might be avenged on Roland and on the friends of Roland, and in a manner which his treachery need never be known, and very rich were the bribes that he offered to the faithless knight.

Thus it came about that Ganelon sold his honour, and bargained with the Saracens to betray Roland and his companions into their hands in their passage of the narrow defiles of Roncesvalles. For more than fifty pieces of silver Marsile purchased the soul of Ganelon, and when this Judas of the Douzeperes returned in safety to Cordova, bringing with him princely gifts for Charlemagne, the keys of Saragossa, and the promise that in sixteen days Marsile would repair to France to do homage and to embrace the Christian faith, the Emperor was happy indeed. All had fallen out as he desired. Ganelon, who had gone forth in wrath, had returned calm and gallant, and had carried himself throughout his difficult embassy as a wise statesman and a brave and loyal soldier.

"Thou hast done well, Ganelon," said the king. "I give thanks to my God and to thee. Thou shalt be well rewarded."

The order then was speedily given for a return to France, and for ten miles the great army marched before they halted and encamped for the night. But when Charlemagne slept, instead of dreams of peace he had two dreams which disturbed him greatly. In the first, Ganelon roughly seized the imperial spear of tough ash-wood and it broke into splinters in his hand. In the next, Charlemagne saw himself attacked by a leopard and a bear, which tore off his right arm, and as a greyhound darted to his aid he awoke, and rose from his couch heavy at heart because of those dreams of evil omen.

In the morning he held a council and reminded his knights of the dangers of the lonely pass of Roncesvalles. It was a small oval plain, shut in all round, save on the south where the river found its outlet, by precipitous mountain ridges densely covered with beech woods. Mountains ran sheer up to the sky above it, precipices rushed sheer down below, and the path that crossed the crest of the Pyrenees and led to it was so narrow that it must be traversed in single file. The dangers for the rearguard naturally seemed to Charlemagne to be the greatest, and to his Douzeperes he turned, as before, for counsel.

"Who, then, shall command the rearguard?" he asked. And quickly Ganelon answered, "Who but Roland? Ever would he seek the post where danger lies."

And Charlemagne, feeling he owed much to Ganelon, gave way to his counsel, though with heavy forebodings in his heart. Then all the other Douzeperes, save Ganelon, said that for love of Roland they would go with him and see him safely through the dangers of the way. Loudly they vaunted his bravery:

"For dred of dethe, he hid neuer his hed."

Leaving them behind with twenty thousand men, and with Ganelon commanding the vanguard, Charlemagne started.

"Christ keep you!" he said on parting with Roland—*"I betak you to Crist."*

And Roland, clad in his shining armour, his lordly helmet on his head, his sword Durendala by his side, his horn Olifant slung round him, and his flower-painted shield on his arm, mounted his good steed Veillantif, and, holding his bright lance with its white pennon and golden fringe in his hand, led the way for his fellow-knights and for the other Franks who so dearly loved him.

Not far from the pass of Roncesvalles he saw, gleaming against the dark side of the purple mountain, the spears of the Saracens. Ten thousand men, under Sir Gautier, were sent by Roland to reconnoitre, but from every side the heathen pressed upon them, and every one of the ten thousand were slain—hurled into the valley far down below. Gautier alone, sorely wounded, returned to Roland, to tell him, ere his life ebbed away, of the betrayal by Ganelon, and to warn him of the ambush. Yet even then they were at Roncesvalles, and the warning came too late. Afar off, amongst the beech trees, and coming down amongst the lonely passes of the mountains, the Franks could see the gleam of silver armour, and Oliver, well knowing that not even the most dauntless valour could withstand such a host as the one that came against them, besought Roland to blow a blast on his magic horn that Charlemagne might hear and return to aid him. And all the other Douzeperes begged of him that thus he would call for help. But Roland would not listen to them.

"I will fight with them that us hathe soughtAnd or I se my brest blod throughe my harnes rynBlow never horn for no help then."

229

Through the night they knew their enemies were coming ever nearer, hemming them in, but there were no night alarms, and day broke fair and still. There was no wind, there was dew on the grass; "dew dymmd the floures," and amongst the trees the birds sang merrily. At daybreak the good Bishop Turpin celebrated Mass and blessed them, and even as his voice ceased they beheld the Saracen host close upon them. Then Roland spoke brave words of cheer to his army and commended their souls and his own to Christ, "who suffrid for us paynes sore," and for whose sake they had to fight the enemies of the Cross. Behind every tree and rock a Saracen seemed to be hidden, and in a moment the whole pass was alive with men in mortal strife.

Surely never in any fight were greater prodigies of valour performed than those of Roland and his comrades. Twelve Saracen kings fell before their mighty swords, and many a Saracen warrior was hurled down the cliffs to pay for the lives of the men of France whom they had trapped to their death. Never before, in one day, did one man slay so many as did Roland and Oliver his friend—"A Roland for an Oliver" was no good exchange, and yet a very fair one, as the heathen quickly learned.

"Red was Roland, red with bloodshed;Red his corselet, red his shoulders,Red his arm, and red his charger."

In the thickest of the fight he and Oliver came together, and Roland saw that his friend was using for weapon and dealing death-blows with the truncheon of a spear.

"'Friend, what hast thou there?' cried Roland.'In this game 'tis not a distaff,But a blade of steel thou needest.Where is now Hauteclaire, thy good sword,Golden-hilted, crystal-pommelled?'Here,' said Oliver; 'so fight IThat I have not time to draw it.'Friend,' quoth Roland, 'more I love theeEver henceforth than a brother.'"

When the sun set on that welter of blood, not a single Saracen was left, and those of the Frankish rearguard who still lived were very weary men.

Then Roland called on his men to give thanks to God, and Bishop Turpin, whose stout arm had fought well on that bloody day, offered up thanks for the army, though in sorry plight were they, almost none unwounded, their swords and lances broken, and their hauberks rent and blood-stained. Gladly they laid themselves down to rest beside the comrades whose eyes never more would open on the fair land of France, but even as Roland was about to take his rest he saw descending upon him and his little band a host of Saracens, led by Marsile himself.

A hundred thousand men, untired, and fiercely thirsting for revenge, came against the handful of wearied, wounded heroes. Yet with unwavering courage the Franks responded to their leaders' call.

The war-cry of the soldiers of France—"Montjoie! Montjoie!"—rang clear above the fierce sound of the trumpets of the Saracen army.

"'Soldiers of the Lord,' cried Turpin,'Be ye valiant and steadfast,For this day shall crowns be given youMidst the flowers of Paradise.In the name of God our Saviour,Be ye not dismayed nor frighted,Lest of you be shameful legendsChanted by the tongues of minstrels.Rather let us die victorious,Since this eve shall see us lifeless!—Heaven has no room for cowards!Knights, who nobly fight, and vainly,Ye shall sit among the holyIn the blessed fields of Heaven.On then, Friends of God, to glory!'"

Marsile fell, the first victim to a blow from the sword of Roland, and even more fiercely than the one that had preceded it, waged this terrible fight.

And now it seemed as though the Powers of Good and of Evil also took part in the fray, for a storm swept down from the mountains, thick darkness fell, and the rumble of thunder and the rush of heavy rain dulled the shouts of those who fought and the clash and clang of their weapons. When a blood-red cloud came up, its lurid light showed the trampled ground strewn with dead and dying. At that piteous sight Roland proposed to send a messenger to Charlemagne to ask him for aid, but it was then too late.

When only sixty Franks remained, the pride of Roland gave way to pity for the men whom he had led to death, and he took the magic horn Olifant in his hand, that he might blow on it a blast that would bring Charlemagne, his mighty army behind him, to wipe out the Saracen host that had done him such evil. But Oliver bitterly protested. Earlier in the day, when he had willed it, Roland had refused to call for help. Now the day was done. The twilight of death—Death the inevitable—was closing in upon them. Why, then, call now for Charlemagne, when nor he nor any other could help them? But Turpin with all his force backed the wish of Roland.

"The blast of thy horn cannot bring back the dead to life," he said. "Yet if our Emperor return he can save our corpses and weep over them and bear them reverently to la belle France. And there shall they lie in sanctuary, and not in a Paynim land where the wild beasts devour them and croaking wretches with foul beaks tear our flesh and leave our bones dishonoured."

"That is well said," quoth Roland and Oliver.

Then did Roland blow three mighty blasts upon his horn, and so great was the third that a blood-vessel burst, and the red drops trickled from his mouth.

For days on end Charlemagne had been alarmed at the delay of his rearguard, but ever the false Ganelon had reassured him.

"Why shouldst thou fear, sire?" he asked. "Roland has surely gone after some wild boar or deer, so fond is he of the chase."

But when Roland blew the blast that broke his mighty heart, Charlemagne heard it clearly, and no longer had any doubt of the meaning of its call. He knew that his dreams had come true, and at once he set his face towards the dire pass of Roncesvalles that he might, even at the eleventh hour, save Roland and his men.

Long ere Charlemagne could reach the children of his soul who stood in such dire need, the uncle of Marsile had reached the place of battle with a force of fifty thousand men. Pierced from behind by a cowardly lance, Oliver was sobbing out his life's blood. Yet ever he cried, "Montjoie! Montjoie!" and each time his voice formed the words, a thrust from his sword, or from the lances of his men, drove a soul down to Hades. And when he was breathing his last, and lay on the earth, humbly confessing his sins and begging God to grant him rest in Paradise, he asked God's blessing upon Charlemagne, his lord the king, and upon his fair land of France, and, above all other men, to keep free from scathe his heart's true brother and comrade, Roland, the gallant knight. Then did he gently sigh his last little measure of life away, and as Roland bent over him he felt that half of the glamour of living was gone. Yet still so dearly did he love Aude the Fair, the sister of Oliver, who was to be his bride, that his muscles grew taut as he gripped his sword, and his courage was the dauntless courage of a furious wave that faces all the cliffs of a rocky coast in a winter storm, when again, he faced the Saracen host.

Of all the Douzeperes, only Gautier and Turpin and Roland now remained, and with them a poor little handful of maimed men-at-arms. Soon a Saracen arrow drove through the heart of Gautier, and Turpin, wounded by four lances, stood alone by Roland's side. But for each lance thrust he slew a hundred men, and when at length he fell, Roland, himself sorely wounded, seized once more his horn and blew upon it a piercing blast:

"... a blast of that dread horn,On Fontarabian echoes borne,That to King Charles did come,When Rowland brave, and Olivier,And every paladin and peer,On Roncesvalles died."

SIR WALTER SCOTT.

That blast pierced right into the heart of Charlemagne, and straightway he turned his army towards the pass of Roncesvalles that he might succour Roland, whom he so greatly loved. Yet then it was too late. Turpin was nearly dead. Roland knew himself to be dying. Veillantif, Roland's faithful warhorse, was enduring agonies from wounds of the Paynim arrows, and him Roland slew with a shrewd blow from his well-tried sword. From far, far away the hero could hear the blare of the trumpets of the Frankish army, and, at the sound, what was left of the Saracen host fled in terror. He made his way, blindly, painfully, to where Turpin lay, and with fumbling fingers took off his hauberk and unlaced his golden helmet. With what poor skill was left to him, he strove to bind up his terrible wounds with strips of his own tunic, and he dragged him, as gently as he could, to a spot under the beech trees where the fresh moss still was green.

"'Ah, gentle lord,' said Roland, 'give me leaveTo carry here our comrades who are dead,Whom we so dearly loved; they must not lieUnblest; but I will bring their corpses hereAnd thou shalt bless them, and me, ere thou die."Go,' said the dying priest, 'but soon return.Thank God! the victory is yours and mine!'"

With exquisite pain Roland carried the bodies of Oliver and of the rest of the Douzeperes from the places where they had died to where Turpin, their dear bishop, lay a-dying. Each step that he took cost him a pang of agony; each step took from him a toll of blood. Yet faithfully he performed his task, until they all lay around Turpin, who gladly blessed them and absolved them all. And then the agony of soul and of heart and body that Roland had endured grew overmuch for him to bear, and he gave a great cry, like the last sigh of a mighty tree that the woodcutters fell, and dropped down, stiff and chill, in a deathly swoon. Then the dying bishop dragged himself towards him and lifted the horn Olifant, and with it in his hand he struggled, inch by inch, with very great pain and labour, to a little stream that trickled down the dark ravine, that he might fetch some water to revive the hero that he and all men loved. But ere he could reach the stream, the mists of death had veiled his eyes. He joined his hands in prayer, though each movement meant a pang, and gave his soul to Christ, his Saviour and his Captain. And so passed away the soul of a mighty warrior and a stainless priest.

Thus was Roland alone amongst the dead when consciousness came back to him. With feeble hands he unlaced his helmet and tended to himself as best he might. And, as Turpin had done, so also did he painfully crawl towards the stream. There he found Turpin, the horn Olifant by his side, and knew that it was in trying to fetch him water that the brave bishop had died, and for tenderness and pity the hero wept.

"Alas! brave priest, fair lord of noble birth,Thy soul I give to the great King of Heaven!

May thy fair soul escape the pains of Hell,And Paradise receive thee in its bowers!"

Then did Roland know that for him, also, there "was no other way but death." With dragging steps he toiled uphill a little way, his good sword Durendala in one hand, and in the other his horn Olifant. Under a little clump of pines were some rough steps hewn in a boulder of marble leading yet higher up the hill, and these Roland would have climbed, but his throbbing heart could no more, and again he fell swooning on the ground. A Saracen who, out of fear, had feigned death, saw him lying there and crawled out of the covert where he lay concealed.

"It is Roland, the nephew of the Emperor!" he joyously thought, and in triumph he said to himself, "I shall bear his sword back with me!" But as his Pagan hand touched the hilt of the sword and would have torn it from Roland's dying grasp, the hero was aroused from his swoon. One great stroke cleft the Saracen's skull and laid him dead at Roland's feet. Then to Durendala Roland spoke:

"I surely die; but, ere I end,Let me be sure that thou art ended too my friend!For should a heathen grasp thee when I am clay,My ghost would grieve full sore until the judgment day!"

More ghost than man he looked as with a mighty effort of will and of body he struggled to his feet and smote with his blade the marble boulder. Before the stroke the marble split asunder as though the pick-axe of a miner had cloven it. On a rock of sardonyx he strove to break it then, but Durendala remained unharmed. A third time he strove, and struck a rock of blue marble with such force that the sparks rushed out as from a blacksmith's anvil. Then he knew that it was in vain, for Durendala would not be shattered. And so he raised Olifant to his lips and blew a dying blast that echoed down the cliffs and up to the mountain tops and rang through the trees of the forest. And still, to this day, do they say, when the spirit of the warrior rides by night down the heights and through the dark pass of Roncesvalles, even such a blast may be heard, waking all the echoes and sounding through the lonely hollows of the hills.

Then he made confession, and with a prayer for pardon of his sins and for mercy from the God whose faithful servant and soldier he had been unto his life's end, the soul of Roland passed away.

"... With hands devoutly joinedHe breathed his last. God sent his Cherubim,Saint Raphael, Saint Michel del Peril.Together with them Gabriel came.—All bringThe soul of Count Rolland to Paradise.Aoi."

Charlemagne and his army found him lying thus, and very terrible were the grief and the rage of the Emperor as he looked on him and on the others of his Douzeperes and on the bodies of that army of twenty thousand.

"All the field was with blod ouer roun"—"Many a good swerd was broken ther"—"Many a fadirles child ther was at home."

By the side of Roland, Charlemagne vowed vengeance, but ere he avenged his death he mourned over him with infinite anguish:

"'The Lord have mercy, Roland, on thy soul!Never again shall our fair France beholdA knight so worthy, till France be no more!

How widowed lies our fair France, and how lone!How will the realms that I have swayed rebel,Now thou art taken from my weary age!So deep my woe that fain would I die tooAnd join my valiant Peers in Paradise,While men inter my weary limbs with thine!'"

A terrible vengeance was the one that he took next day, when the Saracen army was utterly exterminated; and when all the noble dead had been buried where they fell, save only Roland, Oliver, and Turpin, the bodies of these three heroes were carried to Blaye and interred with great honour in the great cathedral there.

Charlemagne then returned to Aix, and as he entered his palace, Aude the Fair, sister of Oliver, and the betrothed of Roland, hastened to meet him. Where were the Douzeperes? What was the moaning murmur as of women who wept, that had heralded the arrival in the town of the Emperor and his conquering army? Eagerly she questioned Charlemagne of the safety of Roland, and when the Emperor, in pitying grief, told her:

"Roland, thy hero, like a hero died," Aude gave a bitter cry and fell to the ground like a white lily slain by a cruel wind. The Emperor thought she had fainted, but when he would have lifted her up, he found that she was dead, and, in infinite pity, he had her taken to Blaye and buried by the side of Roland.

Very tender was Charlemagne to the maiden whom Roland had loved, but when the treachery of Ganelon had been proved, for him there was no mercy. At Aix-la-Chapelle, torn asunder by wild horses, he met a shameful and a horrible death, nor is his name forgotten as that of the blackest of traitors. But the memory of Roland and of the other Douzeperes lives on and is, however fanciful, forever fragrant.

"... Roland, and Olyvere,And of the twelve Tussypere,That dieden in the batayle of Runcyvale;Jesu lord, heaven king,To his bliss hem and us both bring,To liven withouten bale!"

SIR OTUEL.

ROLAND SEIZED ONCE MORE HIS HORN

THE CHILDREN OF LÎR

"Silent, O Moyle, be the roar of thy water;Break not, ye breezes, your chain of repose;While murmuring mournfully, Lîr's lonely daughterTells to the night-star her tale of woes."

MOORE.

They are the tragedies, not the comedies of the old, old days that are handed down to us, and the literature of the Celts is rich in tragedy. To the romantic and sorrowful imagination of the Celts of the green island of Erin we owe the hauntingly piteous story of the children of Lîr.

In the earliest times of all, when Ireland was ruled by the Dedannans, a people who came from Europe and brought with them from Greece magic and other arts so wonderful that the people of the land believed them to be gods, the Dedannans had so many chiefs that they met one day to decide who was the best man of them all, that they might choose him to be their king. The choice fell upon Bodb the Red, and gladly did every man acclaim him as king, all save Lîr of Shee Finnaha, who left the council in great wrath because he thought that he, and not Bodb, should have been chosen. In high dudgeon he retired to his own place, and in the years that followed he and Bodb the Red waged fierce war against one another. At last a great sorrow came to Lîr, for after an illness of three days his wife, who was very dear to him, was taken from him by death. Then Bodb saw an opportunity for reconciliation with the chief whose enemy he had no wish to be. And to the grief-stricken husband he sent a message:

"My heart weeps for thee, yet I pray thee to be comforted. In my house have I three maidens, my foster-daughters, the most beautiful and the best instructed in all Erin. Choose which one thou wilt for thy wife, and own me for thy lord, and my friendship shall be thine forever."

And the message brought comfort to Lîr, and he set out with a gallant company of fifty chariots, nor ever halted until he had reached the palace of Bodb the Red at Lough Derg, on the Shannon. Warm and kindly was the welcome that Lîr received from his overlord, and next day, as the three beautiful foster-daughters of Bodb sat on the same couch as his queen, Bodb said to Lîr:

"Behold my three daughters. Choose which one thou wilt."

And Lîr answered, "They are all beautiful, but Eve is the eldest, so she must be the noblest of the three. I would have her for my wife."

That day he married Eve, and Lîr took his fair young wife back with him to his own place, Shee Finnaha, and happy were both of them in their love. To them in course of time were born a twin son and a daughter. The daughter they named Finola and the son Aed, and the children were as beautiful, as good, and as happy as their mother. Again she bore twins, boys, whom they named Ficra and Conn, but as their eyes opened on the world, the eyes of their mother closed on pleasant life forever, and once again Lîr was a widower, more bowed down by grief than before.

The tidings of the death of Eve brought great sorrow to the palace of Bodb the Red, for to all who knew her Eve was very dear. But again the king sent a message of comfort to Lîr:

"We sorrow with thee, yet in proof of our friendship with thee and our love for the one who is gone, we would give thee another of our daughters to be a mother to the children who have lost their mother's care."

And again Lîr went to the palace at Loch Derg, the Great Lake, and there he married Eva, the second of the foster-daughters of the king.

At first it seemed as if Eva loved her dead sister's children as though they were her own. But when she saw how passionate was her husband's devotion to them, how he would have them to sleep near him and would rise at their slightest whimper to comfort and to caress them, and how at dawn she would wake to find he had left her side to see that all was well with them, the poisonous weed of jealousy began to grow up in the garden of her heart. She was a childless woman, and she knew not whether it was her sister who had borne them whom she hated, or whether she hated the children themselves. But steadily the hatred grew, and the love that Bodb the Red bore for them only embittered her the more. Many times in the year he would come to see them, many times would take them away to stay with him, and each year when the Dedannans held the Feast of Age—the feast of the great god Mannanan, of which those who partook never grew old—the four children of Lîr were present, and gave joy to all who beheld them by their great beauty, their nobility, and their gentleness.

But as the love that all others gave to the four children of Lîr grew, the hatred of Eva, their stepmother, kept pace with it, until at length the poison in her heart ate into her body as well as her soul, and she grew worn and ill out of her very wickedness. For nearly a year she lay sick in bed, while the sound of the children's laughter and their happy voices, their lovely faces like the faces of the children of a god, and the proud and loving words with which their father spoke of them were, to her, like acid in a festering wound. At last there came a black day when jealousy had choked all the flowers of goodness in her heart, and only treachery and merciless cruelty remained. She rose from her couch and ordered the horses to be yoked to her chariot that she might take the four children to the Great Lake to see the king, her foster-father. They were but little children, yet the instinct that sometimes tells even a very little child when it is near an evil thing, warned Finola that harm would come to her and to her brothers were they to go. It may also have been, perhaps, that she had seen, with the sharp vision of a woman child, the thing to which Lîr was quite blind, and that in a tone of her stepmother's voice, in a look she had surprised in her eyes, she had learned that the love that her father's wife professed for her and for the others was only hatred, cunningly disguised. Thus she tried to make excuses for herself and the little brothers to whom she was a child-mother, so that they need not go. But Eva listened with deaf ears, and the children said farewell to Lîr, who must have wondered at the tears that stood in Finola's eyes and the shadow that darkened their blue, and drove off in the chariot with their stepmother.

When they had driven a long way, Eva turned to her attendants: "Much wealth have I," she said, "and all that I have shall be yours if you will slay for me those four hateful things that have stolen from me the love of my man."

The servants heard her in horror, and in horror and shame for her they answered: "Fearful is the deed thou wouldst have us do; more fearful still is it that thou shouldst have so wicked a thought. Evil will surely come upon thee for having wished to take the lives of Lîr's innocent little children."

Angrily, then, she seized a sword and herself would fain have done what her servants had scorned to do. But she lacked strength to carry out her own evil wish, and so they journeyed onwards. They came to Lake Darvra at last—now Lough Derravaragh, in West Meath—and there they all alighted from the chariot, and the children, feeling as though they had been made to play at an ugly game, but that now it was over and all was safety and happiness again, were sent into the loch to bathe. Joyously and with merry laughter the little boys splashed into the clear water by the rushy shore, all three seeking to hold the hands of their sister, whose little slim white body was whiter than the water-lilies and her hair more golden than their hearts.

It was then that Eva struck them, as a snake strikes its prey. One touch for each, with a magical wand of the Druids, then the low chanting of an old old rune, and the beautiful children had vanished, and where their tiny feet had pressed the sand and their yellow hair had shown above the water like four daffodil heads that dance in the wind, there floated four white swans. But although to Eva belonged the power of bewitching their bodies, their hearts and souls and speech still belonged to the children of Lîr. And when

Finola spoke, it was not as a little timid child, but as a woman who could look with sad eyes into the future and could there see the terrible punishment of a shameful act.

"Very evil is the deed that thou hast done," she said. "We only gave thee love, and we are very young, and all our days were happiness. By cruelty and treachery thou hast brought our childhood to an end, yet is our doom less piteous than thine. Woe, woe unto thee, O Eva, for a fearful doom lies before thee!"

Then she asked—a child still, longing to know when the dreary days of its banishment from other children should be over—"Tell us how long a time must pass until we can take our own forms again."

And, relentlessly, Eva made answer: "Better had it been for thy peace hadst thou left unsought that knowledge. Yet will I tell thee thy doom. Three hundred years shall ye live in the smooth waters of Lake Darvra; three hundred years on the Sea of Moyle, which is between Erin and Alba; three hundred years more at Ivros Domnann and at Inis Glora, on the Western Sea. Until a prince from the north shall marry a princess from the south; until the Tailleken (St. Patrick) shall come to Erin, and until ye shall hear the sound of the Christian bell, neither my power nor thy power, nor the power of any Druid's runes can set ye free until that weird is dreed."

As she spoke, a strange softening came into the evil woman's heart. They were so still, those white creatures who gazed up at her with eager, beseeching eyes, through which looked the souls of the little children that once she had loved. They were so silent and piteous, the little Ficra and Conn, whose dimpled baby faces she often used to kiss. And she said, that her burden of guilt might be the lighter:

"This relief shall ye have in your troubles. Though ye keep your human reason and your human speech, yet shall ye suffer no grief because your form is the form of swans, and you shall sing songs more sweet than any music that the earth has ever known."

Then Eva went back to her chariot and drove to the palace of her foster-father at the Great Lake, and the four white swans were left on the lonely waters of Darvra.

When she reached the palace without the children, the king asked in disappointment why she had not brought them with her.

"Lîr loves thee no longer," she made answer. "He will not trust his children to thee, lest thou shouldst work them some ill."

But her father did not believe her lying words. Speedily he sent messengers to Shee Finnaha that they might bring back the children who ever carried joy with them. Amazed, Lîr received the message, and when he learned that Eva had reached the palace alone, a terrible dread arose in his heart. In great haste he set out, and as he passed by Lake Darvra he heard voices singing melodies so sweet and moving that he was fain, in spite of his fears, to stop and listen. And lo, as he listened, he found that the singers were four swans, that swam close up to where he stood, and greeted him in the glad voices of his own dear children. All that night he stayed beside them, and when they had told him their piteous tale and he knew that no power could free them till the years of their doom were accomplished, Lîr's heart was like to break with pitying love and infinite sorrow. At dawn he took a tender leave of them and drove to the house of Bodb the Red. Terrible were the words of Lîr, and dark was his face as he told the king the evil thing that Eva had done. And Eva, who had thought in the madness of her jealousy that Lîr would give her all his love when he was a childless man, shrank, white and trembling, away from him when she saw the furious hatred in his eyes. Then said the king, and his anger was even as the anger of Lîr:

"The suffering of the little children who are dear to our souls shall come to an end at last. Thine shall be an eternal doom."

And he put her on oath to tell him "what shape of all others, on the earth, or above the earth, or beneath the earth, she most abhorred, and into which she most dreaded to be transformed."

"A demon of the air," answered the cowering woman.

"A demon of the air shalt thou be until time shall cease!" said her foster-father. Thereupon he smote her with his druidical wand, and a creature too hideous for men's eyes to look upon, gave a great scream of anguish, and flapped its black wings as it flew away to join the other demons of the air.

Then the king of the Dedannans and all his people went with Lîr to Lake Darvra, and listened to the honey-sweet melodies that were sung to them by the white swans that had been the children of their hearts. And such magic was in the music that it could lull away all sorrow and pain, and give rest to the grief-stricken and sleep to the toil-worn and the heavy at heart. And the Dedannans made a great encampment on the shores of the lake that they might never be far from them. There, too, as the centuries went by, came the Milesians, who succeeded the Dedannans in Erin, and so for the children of Lîr three hundred years passed happily away.

Sad for them and for Lîr, and for all the people of the Dedannans, was the day when the years at Darvra were ended and the four swans said farewell to their father and to all who were so dear to them, spread their snowy pinions, and took flight for the stormy sea. They sang a song of parting that made grief sit heavy on the hearts of all those who listened, and the men of Erin, in memory of the children of Lîr and of the good things they had wrought by the magic of their music, made a law, and proclaimed it throughout all the land, that from that time forth no man of their land should harm a swan.

Weary were the great white wings of the children of Lîr when they reached the jagged rocks by the side of the fierce grey sea of Moyle, whose turbulent waves fought angrily together. And the days that came to them there were days of weariness, of loneliness, and of hardship. Very cold were they often, very hungry, and yet the sweetness of their song pierced through the vicious shriek of the tempest and the sullen boom and crash of the great billows that flung themselves against the cliffs or thundered in devouring majesty over the wrack-strewn shore, like a thread of silver that runs through a pall. One night a tempest drove across and down the Sea of Moyle from the north-east, and lashed it into fury. And the mirk darkness and the sleet that drove in the teeth of the gale like bullets of ice, and the huge, irresistible breakers that threshed the shore, filled the hearts of the children of Lîr with dread. For always they had desired love and beauty, and the ugliness of unrestrained cruelty and fury made them sick at soul.

To her brothers Finola said: "Beloved ones, of a surety the storm must drive us apart. Let us, then, appoint a place of meeting, lest we never look upon each other again."

And, knowing that she spoke wisely and well, the three brothers appointed as their meeting-place the rock of Carricknarone.

Never did a fiercer storm rage on the sea between Alba and Erin than the storm that raged that night. Thunderous, murky clouds blotted out stars and moon, nor was there any dividing line between sky and sea, but both churned themselves up together in a passion of destruction. When the lightning flashed, it showed only the fury of the cruel seas, the shattered victims of the destroying storm. Very soon the swans were driven one from another and scattered over the face of the angry deep. Scarcely could their souls cling to their bodies while they struggled with the winds and waves. When the long, long night came to an end, in the grey and cheerless dawn Finola swam to the rock of Carricknarone. But no swans were there, only the greedy gulls that sought after wreckage, and the terns that cried very dolorously.

Then great grief came upon Finola, for she feared she would see her brothers nevermore. But first of all came Conn, his feathers all battered and broken and his head drooping, and in a little Ficra appeared, so drenched and cold and beaten by the winds that no word could he speak. And Finola took her younger brothers under her great white wings, and they were comforted and rested in that warm shelter.

"If Aed would only come," she said, "then should we be happy indeed."

And even as she spoke, they beheld Aed sailing towards them like a proud ship with its white sails shining in the sun, and Finola held him close to the snowy plumage of her breast, and happiness returned to the children of Lîr.

Many another tempest had they to strive with, and very cruel to them were the snow and biting frosts of the dreary winters. One January night there came a frost that turned even the restless sea into solid ice, and in the morning, when the swans strove to rise from the rock of Carricknarone, the iron frost clung to them and they left behind them the skin of their feet, the quills of their wings, and the soft feathers of their breasts, and when the frost had gone, the salt water was torture for their wounds. Yet ever they sang their songs, piercing sweet and speaking of the peace and joy to come, and many a storm-tossed mariner by them was lulled to sleep and dreamt the happy dreams of his childhood, nor knew who had sung him so magical a lullaby. It was in those years that Finola sang the song which a poet who possessed the wonderful heritage of a perfect comprehension of the soul of the Gael has put into English words for us.

"Happy our father Lîr afar,With mead, and songs of love and war:The salt brine, and the white foam,With these his children have their home.

In the sweet days of long ago,Soft-clad we wandered to and fro:But now cold winds of dawn and nightPierce deep our feathers thin and light.

Beneath my wings my brothers lieWhen the fierce ice-winds hurtle by;On either side and 'neath my breastLîr's sons have known no other rest."

FIONA MACLEOD (WILLIAM SHARP).

Only once during those dreary three hundred years did the children of Lîr see any of their friends. When they saw, riding down to the shore at the mouth of the Bann on the north coast of Erin, a company in gallant attire, with glittering arms, and mounted on white horses, the swans hastened to meet them. And glad were their hearts that day, for the company was led by two sons of Bodb the Red, who had searched for the swans along the rocky coast of Erin for many a day, and who brought them loving greetings from the good king of the Dedannans and from their father Lîr.

At length the three hundred years on the Sea of Moyle came to an end, and the swans flew to Ivros Domnann and the Isle of Glora in the western sea. And there they had sufferings and hardships to bear that were even more grievous than those that they had endured on the Sea of Moyle, and one night the snow that drifted down upon them from the ice was scourged on by a north-west wind, and there came a moment when the three brothers felt that they could endure no more.

But Finola said to them:

"It is the great God of truth who made both land and sea who alone can succour us, for He alone can wholly understand the sorrows of our hearts. Put your trust in Him, dear brothers, and He will send us comfort and help."

Then said her brothers: "In Him we put our trust," and from that moment the Lord of Heaven gave them His help, so that no frost, nor snow, nor cold, nor tempest, nor any of the creatures of the deep could work them any harm.

When the nine hundred years of their sorrowful doom had ended, the children of Lîr joyously spread their wings and flew to their father's home at Shee Finnaha.

But the house was there no more, for Lîr, their father, was dead. Only stones, round which grew rank grass and nettles, and where no human creature had his habitation, marked the place for which they had longed with an aching, hungry longing, through all their weary years of doom. Their cries were piteous as the cries of lost children as they looked on the desolate ruins, but all night they stayed there, and their songs were songs that might have made the very stones shed tears.

Next day they winged their way back to Inis Glora, and there the sweetness of their singing drew so many birds to listen that the little lake got the name of the Lake of the Bird-Flocks. Near and far, for long thereafter, flew the swans, all along the coast of the Western Sea, and at the island of Iniskea they held converse with the lonely crane that has lived there since the beginning of the world, and which will live there until time is no more.

And while the years went by, there came to Erin one who brought glad tidings, for the holy Patrick came to lead men out of darkness into light. With him came Kemoc, and Kemoc made his home on Inis Glora.

At dawn one morning, the four swans were roused by the tinkle of a little bell. It was so far away that it rang faintly, but it was like no sound they had ever known, and the three brothers were filled with fear and flew hither and thither, trying to discover from whence the strange sound came. But when they returned to Finola, they found her floating at peace on the water.

"Dost not know what sound it is?" she asked, divining their thoughts.

"We heard a faint, fearful voice," they said, "but we know not what it is."

Then said Finola: "It is the voice of the Christian bell. Soon, now, shall our suffering be ended, for such is the will of God."

So very happily and peacefully they listened to the ringing of the bell, until Kemoc had said matins. Then said Finola: "Let us now sing our music," and they praised the Lord of heaven and earth.

And when the wonderful melody of their song reached the ears of Kemoc, he knew that none but the children of Lîr could make such magic-sweet melody. So he hastened to where they were, and when he asked them if they were indeed the children of Lîr, for whose sake he had come to Inis Glora, they told him all their piteous tale.

Then said Kemoc, "Come then to land, and put your trust in me, for on this island shall your enchantment come to an end." And when most gladly they came, he caused a cunning workman to fashion two slender silver chains; one he put between Finola and Aed, and the other between Ficra and Conn, and so joyous were they to know again human love, and so happy to join each day with Kemoc in praising God, that the memory of their suffering and sorrow lost all its bitterness. Thus in part were the words of Eva fulfilled, but there had yet to take place the entire fulfilment of her words.

Decca, a princess of Munster, had wed Larguen, king of Connaught, and when news came to her of the wonderful swans of Kemoc, nothing would suffice her but that she should have them for her own. By constant beseeching, she at length prevailed upon Larguen to send messengers to Kemoc, demanding the swans. When the messengers returned with a stern refusal from Kemoc, the king was angry indeed. How dared a mere cleric refuse to gratify the whim of the queen of Larguen of Connaught! To Inis Glora he went, posthaste, himself.

"Is it truth that ye have dared to refuse a gift of your birds to my queen?" he asked, in wrath.

And Kemoc answered: "It is truth."

Then Larguen, in furious anger, seized hold of the silver chain that bound Finola and Aed together, and of the chain by which Conn and Ficra were bound, and dragged them away from the altar by which they sat, that he might take them to his queen.

But as the king held their chains in his rude grasp, a wondrous thing took place.

250

Instead of swans, there followed Larguen a very old woman, white-haired and feeble, and three very old men, bony and wrinkled and grey. And when Larguen beheld them, terror came upon him and he hastened homeward, followed by the bitter denunciations of Kemoc. Then the children of Lîr, in human form at last, turned to Kemoc and besought him to baptize them, because they knew that death was very near.

"Thou art not more sorrowful at parting from us than we are to part with you, dear Kemoc," they said. And Finola said, "Bury us, I pray you, together."

"As oft in life my brothers dearWere sooth'd by me to rest—Ficra and Conn beneath my wings,And Aed before my breast;

So place the two on either hand—Close, like the love that bound me;Place Aed as close before my face,And twine their arms around me."

JOYCE.

So Kemoc signed them in Holy Baptism with the blessed Cross, and even as the water touched their foreheads, and while his words were in their ears, death took them. And, as they passed, Kemoc looked up, and, behold, four beautiful children, their faces radiant with joy, and with white wings lined with silver, flying upwards to the clouds. And soon they vanished from his sight and he saw them no more.

He buried them as Finola had wished, and raised a mound over them, and carved their names on a stone.

And over it he sang a lament and prayed to the God of all love and purity, a prayer for the pure and loving souls of those who had been the children of Lîr.

ONE TOUCH FOR EACH, WITH A MAGICAL WAND OF THE DRUIDS

DEIRDRÊ

"Her beauty filled the old world of the Gael with a sweet, wonderful, and abiding rumour. The name of Deirdrê has been as a harp to a thousand poets. In a land of heroes and brave and beautiful women, how shall one name survive? Yet to this day and for ever, men will remember Deirdrê...."

FIONA MACLEOD.

So long ago, that it was before the birth of our Lord, so says tradition, there was born that

"Morning star of loveliness,Unhappy Helen of a Western land,"

who is known to the Celts of Scotland as Darthool, to those of Ireland as Deirdrê. As in the story of Helen, it is not easy, or even possible in the story of Deirdrê, to disentangle the old, old facts of actual history from the web of romantic fairy tale that time has woven about them, yet so great is the power of Deirdrê, even unto this day, that it has been the fond task of those men and women to whom the Gael owes so much, to preserve, and to translate for posterity, the tragic romance of Deirdrê the Beautiful and the Sons of Usna.

In many ancient manuscripts we get the story in more or less complete form. In the Advocates' Library of Edinburgh, in the Glenmasan MS. we get the best and the fullest version, while the oldest and the shortest is to be found in the twelfth-century *Book of Leinster*.

But those who would revel in the old tale and have Deirdrê lead them by the hand into the enchanted realm of the romance of misty, ancient days of our Western Isles must go for help to Fiona Macleod, to Alexander Carmichael, to Lady Gregory, to Dr. Douglas Hyde, to W. F. Skene, to W. B. Yeats, to J. M. Synge, and to those others who, like true descendants of the Druids, possess the power of unlocking the entrance gates of the Green Islands of the Blest.

Conchubar, or Conor, ruled the kingdom of the Ultonians, now Ulster, when Deirdrê was born in Erin. All the most famous warriors of his time, heroes whose mighty deeds live on in legend, and whose title was "The Champions of the Red Branch," he gathered round him, and all through Erin and Alba rang the fame of the warlike Ultonians.

There came a day when Conor and his champions, gorgeous in their gala dress of crimson tunic with brooches of inlaid gold and white-hooded shirt embroidered in red gold, went to a feast in the house of one called Felim. Felim was a bard, and because not only was his arm in war strong and swift to strike, but because, in peace, his fingers could draw the sweetest of music from his harp, he was dear to the king. As they feasted, Conor beheld a dark shadow of horror and of grief fall on the face of Cathbad, a Druid who had come in his train, and saw that his aged eyes were gazing far into the Unseen. Speedily he bade him tell him what evil thing it was that he saw, and Cathbad turned to the childless Felim and told him that to his wife there was about to be born a daughter, with eyes like stars that are mirrored by night in the water, with lips red as the rowan berries and teeth more white than pearls; with a voice more sweet than the music of fairy harps. "A maiden fair, tall, long haired, for whom champions will contend ... and mighty kings be envious of her lovely, faultless form." For her sweet sake, he said, more blood should be spilt in Erin than for generations and ages past, and many heroes and bright torches of the Gaels should lose their lives. For love of her, three heroes of eternal renown must give their lives away, the sea in which her starry eyes should mirror themselves would be a sea of blood, and woe unutterable should come on the sons of Erin. Then up spoke the lords of the Red Branch, and grimly they looked at Felim the Harper:

"If the babe that thy wife is about to bear is to bring such evil upon our land, better that thou shouldst shed her innocent blood ere she spills the blood of our nation."

And Felim made answer:

"It is well spoken. Bitter it is for my wife and for me to lose a child so beautiful, yet shall I slay her that my land may be saved from such a doom."

But Conor, the king, spoke then, and because the witchery of the perfect beauty and the magic charm of Deirdrê was felt by him even before she was born, he said: "She shall not die. Upon myself I take the doom. The child shall be kept apart from all men until she is of an age to wed. Then shall I take her for my wife, and none shall dare to contend for her."

His voice had barely ceased, when a messenger came to Felim to tell him that a daughter was born to him, and on his heels came a procession of chanting women, bearing the babe on a flower-decked cushion. And all who saw the tiny thing, with milk-white skin, and locks "more yellow than the western gold of the summer sun," looked on her with the fear that even the bravest heart feels on facing the Unknown. And Cathbad spoke: "Let Deirdrê be her name, sweet menace that she is." And the babe gazed up with starry eyes at the white-haired Druid as he chanted to her:

"*Many will be jealous of your face, O flame of beauty; for your sake heroes shall go to exile. For there is harm in your face; it will bring banishment and death on the sons of kings. In your fate, O beautiful child, are wounds and ill-doings, and shedding of blood.*

"*You will have a little grave apart to yourself; you will be a tale of wonder for ever, Deirdrê.*"

LADY GREGORY'S TRANSLATION.

As Conor commanded, Deirdrê, the little "babe of destiny," was left with her mother for only a month and a day, and then was sent with a nurse and with Cathbad the Druid to a lonely island, thickly wooded, and only accessible by a sort of causeway at low tide. Here she grew into maidenhood, and each day became more fair. She had instruction from Cathbad in religion and in all manner of wisdom, and it would seem as though she also learned from him some of that mystical power that enabled her to see things hidden from human eyes.

"Tell me," one day she asked her teacher, "who made the stars, the firmament above, the earth, the flowers, both thee and me?"

And Cathbad answered: "God. But who God is, alas! no man can say."

Then Deirdrê, an impetuous child, seized the druidical staff from the hand of Cathbad, broke it in two, and flung the pieces far out on the water. "Ah, Cathbad!" she cried, "there shall come One in the dim future for whom all your Druid spells and charms are naught."

Then seeing Cathbad hang his head, and a tear trickle down his face, for he knew that the child spoke truth, the child, grieved at giving pain to the friend whom she loved, threw her arms about the old man's neck, and by her kisses strove to comfort him.

As Deirdrê grew older, Conor sent one from his court to educate her in all that any queen should know. They called her the Lavarcam, which, in our tongue, really means the Gossip, and she was one of royal blood who belonged to a class that in those days had been trained to be chroniclers, or story-tellers. The Lavarcam was a clever woman, and she marvelled at the wondrous beauty of the child she came to teach, and at her equally marvellous mind.

One winter day, when the snow lay deep, it came to pass that Deirdrê saw lying on the snow a calf that had been slain for her food. The red blood that ran from its neck had brought a black raven swooping down upon the snow. And to Lavarcam Deirdrê said: "If there were a man who had hair of the blackness of that raven, skin of the whiteness of the snow, and cheeks as red as the blood that stains its whiteness, to him should I give my heart."

And Lavarcam, without thought, made answer:

"One I know whose skin is whiter than the snow, whose cheeks are ruddy as the blood that stained the snow, and whose hair is black and glossy as the raven's wing. He has eyes of the darkest blue of the sky, and head and shoulders is he above all the men of Erin."

"And what will be the name of that man, Lavarcam?" asked Deirdrê. "And whence is he, and what his degree?"

And Lavarcam made answer that he of whom she spoke was Naoise, one of the three sons of Usna, a great lord of Alba, and that these three sons were mighty champions who had been trained at the famed military school at Sgathaig in the Isle of Skye.

Then said Deirdrê: "My love shall be given to none but Naoise, son of Usna. To him shall it belong forever."

From that day forward, Naoise held kingship over the thoughts and dreams of Deirdrê.

And when Lavarcam saw how deep her careless words had sunk into the heart of the maiden, she grew afraid, and tried to think of a means by which to undo the harm which, in her thoughtlessness, she had wrought.

Now Conor had made a law that none but Cathbad, Lavarcam, and the nurse of Deirdrê should pass through the forest that led to her hiding-place, and that none but they should look upon her until his own eyes beheld her and he took her for his wife. But as Lavarcam one day came from seeing Deirdrê, and from listening to her many eager questions about Naoise, she met a swineherd, rough in looks and speech, and clad in the pelt of a deer, and with him two rough fellows, bondmen of the Ultonians, and to her quick mind there came a plan. Thus she bade them follow her into the forbidden forest and there to remain, by the side of a well, until they should hear the bark of a fox and the cry of a jay. Then they were to walk slowly on through the woods, speaking to none whom they might meet, and still keeping silence when they were again out of the shadow of the trees.

Then Lavarcam sped back to Deirdrê and begged her to come with her to enjoy the beauty of the woods. In a little, Lavarcam strayed away from her charge, and soon the cry of a jay and the bark of a fox were heard, and while Deirdrê still marvelled at the sounds that came so close together, Lavarcam returned. Nor had she been back a minute before three men came through the trees and slowly walked past, close to where Lavarcam and Deirdrê were hidden.

"I have never seen men so near before," said Deirdrê. "Only from the outskirts of the forest have I seen them very far away. Who are these men, who bring no joy to my eyes?"

And Lavarcam made answer: "These are Naoise, Ardan, and Ainle—the three sons of Usna."

But Deirdrê looked hard at Lavarcam, and scorn and laughter were in her merry eyes.

"Then shall I have speech with Naoise, Ardan, and Ainle," she said, and ere Lavarcam could stop her, she had flitted through the trees by a path amongst the fern, and stood suddenly before the three men.

And the rough hinds, seeing such perfect loveliness, made very sure that Deirdrê was one of the *sidhe* and stared at her with the round eyes and gaping mouths of wondering terror.

For a moment Deirdrê gazed at them. Then: "Are ye the Sons of Usna?" she asked.

And when they stood like stocks, frightened and stupid, she lashed them with her mockery, until the swineherd could no more, and blurted out the whole truth to this most beautiful of all the world. Then, very gently, like pearls from a silver string, the words fell from the rowan-red lips of Deirdrê: "I blame thee not, poor swineherd," she said, "and that thou mayst know that I deem thee a true man, I would fain ask thee to do one thing for me."

258

And when the eyes of the herd met the eyes of Deirdrê, a soul was born in him, and he knew things of which he never before had dreamed.

"If I can do one thing to please thee, that will I do," he said. "Aye, and gladly pay for it with my life. Thenceforth my life is thine."

And Deirdrê said: "I would fain see Naoise, one of the Sons of Usna."

And once more the swineherd said: "My life is thine."

Then Deirdrê, seeing in his eyes a very beautiful thing, stooped and kissed the swineherd on his weather-beaten, tanned forehead.

"Go, then," she said, "to Naoise. Tell him that I, Deirdrê, dream of him all the night and think of him all the day, and that I bid him meet me here to-morrow an hour before the setting of the sun."

The swineherd watched her flit into the shadows of the trees, and then went on his way, through the snowy woods, that he might pay with his life for the kiss that Deirdrê had given him.

Sorely puzzled was Lavarcam over the doings of Deirdrê that day, for Deirdrê told her not a word of what had passed between her and the swineherd. On the morrow, when she left her to go back to the court of King Conor, she saw, as she drew near Emain Macha, where he stayed, black wings that flapped over something that lay on the snow. At her approach there rose three ravens, three kites, and three hoodie-crows, and she saw that their prey was the body of the swineherd with gaping spear-wounds all over him. Yet even then he looked happy. He had died laughing, and there was still a smile on his lips. Faithfully had he delivered his message, and when he had spoken of the beauty of Deirdrê, rumour of his speech had reached the king, and the spears of Conor's men had enabled him to make true the words he had said to Deirdrê: "I will pay for it with my life." In this way was shed the first blood of that great sea of blood that was spilt for the love of Deirdrê, the Beauty of the World.

From where the swineherd lay, Lavarcam went to the camp of the Sons of Usna, and to Naoise she told the story of the love that Deirdrê bore him, and counselled him to come to the place where she was hidden, and behold her beauty. And Naoise, who had seen how even a rough clod of a hind could achieve the noble chivalry of a race of kings for her dear sake, felt his heart throb within him. "I will come," he said to Lavarcam.

Days passed, and Deirdrê waited, very sure that Naoise must come to her at last. And one day she heard a song of magical sweetness coming through the trees. Three voices sung the song, and it was as though one of the *sidhe* played a harp to cast a spell upon men. The voice of Ainle, youngest of the Sons of Usna, was like the sweet upper strings of the harp, that of Ardan the strings in the middle, and the voice of Naoise was like the strings whose deep resonance can play upon the hearts of warriors and move them to tears. Then Deirdrê knew that she heard the voice of her beloved, and she sped to him as a bird speeds to her mate. Even as Lavarcam had told her was Naoise, eldest of the Sons of Usna, but no words had been able to tell Naoise of the beauty of Deirdrê.

"It was as though a sudden flood of sunshine burst forth in that place. For a woman came from the thicket more beautiful than any dream he had ever dreamed. She was clad in a saffron robe over white that was like the shining of the sun on foam of the sea, and this was claspt with great bands of yellow gold, and over her shoulders was the rippling flood of her hair, the sprays of which lightened into delicate fire, and made a mist before him, in the which he could see her eyes like two blue pools wherein purple shadows dreamed."

Fiona Macleod.

From that moment Naoise "gave his love to Deirdrê above every other creature," and their souls rushed together and were one for evermore. It was for them the beginning of a perfect love, and so sure were they of that love from the very first moment that it seemed as though they must have been born loving one another.

Of that love they talked, of the anger of Conor when he knew that his destined bride was the love of Naoise, and together they planned how it was best for Deirdrê to escape from the furious wrath of the king who desired her for his own.

Of a sudden, the hands of Naoise gripped the iron-pointed javelin that hung by his side, and drove it into a place where the snow weighed down the bracken.

"Is it a wolf?" cried Deirdrê.

And Naoise made answer: "Either a dead man, or the mark of where a man has lain hidden thou wilt find under the bracken."

And when they went to look they found, like the clap of a hare, the mark of where a man had lain hidden, and close beside the javelin that was driven in the ground there lay a wooden-hilted knife.

Then said Naoise: "Well I knew that Conor would set a spy on my tracks. Come with me now, Deirdrê, else may I lose thee forever."

And with a glad heart Deirdrê went with him who was to be her lord, and Naoise took her to where his brothers awaited his coming. To Deirdrê, both Ainle and Ardan swiftly gave their lifelong allegiance and their love, but they were full of forebodings for her and for Naoise because of the certain wrath of Conor, the king.

Then said Naoise: "Although harm should come, for her dear sake I am willing to live in disgrace for the rest of my days."

And Ardan and Ainle made answer: "Of a certainty, evil will be of it, yet though there be, thou shalt not be under disgrace as long as we shall be alive. We will go with her to another country. There is not in Erin a king who will not bid us welcome."

Then did the Sons of Usna decide to cross the Sea of Moyle, and in their own land of Alba to find a happy sanctuary. That night they fled, and with them took three times fifty men, three times fifty women, three times fifty horses, and three times fifty greyhounds.

And when they looked back to where they had had their dwelling, they saw red flames against the deep blue sky of the night, and knew that the vengeance of Conor had already begun. And first they travelled round Erin from Essa to Beinn Etair, and then in a great black galley they set sail, and Deirdrê had a heart light as the white-winged sea-birds as the men pulled at the long oars and sang together a rowing song, and she leaned on the strong arm of Naoise and saw the blue coast-line of Erin fading into nothingness.

In the bay of Aros, on the eastern shores of the island of Mull, they found their first resting-place, but there they feared treachery from a lord of Appin. For the starry eyes of Deirdrê were swift to discern evil that the eyes of the Sons of Usna could not see. Thus they fared onward until they reached the great sea-loch of Etive, with hills around it, and Ben Cruachan, its head in mist, towering above it like a watchman placed there by Time, to wait and to watch over the people of those silent hills and lonely glens until Time should give place to his brother, Eternity.

Joy was in the hearts of the three Sons of Usna when they came back to the home of their fathers. Usna was dead, but beyond the Falls of Lora was still the great dun—the vitrified fort—which he had built for himself and for those who should follow him.

For Deirdrê then began a time of perfect happiness. Naoise was her heart, but very dear to her also were the brothers of Naoise, and each of the three vied with one another in their acts of tender and loving service. Their thrice fifty vassals had no love for Alba, and rejoiced when their lord, Naoise, allowed them to return to Erin, but the Sons of Usna were glad to have none to come between them and their serving of Deirdrê, the queen of their hearts. Soon she came to know well each little bay, each beach, and each little lonely glen of Loch Etive, for the Sons of Usna did not always stay at the dun which had been their father's, but went a-hunting up the loch. At various spots on the shores of Etive they had camping places, and at Dail-an-eas they built for Deirdrê a sunny bower.

On a sloping bank above the waterfall they built the little nest, thatched with the royal fern of the mountains, the red clay of the pools, and with soft feathers from the breasts of birds. There she could sit and listen to the murmur and drip of the clear water over the mossy boulders, the splash of the salmon in the dark pools, and see the distant silver of the loch. When the summer sun was hot on the bog myrtle and heather, the hum of the wild bees would lull her to sleep, and in autumn, when the bracken grew red and golden and the rowan berries grew red as Deirdrê's lips, her keen eyes would see the stags grazing high up among the grey boulders of the mist-crowned mountains, and would warn the brothers of the sport awaiting them. The crow of the grouse, the belling of stags, the bark of the hill-fox, the swish of the great wings of the golden eagle, the song of birds, the lilt of running water, the complaining of the wind through the birches—all these things made music to Deirdrê, to whom all things were dear.

"*Is tu mein na Dearshul agha*"–"The tenderness of heartsweet Deirdrê"–so runs a line in an old, old Gaelic verse, and it is always of her tenderness as well as her beauty that the old *Oea* speak.

Sometimes she would hunt the red deer with Naoise and his brothers, up the lonely glens, up through the clouds to the silent mountain tops, and in the evening, when she was weary, her three loyal worshippers would proudly bear her home upon their bucklers.

So the happy days passed away, and in Erin the angry heart of Conor grew yet more angry when tidings came to him of the happiness of Deirdrê and the Sons of Usna. Rumour came to him that the king of Alba had planned to come against Naoise, to slay him, and to take Deirdrê for his wife, but that ere he could come the Sons of Usna and Deirdrê had sailed yet further north in their galley, and that there, in the land of his mother, Naoise ruled as a king. And not only on Loch Etive, but on Loch Awe and Loch Fyne, Loch Striven, Loch Ard, Loch Long, Loch Lomond and all along the sea-loch coast, the fame of the Sons of Usna spread, and the wonder of the beauty of Deirdrê, fairest of women.

And ever the hatred of Conor grew, until one day there came into his mind a plan of evil by which his burning thirst for revenge might be handsomely assuaged.

He made, therefore, a great feast, at which all the heroes of the Red Branch were present. When he had done them every honour, he asked them if they were content. As one man: "Well content indeed!" answered they.

"And that is what I am not," said the king. Then with the guile of fair words he told them that to him it was great sorrow that the three heroes, with whose deeds the Western Isles and the whole of the north and west of Alba were ringing, should not be numbered amongst his friends, sit at his board in peace and amity, and fight for the Ultonians like all the other heroes of the Red Branch.

"They took from me the one who would have been my wife," he said, "yet even that I can forgive, and if they would return to Erin, glad would my welcome be."

At these words there was great rejoicing amongst the lords of the Red Branch and all those who listened, and Conor, glad at heart, said, "My three best champions shall go to bring them back from their exile," and he named Conall the Victorious, Cuchulainn, and Fergus, the son of Rossa the Red. Then secretly he called Conall to him and asked him what he would do if he were sent to fetch the Sons of Usna, and, in spite of his safe-conduct, they were slain when they reached the land of the Ultonians. And Conall made answer that should such a shameful thing come to pass he would slay with his own hand all the traitor dogs. Then he sent for Cuchulainn, and to him put the same question, and, in angry scorn, the young hero replied that even Conor himself would not be safe from his vengeance were such a deed of black treachery to be performed.

"Well did I know thou didst bear me no love," said Conor, and black was his brow.

He called for Fergus then, and Fergus, sore troubled, made answer that were there to be such a betrayal, the king alone would be held sacred from his vengeance.

Then Conor gladly gave Fergus command to go to Alba as his emissary, and to fetch back with him the three brothers and Deirdrê the Beautiful.

"Thy name of old was Honeymouth," he said, "so I know well that with guile thou canst bring them to Erin. And when thou shalt have returned with them, send them forward, but stay thyself at the house of Borrach. Borrach shall have warning of thy coming."

This he said, because to Fergus and to all the other of the Red Branch, a *geasa*, or pledge, was sacrosanct. And well he knew that Fergus had as one of his*geasa* that he would never refuse an invitation to a feast.

Next day Fergus and his two sons, Illann the Fair and Buinne the Red, set out in their galley for the dun of the Sons of Usna on Loch Etive.

The day before their hurried flight from Erin, Ainle and Ardan had been playing chess in their dun with Conor, the king. The board was of fair ivory, and the chessmen were of red-gold, wrought in strange devices. It had come from the mysterious East in years far beyond the memory of any living man, and was one of the dearest of Conor's possessions. Thus, when Ainle and Ardan carried off the chess-board with them in their flight, after the loss of Deirdrê, that was the loss that gave the king the greatest bitterness. Now it came to pass that as Naoise and Deirdrê were sitting in front of their dun, the little waves of Loch Etive lapping up on the seaweed, yellow as the hair of Deirdrê, far below, and playing chess at this board, they heard a shout from the woods down by the shore where the hazels and birches grew thick.

"That is the voice of a man of Erin!" said Naoise, and stopped in his game to listen.

265

But Deirdrê said, very quickly: "Not so! It is the voice of a Gael of Alba."

Yet so she spoke that she might try to deceive her own heart, that even then was chilled by the black shadow of an approaching evil. Then came another shout, and yet a third. And when they heard the third shout, there was no doubt left in their minds, for they all knew the voice for that of Fergus, the son of Rossa the Red. And when Ardan hastened down to the harbour to greet him, Deirdrê confessed to Naoise why she had refused at first to own that it was a voice from Erin that she heard.

"I saw in a dream last night," she said, "three birds that flew hither from Emain Macha, carrying three sips of honey in their beaks. The honey they left with us, but took away three sips of blood."

And Naoise said: "What then, best beloved, dost thou read from this dream of thine?"

And Deirdrê said: "I read that Fergus comes from Conor with honeyed words of peace, but behind his treacherous words lies death."

As they spake, Ardan and Fergus and his following climbed up the height where the bog-myrtle and the heather and sweet fern yielded their sweetest incense as they were wounded under their firm tread.

And when Fergus stood before Deirdrê and Naoise, the man of her heart, he told them of Conor's message, and of the peace and the glory that awaited them in Erin if they would but listen to the words of welcome that he brought.

Then said Naoise: "I am ready." But his eyes dared not meet the sea-blue eyes of Deirdrê, his queen.

"Knowest thou that my pledge is one of honour?" asked Fergus.

"I know it well," said Naoise.

So in joyous feasting was that night spent, and only over the heart of Deirdrê hung that black cloud of sorrow to come, of woe unspeakable.

When the golden dawn crept over the blue hills of Loch Etive, and the white-winged birds of the sea swooped and dived and cried in the silver waters, the galley of the Sons of Usna set out to sea.

And Deirdrê, over whom hung a doom she had not the courage to name, sang a song at parting:

THE LAY OF DEIRDRE

"Beloved land, that Eastern land,Alba, with its wonders.O that I might not depart from it,But that I go with Naoise.

Beloved is Dunfidgha and Dun Fin;Beloved the Dun above them;Beloved is Innisdraighende; And beloved Dun Suibhne.

Coillchuan! O Coillchuan!Where Ainnle would, alas! resort;Too short, I deem, was then my stayWith Ainnle in Oirir Alban.

Glenlaidhe!   O Glenlaidhe!I used to sleep by its soothing murmur;Fish, and flesh of wild boar and badger,Was my repast in Glenlaidhe.

Glenmasan! O Glenmasan! High its herbs, fair its boughs.Solitary was the place of our reposeOn grassy Invermasan.

Gleneitche!   O Gleneitche!There was raised my earliest home.Beautiful its woods on rising,When the sun struck on Gleneitche.

Glen Urchain! O Glen Urchain!It was the straight glen of smooth ridges,Not more joyful was a man of his ageThan Naoise in Glen Urchain.

Glendaruadh!   O Glendaruadh!My love each man of its inheritance.Sweet the voice of the cuckoo, on bending bough,On the hill above Glendaruadh.

Beloved is Draighen and its sounding shore;Beloved is the water o'er the pure sand.O that I might not depart from the east,But that I go with my beloved!"

Translated by W. F. SKENE, LL.D.

Thus they fared across the grey-green sea betwixt Alba and Erin, and when Ardan and Ainle and Naoise heard the words of the song of Deirdrê, on their hearts also descended the strange sorrow of an evil thing from which no courage could save them.

At Ballycastle, opposite Rathlin Island, where a rock on the shore ("Carraig Uisneach") still bears the name of the Sons of Usna, Fergus and the returned exiles landed. And scarcely were they out of sight of the shore when a messenger came to Fergus, bidding him to a feast of ale at the dun of Borrach. Then Fergus, knowing well that in this was the hand of Conor and that treachery was meant, reddened all over with anger and with shame. But yet he dared not break his *geasa*, even although by holding to it the honour he had pledged the three brothers for their safe-conduct and that of Deirdrê was dragged through the mire. He therefore gave them his sons for escort and went to the feast at the dun of Borrach, full well knowing that Deirdrê spoke truth when she told him sadly that he had sold his honour. The gloomy forebodings that had assailed the heart of Deirdrê ere they had left Loch Etive grew ever the stronger as they went southwards. She begged Naoise to let them go to some place of safety and there wait until Fergus had fulfilled his *geasa* and could rejoin them and go with them to Emain Macha. But the Sons of Usna, strong in the knowledge of their own strength, and simply trustful of the pledged word of Conor and of Fergus, laughed at her fears, and continued on their way. Dreams of dread portent haunted her sleep, and by daytime her eyes in her white face looked like violets in the snow. She saw a cloud of blood always hanging over the beautiful Sons of Usna, and all of them she saw, and Illann the Fair, with their heads shorn off, gory and awful. Yet no pleading words could prevail upon Naoise. His fate drove him on.

"To Emain Macha we must go, my beloved," he said. "To do other than this would be to show that we have fear, and fear we have none."

Thus at last did they arrive at Emain Macha, and with courteous welcome Conor sent them word that the house of the heroes of the Red Branch was to be theirs that night. And although the place the king had chosen for their lodgment confirmed all the intuitions and forebodings of Deirdrê, the evening was spent by in good cheer, and Deirdrê had the joy of a welcome there from her old friend Lavarcam. For to Lavarcam Conor had said: "I would have thee go to the House of the Red Branch and bring me back tidings if the beauty of Deirdrê has waned, or if she is still the most beautiful of all women."

And when Lavarcam saw her whom she had loved as a little child, playing chess with her husband at the board of ivory and gold, she knew that love had made the beauty of Deirdrê blossom, and that she was now more beautiful than the words of any man or woman could tell. Nor was it possible for her to be a tool for Conor when she looked in the starry eyes of Deirdrê, and so she poured forth warning of the treachery of Conor, and the Sons of Usna knew that there was truth in the dreams of her who was the queen of their hearts. And even as Lavarcam ceased there came to the eyes of Deirdrê a vision such as that of Cathbad the Druid on the night of her birth.

"I see three torches quenched this night," she said. "And these three torches are the Three Torches of Valour among the Gael, and their names are the names of the Sons of Usna. And more bitter still is this sorrow, because that the Red Branch shall ultimately perish through it, and Uladh itself be overthrown, and blood fall this way and that as the whirled rains of winter."

FIONA MACLEOD.

Then Lavarcam went her way, and returned to the palace at Emain Macha and told Conor that the cruel winds and snows of Alba had robbed Deirdrê of all her loveliness, so that she was no more a thing to be desired. But Naoise had said to Deirdrê when she foretold his doom: "Better to die for thee and for thy deathless beauty than to have lived without knowledge of thee and thy love," and it may have been that some memory of the face of Deirdrê, when she heard these words, dwelt in the eyes of Lavarcam and put quick suspicion into the evil heart of the king. For when Lavarcam had gone forth, well pleased that she had saved her darling, Conor sent a spy—a man whose father and three brothers had fallen in battle under the sword of Naoise—that he might see Deirdrê and confirm or contradict the report of Lavarcam. And when this man reached the house of the Red Branch, he found that the Sons of Usna had been put on their guard, for all the doors and windows were barred. Thus he climbed to a narrow upper window and peered in. There, lying on the couches, the chess-board of ivory and gold between them, were Naoise and Deirdrê. So beautiful were they, that they were as the deathless gods, and as they played that last game of their lives, they spoke together in low voices of love that sounded like the melody of a harp in the hands of a master player. Deirdrê was the first to see the peering face with the eyes that gloated on her loveliness. No word said she, but silently made the gaze of Naoise follow her own, even as he held a golden chessman in his hand, pondering a move. Swift as a stone from a sling the chessman was hurled, and the man fell back to the ground with his eyeball smashed, and found his way to Emain Macha as best he could, shaking with agony and snarling with lust for revenge. Vividly he painted for the king the picture of the most beautiful woman on earth as she played at the chess-board that he held so dear, and the rage of Conor that had smouldered ever since that day when he learned that Naoise had stolen Deirdrê from him, flamed up into madness. With a bellow like that of a wounded bull, he called upon the Ultonians to come with him to the House of the Red Branch, to burn it down, and to slay all those within it with the sword, save only Deirdrê, who was to be saved for a more cruel fate.

In the House of the Red Branch, Deirdrê and the three brothers and the two sons of Fergus heard the shouts of the Ultonians and knew that the storm was about to break. But, calm as rocks against which the angry waves beat themselves in vain, sat those whose portion at dawn was to be cruel death. And Naoise and Ainle played chess, with hands that did not tremble. At the first onslaught, Buinne the Red, son of Fergus, sallied forth, quenched the flames, and drove back the Ultonians with great slaughter. But Conor called to him to parley and offered him a bribe of land, and Buinne, treacherous son of a treacherous father, went over to the enemy. His brother, Illann the Fair, filled with shame, did what he could to make amends. He went forth, and many hundreds of the besieging army fell before him, ere death stayed his loyal hand. At his death the Ultonians again fired the house, and first Ardan and then Ainle left their chess for a fiercer game, and glutted their sword blades with the blood of their enemies. Last came the turn of Naoise. He kissed Deirdrê, and drank a drink, and went out against the men of Conor, and where his brothers had slain hundreds, a thousand fell before his sword.

Then fear came into the heart of Conor, for he foresaw that against the Sons of Usna no man could prevail, save by magic. Thus he sent for Cathbad the Druid, who was even then very near death, and the old man was carried on a litter to the House of the Red Branch, from which the flames were leaping, and before which the dead lay in heaps.

And Conor besought him to help him to subdue the Sons of Usna ere they should have slain every Ultonian in the land. So by his magic Cathbad raised a hedge of spears round the house. But Naoise, Ardan, and Ainle, with Deirdrê in their centre, sheltered by their shields, burst suddenly forth from the blazing house, and cut a way for themselves through the hedge as though they sheared green wheat. And, laughing aloud, they took a terrible toll of lives from the Ultonians who would have withstood them. Then again the Druid put forth his power, and a noise like the noise of many waters was in the ears of all who were there. So suddenly the magic flood arose that there was no chance of escape for the Sons of Usna. Higher it mounted, ever higher, and Naoise held Deirdrê on his shoulder, and smiled up in her eyes as the water rose past his middle. Then suddenly as it had come, the flood abated, and all was well with the Ultonians who had sheltered on a rising ground. But the Sons of Usna found themselves entrapped in a morass where the water had been. Conor, seeing them in his hands at last, bade some of his warriors go and take them. But for shame no Ultonian would go, and it was a man from Norway who walked along a dry spit of land to where they stood, sunk deep in the green bog. "Slay me first!" called Ardan as he drew near, sword in hand. "I am the youngest, and, who knows, my death may change the tides of fate!"

And Ainle also craved that death might be dealt to him the first. But Naoise held out his own sword, "The Retaliator," to the executioner.

"Mannanan, the son of Lîr, gave me my good sword," he said. "With it strike my dear brothers and me one blow only as we stand here like three trees planted in the soil. Then shall none of us know the grief and shame of seeing the other beheaded." And because it was hard for any man to disobey the command of Naoise, a king of men, the Norseman reached out his hand for the sword. But Deirdrê sprang from the shoulder of Naoise and would have killed the man ere he struck. Roughly he threw her aside, and with one blow he shore off the heads of the three greatest heroes of Alba.

For a little while there was a great stillness there, like the silence before the coming of a storm. And then all who had beheld the end of the fair and noble Sons of Usna broke into great lamentation. Only Conor stood silent, gazing at the havoc he had wrought. To Cuchulainn, the mighty champion, a good man and a true, Deirdrê fled, and begged him to protect her for the little span of life that she knew yet remained to her. And with him she went to where the head of Naoise lay, and tenderly she cleansed it from blood and from the stains of strife and stress, and smoothed the hair that was black as a raven's wing, and kissed the cold lips again and again. And as she held it against her white breast, as a mother holds a little child, she chanted for Naoise, her heart, and for his brothers, a lament that still lives in the language of the Gael.

"Is it honour that ye love, brave and chivalrous Ultonians?Or is the word of a base king better than noble truth?Of a surety ye must be glad, who have basely slain honourIn slaying the three noblest and best of your brotherhood.

Let now my beauty that set all this warring aflame,Let now my beauty be quenched as a torch that is spent—For here shall I quench it, here, where my loved one lies,A torch shall it be for him still through the darkness of death."

FIONA MACLEOD'S TRANSLATION.

Then, at the bidding of Cuchulainn, the Ultonian, three graves were dug for the brothers, but the grave of Naoise was made wider than the others, and when he was placed in it, standing upright, with his head placed on his shoulders, Deirdrê stood by him and held him in her white arms, and murmured to him of the love that was theirs and of which not Death itself could rob them. And even as she spoke to him, merciful Death took her, and together they were buried. At that same hour a terrible cry was heard: *The Red Branch perisheth! Uladh passeth! Uladh passeth!*" and when he had so spoken, the soul of Cathbad the Druid passed away.

To the land of the Ultonians there came on the morrow a mighty host, and the Red Branch was wiped out for ever. Emain Macha was cast into ruins, and Conor died in a madness of sorrow.

And still, in that land of Erin where she died, still in the lonely cleuchs and glens, and up the mist-hung mountain sides of Loch Etive, where she knew her truest happiness, we can sometimes almost hear the wind sighing the lament: "Deirdrê the beautiful is dead ... is dead!"

"I hear a voice crying, crying, crying: is it the windI hear, crying its old weary cry time out of mind?

The grey wind weeps, the grey wind weeps, the grey wind weeps:Dust on her breast, dust on her eyes, the grey wind weeps."

Fiona Macleod.

Made in the USA
Monee, IL
29 June 2023